Evenings With Bryson

A Blackstone Family Novel

TINA MARTIN

"Didn't think you were going to show for a minute there," Bryson said to her. He had already made himself comfortable at the table she'd dubbed as hers.

And he has the nerve to sit at my table. She narrowed her eyes at him. The sight of him sitting there made her nose twitch. Even his sly comment didn't sit well with her, so she responded, "Women usually don't have problems keeping their commitments, unlike your kind."

"Tell me something...are you normally this rude, or did you save all of your frustrations to take them out on me?"

"No, I'm not rude, and don't flatter yourself...you're not important enough for me to take out my frustrations on you."

Bryson smirked. He'd crossed paths with her kind before – the fist in the air, independent woman who had to exude an air about herself in order to assert her self-importance. Kalina, however, had set the bar even higher. One thing was for certain – she never crossed paths with a man like him. Otherwise her attitude would've been checked a long time ago.

The Blackstone Family

PARENTS: Theodore (Theo) Blackstone & Elowyn Blackstone

CHILDREN:

Bryson Blackstone [Age 38]
  -Divorced
  -Owns Blackstone Tree Service

Barringer (Barry) Blackstone [Age 36]
  -Married to Calista Blackstone
  -CEO of Blackstone Financial Services Group

Garrison (Gary) Blackstone [Age 34]
  -Married to Vivienne Blackstone
  -Director of Finance at Blackstone Financial Services Group

Everson Blackstone [Age 32]
  -Married to June Blackstone
  -Business Management Analyst

Candice (Candy) Blackstone [Age 28]
  -Single and looking
  -Manager of Customer Relations at Blackstone Financial Services Group

COUSINS:

Rexford Blackstone [Age 37]
  -Single and *always* looking
  -Police Officer

Colton Blackstone [Age 33]
  -Single
  -Painter, owns Blackstone Painting, LLC

~*~

One of the hardest things to do in life is to love and care for someone who lacks the ability to love you back or, at the very least, show a hint of gratitude.

~*~

CHAPTER 1

Sitting at a table in her aunt's café, the norm for Kalina for years now, she rubbed her weary eyes and stared at the screen of her laptop a little longer, as if the answer she was seeking would somehow magically pop inside her head. How *was* she going to answer this question she received from one of her blog readers – a woman on the brink of ending her marriage:

> Before we married, my husband and I dated for two years. We learned each other. We knew we wanted to be together forever and have a family. We wanted two children. Five years later, we don't have any children. He says he's not ready. That he's busy building his brand to be distracted by a child right now. I'm thirty-four years old. I'm not getting any younger and neither are my eggs. I shouldn't have to beg my husband for a child. My question is, do I stay and continue with my efforts in convincing him that I want a child? Should I leave and seek my own happiness? Or should I give him an ultimatum – give me a baby or I'm out?

Kalina knew she had to be cautiously careful with her response, because even though people hated it when other people tried to *tell* them what to do in a certain situation, they certainly didn't mind having cosigners – people to take their side and agree with them in the course of action they've already decided to take and encouraging them to move forward with it. Kalina wouldn't do that. After all, she didn't want to be the reason this woman, or any woman, decided to leave her husband.

Graduating from college with her bachelors in behavioral science, she looked forward to the opportunity to work with people, helping them through their issues. She was passionate about it, excelled at it and, after graduating at the top of her class, she had a job lined up at the local Social Services department – that is until she realized she could take her passion and make it into her own business, be her own boss and work for herself.

She did this by starting a relationship blog, *The Cooper Files*, a site geared towards helping people, men and women alike, overcome issues in their relationships. While *The Cooper Files* began as a hobby, the site was becoming increasingly popular, even ranking among the top relationship advice websites on the Internet. Just last year, it landed the number twelve spot for the top fifteen relationship blogs on the Internet.

"Kalina, are you stumped again? I know that look?" Edith asked, standing behind the counter, her short stature competing with the pastry display.

Kalina yawned, glanced up at her aunt, using the

temporary distraction to stretch her arms up in the air and pop her knuckles. "This is a tough one, Edith…think I need a cup of the dark roast tonight."

Edith shook her head. "Honey, I don't know how you do it. If I drank coffee this late in the evening, I wouldn't get a minute of sleep."

"Sleep…what's that?" Kalina joked. But, all kidding aside, she lost her relationship with sleep a long time ago. Running her business was of the utmost importance. Most nights when she left the café, she'd go home and head straight for her office. She'd converted the studio apartment above her garage into *The Cooper Files'* headquarters, a convenient space attached to her home where she did most of her work during the day. She spent many long, stressful nights in that studio – so many nights that she'd bought a comfortable brown sofa that complemented the mint, white and brown color scheme of the workspace. When she was up working late and didn't have the energy to go downstairs to her bedroom, she would crash right there. In her *headquarters*, on a brown sofa with her trusty friend nearby – her laptop.

"Are you sure you want the dark roast?" Edith asked.

"Yes. I'm positive," Kalina answered. "I don't plan to get much sleep tonight anyway. I'm drowning in emails again. I can't get to them fast enough."

"All right. One cup of kick-your-butt coming right up," Edith said, then grinned.

Kalina smiled lazily, but her little joy turned into exasperation when she looked up at her computer screen and quickly scanned the email again, still uncertain of how to answer it.

Bummer...

Kalina rubbed the stiffness of her aching neck, then leaned her head from side-to-side, stretching. Threading her fingers in her wild, wind-tossed hair, she groaned loudly.

"Here you go, honey." Edith set the cup on the table, away from Kalina's laptop. She remembered how Kalina almost had a stroke the last time she placed the cup too close to her computer. "Looks like I'm right on time with it too."

Kalina took a sip of coffee. "Mmm. Perfect. This is exactly what I need right now." She gulped down more of the coffee, inhaling an aromatic breath of it and slowly breathing out in a paced, gratifying sigh.

"I thought you were looking into bringing on an intern," Edith said. "What happened with that?"

"I have to wait until the summer if I want to get a legitimate college student whose major is in this field, and even after waiting, there's no guarantee I will get approved for one." Kalina sipped more coffee.

"Well, you need to get some help, even if that means hiring somebody off the street at this point."

Tickled, Kalina covered her mouth with her hand preventing herself from spewing coffee all over the table and thus, her laptop. Once she could swallow, she laughed and said, "Edith, it's not *that* serious."

"It is...your body can't survive without sleep."

"As long as I got this caffeine it can. Look at me, Edith...I'm living. I'm alive...I'll be fine."

"You know, if I wasn't running this café, I'd

help you, but—"

"I know you would, but I'll be fine. Everything will work out." Kalina glanced around the café for the first time this evening, her eyes settling on a man, as dark as her coffee, standing in front of the coffee dispensers, holding a cup as if he was at a quandary – unable to decide between regular and decaf. *He's so not a decaf kind of guy.* A man of his size and muscle definition, in her opinion, needed something stronger than decaf, or as she like to call it, hot water. Finally, she watched him settle for the regular just as she suspected he would, and thought to herself, *Man, I'm good. Now if only I can answer this woman's email...*

She glanced at the computer screen, then up at Edith before she got the nagging urge to check out Mr. Coffee again. Why was she checking him out? It's not like she was interested. Still, she couldn't stop her head from turning in his direction. How tall was this guy? Six feet, two inches? One of his hands were the size of both of hers put together and his style of dress spoke volumes to his character and maturity level. Yes, people still judged you by what you wore, and he was wearing a long-sleeved, light blue, striped Oxford shirt, neatly tucked inside a pair of tan khakis with a pair of expensive, honey-brown leather shoes on his feet. Distinguished. His outfit was as clean and neat as his low cut fade. The only thing he seemed to be missing was a Kangol cap and a driving iron. *I bet he's the golf type...*

She cracked a half smile and looked at her computer screen again. She couldn't remember the last time she'd given a guy a double-take. Actually, she'd never given a man a double-take before now. There was just something about *this* man that deserved a second look.

"Kalina Cooper, do you hear me?"

"Oh, um…you said something, Edith?" Kalina said with raised brows.

"I asked you if you were going to see your mother tomorrow." Edith was aware that Kalina usually visited her mother every Saturday, but with her work schedule being so hectic, she didn't know if she would be able to make it.

"Tomorrow? Why would I go tomorrow?" Kalina asked. "You know I visit mom on Saturdays."

"Tomorrow *is* Saturday."

"What? I thought today was Thursday." She looked at the date and time display in the bottom right corner of her laptop and confirmed it wasn't Thursday. It was Friday! Friday? Where had the week gone?

"It's Friday, Kalina. See…that's what I'm talking about. You don't even know what day of the week it is and—"

Kalina shushed her aunt by saying, "Well I'm going. I may not have time for much else, but I will make time for mom."

Edith smiled. "I sure do miss Madeline…you know, the way she used to be."

"I do, too. She used to be so alive and was one of those mothers who would stay up all night and help me with my silly science projects." Kalina chuckled. "I remember how she would be so excited to try out a new recipe, and while I helped her cook, we would be dancing and singing…it was awesome. It really was. Then Alzheimer's happened."

Downcast, Edith said, "Yeah…then Alzheimer's happened." Edith shook her head and sighed heavily. Madeline was alive, but in a way, it felt like she had already died. The sister she used to know ceased to exist. This *new* person Madeline became, after being diagnosed with early onset Alzheimer's disease, was a stranger to her – a helpless, disoriented, frail stranger. Edith was certain that Madeline didn't know her. Didn't recognize her. Her memories were gone, stolen from her by a dreadful disease that had come out of nowhere.

Edith glanced up at the clock and said, "Two more hours until closing time."

Kalina eyes rolled to the time display on her laptop. It was already 7:00 p.m. Had she really been sitting here for a full hour, trying to figure out a way to respond to this email? What was it about this particular email that had her stumped?

"Let me get up from here before I fall asleep," Edith said, grunting and blowing breaths as she stood up.

Looking at her computer screen again, Kalina scanned the email from this anonymous woman:

Before we married, my husband and I dated for two years. We learned each other. We knew we wanted to be together forever and have a family. We wanted two children. Five years later, we don't have any children…do I stay and continue with my efforts in convincing him that I want a child? Should I leave and seek my own happiness? Or should I give him an ultimatum – give me a baby or I'm out?

Kalina sighed and scrubbed her hands down her face again. *Married people and their marital problems...*

Aside from her distrust of men, that was another reason she didn't want to marry. She had enough problems of her own without having to deal with, and worry about another person's issues. There was no need for the extra stress that came with marriage. That's why there were so many divorced people out here today. Marital problems. Financial problems. Baby problems. Communication problems. I'm-sick-of-you problems. Problems on top of problems. The glitz and glamour of the wedding day is long forgotten when two people grow to hate each other over the years.

She sighed, wiggled her fingers as they hovered over the keyboard and whispered, "Focus Kalina. Let the words flow and...go." She began typing:

Dear Anonymous,

...and that's as far as she had gotten.

"All right, Kalina, what's the question?" Edith asked from behind the counter. "I meant to ask you when I was over there."

Usually when Kalina found herself stuck on a question, she would discuss it with her aunt to get varying perspectives, then she could formulate an answer which, would not only satisfy her but would be the best advice she could offer the person who'd asked. This time, she wanted to answer it on her own. Why did she go to college for four years if she was going to use her aunt's gray-headed wisdom for the tough questions?

"I got it, Edith. It'll come to me sometime this year."

"Are you sure about that? You've been stuck on this one for a long time and I know you don't like to skip questions, so the faster you answer it, the quicker you can move on to the next one."

Kalina sighed and said, "Okay. Here's the situation…this woman has been married for five years. Before she married, her husband said he wanted kids. Now she's not sure if he wants children or not, but she does. So her question is threefold. She wants to know whether she should beg him for a child, if she should leave him to seek her own happiness, or if she should give her husband an ultimatum – if they don't get pregnant soon, she's leaving."

Edith blew a breath. "Good grief. That's a lot."

"And now you know why I've been sitting here for an hour…" Kalina took a sip of coffee. "I hate it when readers send these multiple-choice options, because my issue is, I can't decipher which option they're already leaning towards to know how I should tailor my answer. I can't necessarily *tell* her what to do, of course, but I can offer my opinion. And I do have an opinion in this case, by the way…"

"Which is?"

"Well, if her husband said he wanted to have babies before they married and now he's changed his mind, wouldn't that be a breach of contract?"

"Hmm…" Edith thought for a moment. "That's

an interesting take on things."

"I think it would," Kalina continued, "Because that's what marriage is, right? A contract, bound by a legal document? And if he was all for having kids before they married and then after they married, he changed his mind, it *would* be a breach of contract, sort of like marrying under false pretenses, and therefore the marriage is null and void."

A man's loud chuckle took Kalina's attention away from her aunt. She looked over at the source of the laughter and it was him, *Mr. Coffee* himself, sitting a couple of tables away from her.

He looked at her and said, "Sorry…didn't mean to laugh out loud at your conversation. That was rude of me." Still amused, he flipped through the magazine he'd obviously been reading while a smug smile remained on his face.

"What was so funny about my conversation?" Kalina asked, watching him shift his body in her direction and for the first time this evening, she got a full look at his face – a handsomely carved face that made her heart skip a beat. For a moment, she'd forgotten what she asked him until she saw his slender, attention-grabbing, firm lips move. And his voice was deep, dark and thunderous; a voice that could talk a woman into just about anything.

"Well, for one thing, nowhere in the marriage vow does it say that a man is obligated to give a woman a child or vice versa."

One eyebrow raised, Kalina said, "Your point?"

"My point is, your argument that the marriage would be a breach of contract, because the man doesn't want children, does not stand."

Edith nodded. "Bryson has a point, Kalina."

Bryson? A frown ripened in Kalina's forehead. "You know this guy, Edith?"

"I know Ms. Edith well," Bryson answered before Edith could respond. "I've been a patron of this café for years, but I've only been coming here at around this time for the last three weeks. Have you not seen me here before? I'm not difficult to miss."

You arrogant... "No, I haven't seen you here before, but it's not like I was looking for you either."

"I wasn't looking for you, but I see you here every evening around this time, talking to your laptop. You know, I've never heard anyone refer to a computer as their best friend..." He looked amused before his lips grew into a smile, one that showed off a mouth full of blindingly white teeth – like the sun rays reflecting off of a fresh snowfall.

"And on that note," Kalina said, turning away from Bryson and back towards her laptop, "I have work to do."

"Speaking of work, that's why you haven't seen me before," Bryson said. "Your eyes are glued to your computer screen twenty-four, seven."

Edith quickly hurried from behind the counter when she saw Kalina's frown deepen. Standing next to her niece now, she said, "Um, let me properly introduce you two. Kalina, this is Bryson Blackstone. Bryson, this is my niece, Kalina Cooper."

Bryson stood up, walked to Kalina's table and extended his hand to her. "Nice to meet you,

Kalina."

"I don't shake hands," Kalina said snippily. "And since my eyes are *glued* to my computer screen twenty-four seven, I better get back to work."

Bryson smirked, lowering his hand. Her attitude certainly didn't match her beautiful face and that silky, chocolate skin tone of hers. And her eyes – those gorgeous, black, almond-shaped eyes nearly quieted him – they almost stole his voice by making him lose his train of thought. And while he was standing there, stricken by her beauty, he'd forgotten what his next plan of action was. Oh yeah, that's right – he would way something to get under her skin. So finally responding to her, he said, "You mean, you have to get back to answering an email on a topic in which you obviously know nothing about?"

"Excuse me?" she asked, her head cocked to the side.

Well, that didn't take long, Bryson thought. Even the frown in her forehead couldn't distort her natural beauty.

Edith sauntered on back behind the counter when she saw a new customer come in. Besides, she wasn't about to get in the middle of this argument.

"Marriage," Bryson said. "You don't have a ring on your finger, and I don't see any indication of one ever being there, which tells me you've never been married. So what advice are you going to give this poor woman who's on the brink of ruining her life *and* marriage to a man she's probably head over heels in love with, simply because he's changed his mind about wanting children?"

"Okay, first of all, I didn't ask for, nor do I need your help, advice or opinion on—"

"So what's your reply?" he interrupted, inviting himself to her table by taking the empty chair across from her. "What are you going to tell this woman?"

The nerve of this conceited, self-centered...

Kalina leaned back in her chair, staring at the self-satisfied look on his face. Who did he think he was, barging his way into her conversation like he had a right? And who was he exactly? Some creepy coffee shop stalker? He did say he'd been coming there for three weeks. How did she not remember him? And how on earth was her aunt on a first name basis with this jerk of a man?

"I'm waiting," he said, then crossed his arms over his chest.

The motion had her glancing at his hand. He wasn't wearing a wedding band, so what did he know about marriage? Or maybe he was married, but kept his ring in his pocket...one of *those* men. And if he was one of those men, how was he in any position to offer anyone advice about anything.

"Okay, then," Kalina said, sitting straight up in her chair again. If this Bison, Bryson or whatever his name was, thought he was going to have the upper hand with her, he had another thought coming. "How would you respond to the woman?"

"How would *I* respond?" Bryson asked.

"Yes, since you're an expert on marriage and all. The *private* conversation I was having with my aunt has somehow intrigued you enough to interrupt us, so tell me, Bison—"

"Bry-son," he corrected.

"Whatever…what would be your perfect response to this woman. I'm dying to know."

"I'm not sure," Bryson responded.

"Well, would you look at that?" Kalina said with raised eyebrows. "Now you're not sure."

"Only because this is not something I can answer on a whim. Sensitive topics such as this requires careful consideration."

Kalina nodded and flashed a phony smile. "You're right. It does, which is why I've been stuck on this question all day long, and the reason why I was discussing it with my aunt. But, I tell you what Bry-son…" Kalina took one of her business cards from a side pocket on her laptop bag. Handing it to him, she said, "Since you don't think I have what it takes to answer the question, you do it."

She watched him smile wide, his teeth a stark contrast to his dark chocolate skin tone. He took the card from her grasp.

"My email address is on the card. I will expect your email reply by tomorrow night."

Bryson scanned over her business card, then looked up at her again. "You don't include a phone number on your business cards?"

She smirked. "Sure don't. There are a lot of crazies out here." *Case in point…*

With a smile on her face, Edith, watching from behind the counter, shook her head. Kalina had no patience for men, she knew, but Bryson Blackstone wasn't just any man and he seemed to have taken an interest in her.

"All right. I'll send you an email then, boss

14

lady."

Short of rolling her eyes, Kalina said, "You do that. Now if you would excuse me, I have to glue my eyes back to my computer screen."

"Right." Bryson stood up tall, towering over her table with a set of long legs and broad shoulders like that of a football player. He slid her business card into his shirt pocket. "It was nice meeting you, Kalina."

Ugh. Go away already...

She flashed him the phoniest smile she could muster and returned her attention back to her inbox. She had a hundreds of emails to answer and she wanted to get through at least fifty of them before the shop closed, especially since she needed to get some sleep tonight. She was going to visit her mother in the morning and that experience was tiring enough in itself. She didn't want to arrive exhausted and quick-tempered, so sleep was a must. It was going to be a long day.

CHAPTER 2

Bryson stepped inside the foyer of his home, looking around like it was his first time at his own house. He was tired of being here, being reminded of his ex-wife, Felicia, and her infidelity. Seemed everywhere he turned, something reminded him of her – the Persian rug in front of the fireplace, the chandelier they picked out together hanging above the dining room table and the blank space on the wall where their wedding picture used to occupy – there was always something.

He shook his head and continued upstairs to one of the guest bedrooms where he'd been sleeping for the two years he'd been divorced. The master bedroom was off limits. He couldn't bring himself to sleep there. They'd shared that room and even after having all the furniture replaced – the bed, nightstand and dressers – he still didn't want to spend any significant amount of time there. Memories of woman who cheated on him needed to cease, even if it meant he had to inconvenience himself to make that happen.

He often thought about the day he found out about Felicia's infidelity. After dinner one day, Felicia had gone to the gym with his sister-in-law, Calista. He ran upstairs to change into some workout clothes since he wanted to go for a jog through the neighborhood. In the walk-in closet they shared, he saw a sheet of paper hanging out the top drawer of her dresser. Her panty drawer. Thinking that it looked odd, because Felicia was a neat freak and she for sure would've fixed this herself, he walked over to it, pulled the paper out and realized it was an email Felicia had printed out – an email she had anonymously sent to a woman named Kalina Cooper, an editor at *The Cooper Files*, whatever that was…

From: Anonymous
To: Kalina Cooper
Subject: Torn

I hope you can help me. I'm 35 years old and have been married to my husband for 6 years. I'm a housewife, taking care of the bills, scheduling, shopping and basically running the house while he works full-time. When I'm not at home, I'm usually at the gym, getting facials, manicures, pedicures and massages. My husband and I have shared some good times together and I love him dearly, but lately, I'm feeling like the romance isn't there. I need excitement. Adventure. That's why I've been seeing someone else. We've only been on a few dates, but I feel a level of excitement whenever I'm with him. Still, I don't want to leave my husband, but even though my husband spoils me, I don't get excited to see him anymore. I don't know what to do at this point.
--
Confused in Wilmington

———

Felicia's email hit him so hard, he had to take a seat to keep from falling over. His wife of six years was on the verge of cheating, or since the email was dated months ago, maybe she already had. She'd given him no indication that she thought he was *boring* or that she didn't feel excited to see him. How was he supposed to know she'd been feeling that way? Who was this man she'd been dating? And where was the reply from this Kalina Cooper person? Did she reply at all?

Frantically, he walked back over to the dresser, tossing her panties around, looking for another email. The response email. He grabbed another paper, a folded one, and unraveled it. It had been exactly what he was searching for:

From: Kalina Cooper
To: Anonymous
Subject: Torn

Hi Confused in Wilmington,

I can't say I understand exactly what you're going through, but I will say this. You've been married to this man for six years. That has to count for something. All too often people, men *and* women, are so quick to walk away from their relationships when they think that someone else can give them what they're 'missing' in their current situation. And guess what...a few years from now, you're going to be feeling the exact same way about this *strange* man you've been dating. If you're bored within your marriage, you need to look within yourself, not into the eyes of another man to give you a feeling of excitement. Why don't you try to go away with your husband? You said you manage the household finances, so schedule a trip together. You better believe there are plenty of women out here who would want a man like you have. Why not take the time to show your husband that you appreciate his hard work – providing you with the financial stability that enables you to get massages and manicures whenever you want? When was the last time you cooked a meal for him? Or surprised him at his office with lunch? Better yet, when was the last time you had an actual conversation with him, looked into his eyes and really asked him if he was okay? When was the last time you told him you loved him? Try it. If nothing else I said has struck a chord with you, remember this – don't throw your marriage away because you *think* someone else can make you happy. Happiness starts within.

All the best,

--
Kalina Cooper
Editor | CEO
The Cooper Files

———

The response from this woman had come a couple of weeks after Felicia had sent her email. Obviously, Felicia had read it, even though she hadn't taken any of the advice that was clearly laid out in the email. She still cheated.

That was two years ago…

It wasn't until a few *months* ago that Bryson stumbled upon this email again, reread it and wondered who this Kalina Cooper was, and what *The Cooper Files* were all about. So, sitting in his office one day during a quiet period in an otherwise chaotic office building, he pulled up her website and started his research on her, reading about how she studied and analyzed people and offered relationship advice. And she was stunning, absolutely breathtaking in his opinion, but what caught him by surprise was her admission in her biography that she wasn't in a relationship, wasn't married, had never been married and had never planned to marry. Her *purpose* was to help other people in this space, not herself.

And that's what she did with her white laptop,

her *friend* – sat in Edith's Café every night and helped people with their relationship issues, one email at a time. That was her purpose.

His *purpose* was getting to know her better. The email she sent to his now, ex-wife had been on point. It came from a woman who knew and appreciated the traits of a good man. A real man. And he was a man who appreciated the intelligence of a beautiful woman. Yes, he had pretended she wasn't capable of giving advice about marriage since she had never experienced marriage, but that was just to get his foot in the door, to stare into her dark brown eyes. It had been a way for him to meet her, ruffle her feathers a bit and make himself a permanent entry into her memory bank. Once she got to know him, she'd see what kind of man he really was. He would make sure of it.

CHAPTER 3

Kalina managed to get seven hours of sleep last night. It wasn't enough to catch her up from the little sleep she had during the course of the entire week, but it was good enough to make her alert to the point where she could sit quietly without nodding off. That's what she was doing now – sitting quietly in her mother's bedroom, watching her sleep. Madeline had been a resident at this assisted living facility for years. When Edith realized she couldn't properly take care of Madeline any longer, she filled out the necessary paperwork to get Madeline an apartment here and footed the money, over thirty grand a year, to keep Madeline here – safe, cared for and protected.

Kalina was grateful for the success of her blog, especially since the money she made allowed her to pay her aunt back every cent. And now, she takes care the monthly bills for her mother's residency. The prices were absurd. It was like paying a mortgage, but at least there was a team of nurses at the facility who could help her, give her medication and make sure she had everything she needed at any given time.

As for the apartment, it wasn't bad. It was all her mom needed – a small kitchen that was open to a spacious living room, one bedroom and one bathroom. Simple. That made it easy for Kalina to clean up and organize some things while she was there on her Saturday visits. Before she sat down next to her mother's bed, she'd dusted, mopped the kitchen floor, wiped down the counter and thoroughly cleaned the bathroom. Afterwards, she disinfected the place with Lysol.

Kalina sighed and shook her head. She couldn't wrap her mind around how her mother had gotten Alzheimer's disease. Where did it come from? She was thirteen when her mother, then forty, was diagnosed, but she didn't know what Alzheimer's entailed as a teen. She only knew that her mother was changing – forgetting little by little every day. She began losing things – a red flag for Kalina because since when does the queen of organization lose things? Her mother was always on point with everything, but suddenly, she began misplacing her keys nearly every day.

One day, Kalina came home from school to find her mother, sitting in a pile of laundry on the living room floor in tears, upset that she couldn't fold a shirt. She'd forgotten how, didn't have the coordination to perform the task. Kalina scooped her mother in her arms, then folded the clothes while her mother watched on. Sometime after that, her father deserted them…

Madeline moved a little, readjusting herself on the bed. She opened her eyes wide, staring at Kalina and said, "Hi."

Kalina smiled warmly. Most words her mother said were hard to understand because she was also losing speech among everything else. But her greeting was something clearly understandable. "Hi, mom."

Madeline frowned.

Every Saturday was the same routine. She would have to tell her own mother who she was. The doctors and nurses encouraged her, and Edith, to talk to Madeline, and if they had to explain who they were in relation to her, then so be it. So, taking her mother's soft hand, Kalina said, "It's me, mom. It's Kalina. Your daughter."

Madeline looked confused.

Kalina spoke up a little louder and said, "It's Kalina. Your daughter."

Madeline sat up as best as she could on the bed. There was a mess of pillows behind her back.

"Do you remember who I am?" Kalina asked.

Madeline frowned. "Uh…ye…ye…you."

Kalina smiled. She'd been having this exact conversation with her mother for years. Not once had Madeline got it right. "I'm your daughter, Kalina. Remember?"

Madeline chuckled loudly, completely out of place for the conversation they were having and said, "Oh." She then stood up from the bed, taking a moment to stabilize herself, then stiffly began walking towards the closet, like a baby taking its first steps.

"Mom, where are you going?" Kalina asked, when she saw her mother attempting to take a coat from the hanger. The weather was nice today, in the mid-seventies. Even if she was capable of going somewhere, she wouldn't need a jacket.

"Tine go," Madeline said. "Tine go."

Tine go…

Kalina knew what she was trying to say, so she asked, "*Time* to go where, mom?"

"Go…yee…ye…go," Madeline said, attempting to point her index finger, but she couldn't do that either.

"Okay, mommy," Kalina said, taking her mother by the arm and guiding her back to the bed. "We're not going anywhere today. That's the good thing about living here. You have everything you need right here, and these good people working at this facility take good care of you."

"Oh," Madeline said, frowning.

After Kalina helped her sit on the bed, she went back over to the closet, threaded her mother's coat onto a hanger, then sat next to her on the bed. She took a photo album from her bag to share pictures with her mother, an activity one of the nurses had recommended. Since there wasn't a cure for Alzheimer's, one way for patients to interact with their loved ones and possibly learn to remember things, was to look at photos of family and friends. It was a long shot, but every little bit of brain stimulation mattered.

Flipping to photos of her mother when she was younger, in her thirties, Kalina pointed to a picture and asked, "Do you know who this is?"

"Uh…yee…ye…" Madeline said.

"That's you, mom," Kalina said as upbeat as she could, watching the confusion wash over her mother's face. She turned the page, but before she could ask her mother who the baby was in the pictures, Madeline had stood up from the bed,

24

stabilized herself, and stumbled back to the closet, taking out a pair of mismatched shoes. She returned to the bed with them. "Mom, we're not going anywhere. You don't need your shoes."

"Stanley…co…get…hmmm," she said.

Kalina frowned and shook her head. "No, mom. Stanley is not coming for you. You have to stay here today, okay."

"Oh."

"How about we go watch TV? You want to watch TV for a little while?"

"TV."

"Okay." Leaving the shoes by the bed, Kalina took her mother's hand and guided her into the living room. When Madeline was sitting comfortably on the couch, Kalina took the remote from the coffee table and powered on the TV. "I'm going to get you a cup of water."

Madeline didn't respond. She just sat there, motionless.

Kalina stepped over to the kitchen, took a cup from the cabinet then filled it with tap water. As she did so, she watched her mother take the remote from the table and rub it across her hair in a brushing motion. She walked over to her, set the cup of water on the coffee table and said, "Mom, this is not a brush. This is the remote control that turns the channels on the TV."

Madeline attempted to take the remote from Kalina.

Kalina placed the remote back on the table and said, "We'll let it stay there for now."

"Stanley…co… get," Madeline said.

"No, mom. Stanley is not coming. He hasn't been here since you checked in thirteen years ago, and he ain't coming now." Kalina hated her father. He left her mother seventeen years ago when she was first diagnosed with Alzheimer's. Before she was diagnosed, and the thought was that she had a case of amnesia, he was there, trying to help her. But when the doctor explained how she was losing her memory and would eventually forget who he was and Kalina for that matter, he left. Kalina overheard him telling Edith that he couldn't take it. Couldn't handle it. Said he refused to watch a woman he loved deteriorate into nothing and that his life, what little he had left of it, didn't have to be over because Madeline's was. He said it wasn't fair to her and it wasn't *fair* to him. But how could he leave a woman he claimed to love? How much of an oxymoron is it to say you love someone, but when they fall ill, you leave them while still claiming to love them? On what universe was that acceptable?

And that's the man Kalina had as a role model to use as the standard for all men. A coward. A man who abandoned his family when life didn't go as planned. And now, he was living in Fayetteville, North Carolina with his *new* wife, like his past was nothing but a lost memory – as lost as the memories that were once stored in Madeline's mind.

"Here, mom," Kalina said, taking the cup from the table. "Take a sip of water." When she brought the cup up to her mother's mouth, she watched her lips tremble.

After Madeline took a sip, she swatted the cup away, causing Kalina to lose grip of it. The cup fell to the table, water spilling everywhere. Kalina jumped up, ran to the kitchen to grab some paper towels to clean up the spill, and when she turned around to come back to the table, she saw her mother with the remote control, brushing it against her hair again.

Kalina shook her head and threw her hands in the air. She was frustrated as she usually was whenever she came to see her mother. But how could she get frustrated with her sick mother? It was comparable to being angry at a baby because it was crying. Still, it bothered her to know that every week, she'd have to watch her mother do mindless things. It was enough to drive her completely insane, and that's why she didn't visit more often. In the beginning, she visited three times a week. Now, she could only tolerate once a week. It was difficult to visit someone who didn't recognize you. Someone you had to introduce yourself to every time you saw them. Most of all, it was mind-boggling that her mother didn't recognize her when she was the one who birthed her into the world and raised her from a baby.

After she cleaned up the spill and threw the paper towels in the garbage can, Kalina took her mother by the hand and said, "Come on, mom. Let's take you back to the bed so you can rest."

She gripped her mother's arm and helped her walk back into the bedroom. Madeline could walk on her own, but not very far distances. In fact, the nurses had already instructed Kalina that, soon, she would need a walker.

Watching her mother get into the bed now, she

adjusted the pillows to help her get as comfortable as possible, then planted a kiss on her cheek.

"Love you, mom."

Madeline suspired softly. She closed her eyes, then opened them wide and said, "Stanley...co—"

"Shh. Just rest mom."

Kalina watched her mother rest, making sure she was sound asleep before she left the room. Once she was standing in the living room, she quietly closed the door, then closed her eyes tight and took a deep breath, willing herself not to cry. Watching her mother die this slow, mentally agonizing death was rough on her – taking little pieces of her soul away as she thought about the torture her mother was going through.

A few minutes later, Kalina quietly opened the bedroom door, peeping in to make sure her mother was still on the bed and resting. She was. She closed it back, then opening the front door to the apartment, she called her mother's nurse, Joan, to the apartment.

"Hey, Kalina. Everything okay," Joan asked.

"As okay as it can be, I guess. Can you come in for a minute?"

"Sure. I have a few minutes," Joan said, walking in, following Kalina to the couch.

"So, how has she been, Joan?"

Joan shook her head. "Not too good, Kalina. She's not eating like she's supposed to. She's lost a lot of weight. Did you make any progress with her today?"

"No," Kalina said. "I try to remain hopeful, but deep down, I know the days of her making progress are not coming."

"And that leads me to her need for a walker. I don't know if you noticed, but she's very unstable now."

"Yes, I noticed. Do I just go to a pharmacy and pick up a walker? How does that work?"

"Well, you could pick up one from a pharmacy, or we could order it here and bill you for it if it would be more convenient?"

"Yes, please do. My schedule has been so hectic, I haven't had time to look into it."

"Okay. No problem. We'll take care of it."

Kalina sighed. "She hasn't been wandering the halls again, has she?"

"No, not this week. With her limited mobility, I don't foresee it being an issue going forward. She's been asking for Stanley almost every day, though."

"Yeah. I know," Kalina said. "She told me he was coming to get her or something."

"Stanley is her husband, correct?"

"*Was* her husband. My father left us when mom was diagnosed with Alzheimer's."

Joan shook her head.

"You know what I find amazing and sad all at the same time?" Kalina asked.

"What's that?"

"I've been coming here every week since she was admitted and she doesn't know my name, doesn't know who I am, but she knows the name of the man who left her high and dry when things got complicated."

Joan shook her head again.

Kalina sighed. That was baffling to her. It's not

like her father came to visit the woman he said he'd love forever. He cut Madeline and Kalina out of his life and didn't have a problem with moving forward and starting his own life. The more Kalina thought about it, the angrier she became. If her father was worth anything, he would've stayed, helped his wife through the process and maybe he would've been what she needed to hang on to her memories a little while longer.

Kalina rubbed her eyes. There was no need to ask herself why bad things happened to good people, or why this adversity had to strike her family. All she could do was cope with it the best way she knew how – by keeping herself excessively occupied so her mind couldn't think on other things. Depressing things. It was her only coping mechanism at this point.

CHAPTER 4

When Kalina left the facility, she drove to her aunt's house. Edith had hired a few college students to run the café on the weekends so she could have a break from working Monday through Friday.

Kalina tapped on the front door and said, "Edith, it's me," turning the knob and pushing the door open.

"Come on in, Kalina," she heard her aunt say from the kitchen.

She could smell chicken and dumpling soup, one of her aunt's specialties. The aroma took her back to her teenage years, especially around the time when Edith had decided to take her and her mother in. For two years she struggled to assist Madeline. She cooked for her, helped her bathe and do simple personal care tasks such as brush her teeth, help her dress and comb her hair. But when it got to be too much for her to handle, she made the painful decision to place Madeline in an assisted living facility. Even though it was the right decision to make, it still broke her heart.

"Smells good in here," Kalina said, peeping around the door, watching her aunt work. Edith had on a flowery dress with a plain, white apron tied around it.

"Have a seat so you can get yourself some of this soup, sweetie."

"I sure will. I need some comfort food right about now." Kalina pulled out a chair, sat down and rubbed her eyes.

"So I take it your visit didn't go too well today."

Kalina blew a breath. "That's an understatement."

"Was she asking for Stanley again?"

"Sure was…all the while I'm thinking if she knew how much of a jerk her *precious* Stanley really is…"

"Now, now, Kalina. He's still your father."

"Father or not…I don't claim him and I never will. I mean, how do you just pack up and walk out on your family? Are men really that selfish?"

"People grieve in different ways, dear," Edith said, placing a bowl of soup in front of Kalina before returning to the stove.

With raised eyebrows, Kalina said, "Grieve? He deserted me and my mother, then had the audacity to marry another woman. How is that grieving? That's not grieving. That's called being selfish."

Edith joined her at the table with a bowl of her own soup. "Well, rest assured…not all men are like that."

"How can you be so sure?"

"Because some people take their vows seriously."

Kalina took a spoonful of soup to her mouth, savoring it. "This is delicious as always, Edith. Thank you."

"You're welcome."

Kalina shoveled a few more spoonfuls in her mouth and then asked, "You know, I've been wondering something about you."

"What have you been wondering about me?" Edith asked, giving Kalina an inquisitive stare.

"Why didn't you ever marry and have kids, Edith?"

Edith chuckled. "That's an easy answer. It wasn't in my plan."

"Your plan?"

"Yes. I never had the desire to have children or a family. Most people thought I was strange for not wanting that kind of life, but I didn't want to go down that path."

"So what *did* you want?"

"I wanted my own business. I wanted to be successful. Now don't get me wrong...when you came along, not only was it one of the happiest days of Madeline's life. It was one of the happiest of mine, too."

Kalina smiled.

"When you were a baby, you had the biggest cheeks ever known to man, and that dimple of yours made people gush over you."

"I still have that dimple. See." Kalina worked up an intentional smile so Edith could see it.

"You sure do...and you grew up to be such a beautiful woman. Madeline would be so proud of you if she had the capacity to comprehend all you have accomplished."

Kalina's smile turned to sadness as long streaks of tears ran down her cheeks. It had already been a rough day of seeing her mother so disoriented and out of it. All the tears she held in from earlier in the day were finally escaping her sad eyes.

"Oh, Kalina, sweetie," Edith said, reaching to place a hand on Kalina's forearm.

"It's just not fair," Kalina cried. "And I know it sounds so…juvenile to say something like that, but I struggle with this, Edith. I don't understand why this had to happen to my mother. She doesn't even know me." Kalina dabbed her nose. "She doesn't know who I am and she will die not knowing who I am."

"Trust me, Kalina. I know how you feel, honey. Over the years, I thought it would get easier, but it hasn't. It has only gotten more difficult."

Kalina sniffled and wiped tears from her face with a napkin. "It's like watching her die a little every day. Now, she needs a walker. Pretty soon, she probably won't be able to walk at all, even *with* a walker…"

Edith nodded.

"I can't wrap my head around this disease. I see what it has done to her, and it's still hard for me to understand. And, for the life of me, I can't figure out how mom still knows Stanley's name, but not mine."

"Well, once upon a time, your father was special to her. And boy did she love that man."

Kalina dabbed her eyes. "Yeah…too bad he didn't love her."

Edith shook her head. "Is that why you've chosen to stay single all of these years, Kalina? You're afraid someone is going to do that to you?"

"I wouldn't say I'm afraid…I just don't trust men and I promised I would never put myself in that predicament."

"But you can't predict the future, honey, nor can you judge a whole gender of people by the actions of one person."

"But I can. How a girl is treated by her father is how she will view men in general. I can't remember most of my childhood. I do recall some happy occasions with my father, but what I remember, as a teen, was him saying he couldn't do it anymore….couldn't live with her, which meant he also couldn't live with me. I don't even think he hugged me before he walked out the door. He just left. That's what I remember about him…watching him walk away."

"But, Kalina—"

"And," Kalina interrupted, holding up her index finger. "Studies have shown that women tend to fall for men who have personalities and behaviors similar to that of their father. My father proved himself to be distrustful, unfaithful, disloyal and incapable of displaying real love. I don't want to fall for a man like that. So, for my own sake, I need to avoid men altogether since I don't know how to choose a man for myself. My father ruined that for me."

Edith shook her head. "You and that behavioral degree…"

Kalina chuckled. Her tears had since dried up. "I'm serious though, Edith. Why would I fall in love with a man, only for him to walk out of my life? I'm perfectly fine being single. I like my life like this, and honestly, I don't have room for a relationship. I don't even have the mindset to *think* about a relationship. I have enough on my plate with my mother, her living expenses, medical supplies, medication…I have to focus on my job so I can to make the money required to handle all of this. I have close to two-hundred emails to answer as we speak." Kalina took a sip of water.

"You should really try to get someone to help you with the emails, Kalina. You can't be stressed out like this all the time."

"I know. I'm keeping my fingers crossed for this intern."

Edith took a sip of tea then said, "Hey, did Bryson ever get back to you?"

"Bryson?" Kalina rolled her eyes. "Did you really just bring him up over dinner?"

"Well, I overheard your conversation with him and was curious."

Kalina dropped her spoon in the bowl. "Edith, how…on…earth do you know that man?"

"He answered that for you…he's a regular."

"Well, he didn't have to *invite* himself into our conversation. That was beyond rude."

"He was probably bored. He usually comes in and reads the paper or play around on his iPad. I've never seen him come in with anyone else. He's always alone."

Kalina took her phone from her purse and checked her emails. She told Bryson to respond to her reader's question by tonight, but she hadn't given him a specific time. It was already after seven and she didn't see an email from him. "And no, he hasn't responded, not like I expected him to. He looked like he was nothing but talk, anyway. No action."

"Well, the night isn't over yet, Kalina. He may surprise you."

"I won't hold my breath."

"So you don't think he'll respond?" Edith asked.

"I don't. I think he butted into our conversation just to meet me for some reason. You know, you should probably start locking the doors to the café at night."

Edith laughed. "Honey, Bryson is harmless."

"To you, he is. You know him. I don't. All I know about him is that he's rude, nosy and he thinks he knows more about relationships than I do."

"Hmm..."

"Uh oh...what was that for, Edith?"

"I just had the perfect idea. Why don't you get Bryson to help you with your emails?"

Kalina shook her head. "No way."

"Come on, Kalina. Why not?"

"How about because I don't *know* him? He does not have what it takes to do what I do. Everybody thinks my job is so easy, but it's not. That's why I told him to email me. I wanted to prove a point. I knew he would back out."

"Technically he hasn't backed out."

"Sure looks that way to me," Kalina said, scrolling through her email inbox on her cell phone.

"Okay, then I'll make a little bet with you."

"A bet? Since when do you make bets, Edith?"

Edith chuckled. "Never, but I'm going to make an exception this time. If Bryson sends a response to your reader's question by midnight, then you will agree to let him help you answer further emails until you get your inbox under control."

Amused, Kalina asked, "Are you serious?"

"I sure am. Now, do we have a deal?"

Kalina shook her head.

"What do you have to lose, Kalina? You said he wasn't going to respond, right? So you have nothing to worry about, right?"

"If I agree to this and Bryson responds to the email, what if his answer is unacceptable?"

"I'll review his answer, and if it passes my inspection, you will let him help you with the other emails. Okay?"

"Deal."

CHAPTER 5

Kalina returned home after finishing another bowl of soup. And, instead of spending her Saturday night hanging out with Lizette, a friend who also doubled as her employee, she was busy in her home office, replying to emails:

Question: We've been together for a year. I know he's *not* the one, but why is it so hard for me to leave?

Kalina quickly typed a reply. She'd answered this same question so many times before, the answer came automatically:

It's hard for you to leave because you've established a relationship with this man. If you're absolutely certain he's not the one, then not only are you hurting yourself. You're hurting him, too and wasting precious time. You need to sit down, have a conversation with him, let him know how you really feel and go from there.

She quickly went on to the next question:

Question: I've been dating this guy for three years and he will not make a commitment. Every time I bring it up, he tells me he's not ready. I feel like I'm wasting my time. Should I stay or go?

Kalina's response:

I think you know what you need to do. Instead of seeking validation, you should let him know you're serious about a commitment. He's been able to push it off for three years, so in his mind, he's thinking, what's another three years? If he wants you, he will not let you stay 'out there' and risk the possibility of someone else snatching you up.

Kalina took a breath, leaned back in her office chair and swiveled around to the television where the ten o'clock news was airing. The meteorologist was forecasting rain most of next week. More rain equaled more emails. Seemed the gloominess of miserable, rainy days made women, and men alike, ponder their relationship woes. The last stretch of rain had produced nearly eight hundred emails. Kalina was already behind. How would she ever catch up if all she ever did was fall behind?

Okay, Kalina. Focus.

She turned back to her computer screen, popped her knuckles and said, "All right. Who's next?"

Question: I've been seeing this guy for three months now and he will not take me out in public. I tried to recommend a restaurant last weekend, and he found a reason why he couldn't go, canceling at the last minute. Does this mean he's ashamed to take me out in public, or does he already have a girlfriend and doesn't want anyone to see him with me?

Kalina quickly replied:

It could mean that he is ashamed of you, but most likely, he's seeing someone else and doesn't want to get caught. Sweetie, if you're with a man and you feel he doesn't want to take you out and be seen with you, then this is not the man for you.

She clicked *send* then, as she was about to click on the next email, she saw a new email arrive in her inbox:

FROM: Bryson Blackstone
TO: Kalina Cooper
SUBJECT: Answer

Hi Kalina.

I used most of the day to think about the question from your reader, and I've finally come up with an answer. So, here goes:

It may be painful, but there is no reason why you should leave a man you love – a man that's been faithful to you, a man you married – because he's not ready to have a baby right now. Marriage is about making sacrifices. If you make this sacrifice for him, then surely, when the time is right whether it be two years or five years, he'll make the same sacrifice for you if the love and respect is mutual. Why don't you forgo the baby talk for now to help him chase his dreams? Let him know you're willing to put off having children a little while longer, but that you are serious about having a baby. Take it one day at a time. When the time is right, it will happen. Whatever you decide to do, please do not give him an ultimatum. Men hate those.

Good luck.
--
B. Blackstone

———

Kalina sat back in her chair, thinking that, not only was his answer brilliant, but it was well thought-out, well said. She couldn't have said it better herself. Where had Bryson gotten so much insight into relationships? Steve Harvey? Or did he learn a lot from his own experiences of jumping in and out of relationships? Probably the latter. He looked like the player type.

Kalina closed her eyes, thinking about her aunt's bet. Why did she agree to it? When Edith read his response, she would automatically declare herself the winner of the bet. *And then I would have to let Bryson help me out with these emails. Ugh. I'd rather just do it myself.* Then it dawned on her – what if Bryson didn't want to do it. Surely the man had some sort of a day job. Maybe he wouldn't have the time to do this anyway. That would make her day.

FROM: Kalina Cooper
TO: Bryson Blackstone
SUBJECT: Re: Answer

Sounds good. I'll send your reply her way. Thx.

--
Kalina Cooper
Editor | CEO
The Cooper Files

———

Kalina answered another question then she saw a reply from Bryson. Was the man sitting in front of his computer or what?

FROM: Bryson Blackstone
TO: Kalina Cooper
SUBJECT: Re: Answer

I thought we could discuss it before you sent it. You're the expert. Not me. I want you to tweak it if some things are a little *off*. Will you be at Edith's Café Monday evening?

--

B. Blackstone

———

Kalina rolled her eyes. Nothing about his email needed to be tweaked, and she had a feeling he knew that already. Was he doing this to see her again? Trying to set up a date on the sly just so they could discuss his email? Kalina wasn't buying it. Still, she knew she would be at the café. Normally, she was there every weekday after work. So she responded back, told him they could discuss it on Monday evening. He replied again, confirming, then had the audacity to tell her to relax and put the laptop down. She could see that sneaky grin on his face now.

She stood, left her office, then went to the kitchen to grab a wine cooler. When she saw Lizette calling, she quickly answered the phone.

"Hey, Lizzie."

"Hey, woman. How'd it go with your mom?"

"Oh my gosh...I don't even want to talk about it."

"That bad, huh?"

"Yes. Bad. She kept asking for my no-good-father again and she's losing her balance now, so I had the facility order a walker for her. That about sums it up. What have you been up to today?"

"Nothing much...the usual Saturday stuff. Did some shopping, laundry—"

"That reminds me...I have to do laundry tomorrow," Kalina said, popping the top off the Sangria cooler and taking a quick swig. "I swear I need a personal assistant. There just isn't enough time in the day."

"Girl, I hear you. By the way, did you put a dent in those emails yet?"

"I'm getting there. I answered about fifty today. I still need to get an intern, although my aunt seems to have another idea."

"What do you mean?"

"Okay, so there's this guy she knows from her coffee shop. Apparently, he's a regular customer. So he overheard me discussing one of the reader questions with my aunt and he decided to call me out, saying that I didn't know how to answer the question, correctly. So I tossed it back to him, gave him my card and told him to email me with what *his* response would be, you know, just to shut him up and prove my point. I knew he wouldn't email me back. So my aunt decides to bet me that if he *did* email me, and she found his answer to be acceptable, then I would *have* to let him help me answer other emails which would help me get my inbox under control. Which would, in turn, eliminate my need for an intern."

"Girl, don't tell me he actually emailed you?"

"He sure did."

"And was his answer any good."

"It was...spoken like a true professional, but I don't have time to baby-sit anyone, especially a man. You know me...I don't do small talk, chit chat...none of that nonsense."

"Well, you said he answered the question professionally, right, so maybe he's a professional...a get-right-down-to-business type of guy who doesn't like small talk either."

"I can only hope." Kalina took another sip.

Lizette grinned. "What's his name, by the way?"

"Bryson Blackstone," Kalina responded in an exasperated sigh.

"Oh. I know a few Blackstones."

"As do I...doesn't mean I want to know him, though."

"So what are you going to do? Tell your aunt he didn't respond?"

"Nah...I can't lie to my aunt. The only thing I can do is try to convince this guy that doing this would be a waste of his time. It's not like I'm going to pay him anything."

"What if he doesn't care about being compensated?"

Kalina shrugged. "Then I guess I don't have a choice but to work with him....and saying that out loud just made my stomach hurt."

"It won't be that bad, Kalina. Besides, you don't even know if he'll accept."

"Whatever the case, my stomach still hurts."

Lizette chuckled.

"Anyway, did you finish the blog post for Monday?"

"I did. I left it in draft form for you. You will see it on your dashboard when you log in."

"All right. Thanks, girl."

"No problem. Now try to get some sleep."

"Okay. See you Monday."

After setting her phone on the countertop, Kalina turned up the bottle to her mouth and finished the wine cooler. Then she quickly ran upstairs, grabbed her laptop before retreating to her bedroom. She sat on the bed with a few pillows behind her back for support. Then she opened the laptop and positioned it on top of her thighs. She didn't know how she would do it, but she made it a goal to get through at least fifty more emails before she fell asleep.

CHAPTER 6

Brnnng. Brnnnng!

"Huh?" Kalina said, startled, sitting straight up in her bed, her hair all over the place, even falling in front of her face, restricting her vision. She looked like a sleep-deprived *Cousin Itt*. Using her fingers, she brushed her hair from her face then looked around for her cell phone. She usually remembered to set her phone to silent before bed, but since she'd fallen asleep while working, she'd completely forgotten about it.

Brnnng. Brnnnng!

"Give me a flippin' break," she said when she couldn't find her cell. It was somewhere in the bed. Under a pillow? Between the sheets? Tangled in the comforter?

Brnnng. Brnnnng!

Frustrated, Kalina raked all the pillows off the bed and there was her phone. It had since stopped ringing.

Figures...

She took a moment to collect herself. She didn't know what time she had fallen asleep in the wee hours of the morning, but what she *did* know is that she wasn't ready to get up right this instant. If she'd set the phone properly, she'd still be sleeping.

She pressed a button to turn on the screen and

when she realized the missed call was from Edith, she dialed her right back.

"Good morning, Kalina," Edith answered cheerily.

"Good morning, Edith," Kalina said, followed by a long yawn. "What's going on?"

"Just wanted to see if you would like to do breakfast, or shall I say brunch, this morning. It's shaping up to be a gorgeous May day."

"Umm…what time is it?"

"It's a little after eleven. What's wrong? Did you not get any sleep last night?"

"I did. I'm fine, and yes, we can meet for brunch. Did you have a place in mind?"

"What about the Omelet House? You want to meet me there in…let's say thirty minutes?"

"Sure," Kalina responded, raking her hair from her face again. "I'll meet you there."

"Okay, sweetie. See you soon."

Kalina placed her phone on the nightstand, rubbed her eyes, let out another long yawn and said, "I so need a personal assistant. Ugh." She fell back on the bed, staring up at the ceiling, dreading the day already.

* * *

When she arrived at the Omelet House, Kalina spotted Edith sitting at a booth next to the windows. Sleepy and all, she managed to work up a sincere smile for the woman who raised her when her mother wasn't able to. And it amazed her how much Madeline and Edith looked alike, well before her mother became ill. Edith had gray hair all over, cut and cropped into a short style of curls that blended well with the oval shape of her face.

Kalina gave Edith a kiss on the cheek and said, "Don't you look lovely this morning." Edith was wearing a ruffled, coral top and a white blazer with a pair of dark brown slacks.

"I try," Edith responded.

"I know I look a hot mess. I need some coffee. Has a server been by yet?"

"Yes. I told her to bring two cups of coffee."

"Good," Kalina said, picking up the menu, browsing through the breakfast side of it.

A few minutes later, the server returned with the coffee. Edith and Kalina went ahead and ordered their breakfast, then Edith asked, "So, did Bryson email you back?"

Kalina glanced up at her aunt. "He did."

"And?"

"What do you mean?"

"Was his answer any good?"

"You were supposed to be the judge of that, remember?" Kalina took out her phone, pulled up her email account then clicked on Bryson's email, handing the phone to Edith and watching her read it. When she saw the smile grow on Edith's face, she knew she was in trouble.

"Yes. That's perfect. Now, tomorrow when you're at the café, ask him to help you answer some of the emails. He's obviously a smart man."

"How do you know he's smart? Just because he can answer an email doesn't make him smart."

"Well, he does own his own business."

"Doing what?"

"He owns a tree service."

Unenthused, Kalina said, "Well, I'll ask him about the emails, but only because I'm a woman of my word and a bet is a bet."

Edith smiled. "Good. Hopefully he says yes. You need all the help you can get."

Kalina took a sip of coffee.

"If your father had stayed around, do you think your life would be different?" Edith asked.

"Different, how?"

"Well, do you think you would view men differently? Maybe had gotten married, had some children and—"

"I don't know, but I don't want to speculate, because I don't want those things anyway so…"

"You don't want to get married and have children?"

"No…guess I got that from you. I like waking up and working without the distraction of a child."

"But there's more to life than working yourself to death, Kalina."

Kalina chuckled. "Spoken by a woman who works herself to death."

"At least I take the weekends off. You work all the time."

"Hence, the reason a baby wouldn't fit into my life."

Edith sighed.

"Seriously, Edith…what would I do with a baby?"

"Love it. Nurture it. Take care of it and—"

"Wait, where is all of this coming from?"

"I've been thinking about it for a while now. You're such a beautiful, intelligent woman and I don't want you to grow up and be a lonely, old lady like me. I doubt it's what Madeline would've wanted for you."

"Edith…"

"Hear me out, Kalina. Now I know I told you that this is the life I wanted, but while I am happy with my success, I can't lie. It's been lonely. Extremely lonely."

"But you have friends."

"I do, but I'm at home alone. I go to bed alone, and I wake up alone. I don't have anyone to share my life with. To sit on the front porch, on a damp Saturday morning, and share a cup of coffee with. To go for a walk on these beautiful days ahead of us. When I'm sad, when I feel overwhelmed and even when I just want to feel loved, I—" Edith paused, gathering her thoughts as her lips trembled.

Kalina reached across the table and clutched Edith's hand. She didn't know how touchy this subject was for her until now – until she watched her normally impassive, strong-minded aunt, who rarely displayed any emotions, almost break down right before her eyes.

Edith swallowed hard, her eyes glazed over and continued, "I don't have anyone there to throw their arms around me and tell me everything will be all right. And I'll admit that I do manage to keep myself busy most days, but it would be nice to have someone there. Are you telling me you don't want that?"

Kalina sighed. No, she didn't want that, but she

would be lying if she said she hadn't thought about settling down with someone special and having children. The only problem was, she couldn't trust a man, and she'd never let a man claim ownership of her heart. "I have thought about it, Edith, but I have trust issues which prohibits me from acting on that thought, and I know I could never trust a man to fulfill that role in my life."

The waitress brought their food over and, after making sure they had everything they needed, she told them she'd be right back to refill their coffee then walked away.

Edith took a napkin, dabbed the corner of her eyes and let go of a slight chuckle. "You were always a stubborn girl."

Kalina grinned. "I remember mom saying that about me when I was like…ten years old."

"She was telling the truth, honey. I'll be the first to let you know that right now."

"Well, there are some issues I can bend on, but I do not want to be connected to a man, especially not at this point in my life. I'm doing good on my own. If the blog continues increasing in popularity, I'll be close to two-hundred thousand dollars this year. I don't need a man to share that success with. I'm perfectly fine with popping champagne with you and Lizette, thank you very much."

Edith chuckled while simultaneously shaking her head. "Stubborn or not, you grew up to be an amazing woman. Madeline would've been so proud."

"Thanks Edith." Kalina cut a slice of her omelet, stabbed it with a fork then took it to her mouth. She glanced around the restaurant. The place was crowded to the point where every table was occupied. And the sunlight peering through the windows was a beautiful reminder that summer was just around the corner.

She remembered how the last few summers had been stressful for her. Still building her company, she'd devoted a lot of time into making the blog work. It had her thinking that maybe if she had someone special in her life, she wouldn't have to worry about the day-to-day struggles. She would have a helper. She wouldn't be lonely. She would have someone to walk with on the beach and share intimate, romantic dinners. She would have a shoulder to lean on when times were tough. Then she snapped back into reality…

Her mother thought she had someone to lean on, but that proved to be a sham. Kalina couldn't let that happen in her own life. It was better to be single with no expectations, than to be in a relationship filled with expectations that went unfulfilled and possibly ended when the *man* decided he'd had enough.

CHAPTER 7

Bryson watched as Kalina stepped into the café wearing a pair of ripped jeans, a low, V-neck purple T-shirt and a pair of black flats. She was five-feet, eight inches if he had to guess, and her milk chocolate skin tone was a shade lighter than his own. Her long, black hair was tussled about – looked like someone had been playing in it, or better yet, like she'd driven across town with all the windows down on her car. Still he liked it – the way it framed her face and fell all around her shoulders. The look suited her well. Then there was her dainty nose and those plump lips he couldn't seem to keep his eyes off of – lips that had probably never been kissed.

"Didn't think you were going to show for a minute there," Bryson said to her. He had already made himself comfortable at the table she'd dubbed as hers.

And he has the nerve to sit at my table. She narrowed her eyes at him. The sight of him sitting there made her nose twitch. Even his sly comment didn't sit well with her, so she responded, "Women usually don't have problems keeping their commitments, unlike your kind."

"Tell me something…are you normally this rude, or did you save all of your frustrations to take them out on me?"

"No, I'm not rude, and don't flatter yourself…you're not important enough for me to take out my frustrations on you."

Bryson smirked. He'd crossed paths with her kind before – the fist in the air, independent woman who had to exude an air about herself in order to assert her self-importance. Kalina, however, had set the bar even higher. One thing was for certain – she never crossed paths with a man like him. Otherwise her attitude would've been checked a long time ago.

Before she said anything further to him, she walked to the counter to speak to Edith.

"Hi there, Kalina," Edith responded, all smiles. She quickly gave Kalina the thumbs up because Bryson was there. "How do you want your coffee?"

With a double shot of liquor. "Surprise me." Kalina returned her attention to the table, looking at Bryson.

What in the world have I gotten myself into?

She continued to the table and placed her laptop bag next to the chair as she sat down. Unzipping her bag, she removed her laptop, placed it on the table and folded the screen up, looking up at Bryson at the same time.

"I know you're eager to get this over with," Bryson said, "So I'll tell you the part of my response that I was questioning. Do you think it was right for me to tell your reader to forego the baby talk and help her husband build his dreams?"

Kalina quickly pulled up his email again and scanned through it. "Um…that's one approach. You have to remember…just because you suggest something to someone doesn't necessarily mean they're going to take your advice."

"I'm well aware of that."

"And honestly, I think your entire email was a good, solid answer to the woman's question."

"Even the part about men not liking ultimatums?"

"Yes. Especially that part. Men *don't* like ultimatums. Women neither."

"All right. I guess my job here is done," he said, reaching across the table for a handshake. "Oh, that's right...you don't shake hands."

"No, I don't, and while you're still sitting here, I need to..." Kalina braced herself. *Stupid bet.* "Um, since you're pretty much at the café in the evenings, I was wondering if you would be available to help me answer more emails like this for the next month until I'm caught up."

"I'm sorry, I don't think I heard you correctly. You want *me* to help you answer these?"

No. "Yes. Only if you have the time and if you want to. I won't be able to pay you anything though."

"Hmm," he said, sitting back in his chair, not believing what he was hearing. She was asking him for help when normally, she acted like she couldn't stand the sight of him. If Edith hadn't called him and given him the heads up about the bet she made with Kalina, he would be completely in the dark. And since he knew Kalina couldn't pay him, especially being that she already had one full-time employee, her mother's expenses and her own bills, he would use it to his advantage. So sitting up in his chair again, he asked, "You've already taken compensation off the table, so what's in this for me?"

Kalina shrugged. "The satisfaction of knowing you're helping someone with their issues...I don't know."

"Or helping you," he said.

"If you want to look at it that way..."

"Yes. I do want to look at it that way."

No. No. No! This can't be happening. "Okay so, to be clear, you're agreeing to do this."

He nodded and said, "I am, but I want to lay down some ground rules."

One eyebrow raised, Kalina asked, "And what might those be?"

"We will sit together, side-by-side so you can see my computer screen and—"

"That won't be necessary," she interjected. "In fact, we don't even need to sit together, period. I will forward the emails to you and all you have to do is send your responses back to me."

Bryson shook his head. Clearing his throat, he repeated, "We will sit together, side-by-side so you can see my computer screen and we will work together."

Jerk. "You're being difficult."

He chuckled. "That's what you call it when someone doesn't play by your rules, huh?"

"No. That's what I call it when someone is trying to be controlling."

"Controlling?" he repeated, amused.

"Yes. Controlling."

"Call it what you will, but this is how it's going

to go, or you can count me out. Oh, and another thing," he said, standing. "I shake hands with people I do business with." He extended his hand to her and said, "Now, are we doing business?"

"Yes. I guess we are," Kalina said caving into his wishes by reaching for his hand, accepting his grasp, feeling his strong hand firmly squeeze her small, dainty one. Had she ever shaken a man's hand before?

"Good. Now, I can't stay this evening. I have a prior engagement, but we'll start tomorrow evening if that's good with you."

"Yeah. That's fine. Can I have my hand back now?"

"Sure," he said releasing his grip on her hand. "See you tomorrow, Kalina."

"All right then. See you tomorrow, Kalina."

With that, he walked away, waving at Edith before he exited.

Kalina hung her head. What had she gotten herself into?

* * *

Edith smiled at the exchange she witnessed between Kalina and Bryson. Unknown to Kalina, it wasn't a coincidence she made the bet. It was a bet she knew she would win. Bryson was an intelligent man. Edith remembered when she first met him. It was three years ago when a hurricane has brushed the North Carolina coast, leaving downed trees in her front yard. Short staffed at the time, Bryson had personally made the trip to her house to clean up the trees.

Later that week, he'd stopped by her café on a whim, surprised to see Edith again. And since that day, he'd been coming back to the café, every now and then, as a place to relax after work. His visits became more frequent around two years ago, when he divorced his wife. He'd spoken briefly to Edith about it and said nothing more of it. It was a topic he preferred to avoid, which is probably the reason why he began limiting his trips to her café. He didn't want her to bring up the subject.

It wasn't until recently, about a month ago, that Bryson had begun frequenting the café again, enquiring about the woman who showed up there every evening with her laptop, discussing relationship issues with Edith. And a delightful smile came to Edith's face when he had inquired about Kalina. She told him that Kalina was her *single* niece who wasn't interested in dating if that's what he had in mind. Still, he came in every weekday for the last four weeks to watch Kalina work. He didn't tell Edith he was somewhat aware of who Kalina was, especially since finding an email she had written to Felicia. It was *that* email that made him want to meet Kalina...made him want to know her.

Edith, aware of Bryson's situation, knew he had no plans to ever marry again. He wouldn't tolerate another woman doing to him what his ex-wife had done. So why was he so intrigued with Kalina? At any rate, Edith saw a way to use his curiosity to her advantage. What better way was there for Bryson to get to know Kalina than to work with her every day? To help her? Surely she would appreciate the help and he would, no doubt, enjoy her company. A woman who doesn't believe in love meets the man who'd given up on love – what was the worst that could happen?

"Here you go, sweetie," Edith said, placing a cup of house blend with cream and sugar on the table.

"Thanks, Edith," Kalina said, downcast.

"You're welcome." Edith sat across from her. "You look upset."

"I'm not sure I can do this, Edith. Can you call off the bet?"

"Why would I do that? You need the help, sweetie. Let the man help you."

Kalina took a deep breath. "I don't have time in my life for anything or anyone extra. He's already puffing his chest out and being demanding and—"

"It'll be fine. Just wait until you get those emails under control. You'll be thanking him in no time. Where did he go anyway?"

"He claimed he had somewhere to go…said he'd be back tomorrow." Kalina shook her head. "Maybe if I work through the night, I'll finish all these emails then I won't need his help."

"No, you are not working through the night. You need rest like everybody else. You are not superwoman, Kalina Cooper."

When the bell chimed, Edith glanced up and saw a few customers come inside the café. "Let me help them."

Kalina took another sip of coffee and began reading and answering emails. She would worry about Bryson later. Right now, she had work to do.

CHAPTER 8

"This steak is phenomenal, Barringer," Bryson said to his brother as he cut another chunk of it. The family dinner, this month, was at Barringer's house. And, as a part of the tradition, all the food had to be home-cooked – no store-bought items, even down to the dessert. Barringer and his wife, Calista had prepared the entire meal.

"It really is, Barry," Candice said. "It's juicy and tender."

"I'm glad you like it, but I can't take credit for it. Calista cooked it," Barringer finally said, glancing up at Calista. She hadn't bothered looking up at him, still fuming from an argument that erupted between them before everyone had arrived. Thank goodness his parents were out of the country. Surely they would have noticed Calista's cold attitude right away.

There were four boys and one girl in the Blackstone family. At thirty-eight, Bryson was the oldest. Then came Barringer at thirty-six, married to Calista. Garrison, thirty-four was married to Vivienne. Everson, thirty-two was married to June. And the only girl, Candice, twenty-eight, was single. If her brothers had their way, she would stay single. They were overly protective of their sister, especially Bryson.

"Well, it's delicious, Calista," Candice reiterated.

"Thank you, guys," Calista finally responded, forcing a smile to her face. She didn't want to do this family dinner tonight. She wanted to retreat to her bedroom, cry herself to sleep as she'd done most of the week, but Barringer had begged her to be here. He didn't want the family to know they were having issues. His mother nearly had a stroke when Bryson divorced Felicia. If Elowyn Blackstone thought another divorce was on the horizon, she would probably have a heart attack.

Barringer cleared his throat to the take the attention away from Calista's fake smile. He said, "So, first things first…we need to figure out who's hosting next month."

"We can't," Everson spoke up. "June and I are going on vacation for a couple of weeks and I have a lot of business travel coming up."

"What about you, Candice?" Garrison asked. "It's been a while since we were all at your apartment."

Already shaking her head, Candice said, "Can't do it. I may be able to in the fall. It's Bryson's turn to host anyway."

The dining room went quiet. Forks and spoons had ceased clanking against ceramic plates. Side conversations stopped and, for a moment, it seemed as if time stood still. All eyes were on Bryson. He hadn't hosted a family dinner at his home since the divorce. Candice knew that. Everybody knew that. It was the reason no one ever asked him to host dinner because they already knew the answer. They also knew the divorce was a touchy subject for him.

Remaining calm, something he had perfected over the years, Bryson looked up at his sister and said, "I'm not hosting. I don't have a wife at home to help me cook, remember?"

"Well, I don't have a husband," Candice tossed back.

"That's because you're not mature enough for one," Bryson told her. He wasn't trying to be mean-spirited. He truly believed his sister wasn't ready for a real relationship which could eventually lead to marriage, especially based on the men she chose to date – men who proved to be unworthy of her time.

"Well let's just hope I do a better job of choosing a husband than you did at choosing your trifling wife," Candice shot back. It irked her when her brother tried to act more like a father than a brother. She didn't need that from him.

"Come on, guys," Garrison said. The family dubbed him the mediator of the bunch because he always tried to find a solution to problems where his family was concerned. "Let's not get into this right now. Jeez. Me and Vivienne hosted last month and, if need be, we'll do it again next month. Okay. Problem solved."

Bryson took a sip of wine. "You know what...I'll do it. Family dinner at my house next month. There."

"You don't have to do that, Bryce," Garrison told him.

"No, I got it, and whoever feels so compelled to

come over and help me cook, be my guest. And if no one shows up, I'll do it all on my own."

Silence.

No one had a word to say after Bryson had offered to host the dinners for next month. They knew how hard the divorce had been on him – at least the brothers did. Candice was still in college at the time.

"Well, we would host," Garrison said, "But certain smells makes Vivienne queasy now since we're expecting."

Vivienne smiled wide and kissed Garrison on the cheek.

The room suddenly erupted in congratulations and cheers.

"I'm only two months along," Vivienne said. "I know you're technically not supposed to tell anyone until you're out of the woods as they say, but I couldn't hide it anymore."

Bryson stood up and walked over to his brother, giving him a pat on the back. "Congrats man."

Barringer and Everson followed suit while Garrison leaned back in his chair.

The women walked over to Vivienne and gave her a hug – well all the woman except for Calista. She was happy for her sister-in-law, but she was struggling with her own issues when it came to having babies. She wanted them, but Barringer seemed to be having second thoughts.

Fighting back tears, Calista left the dining room. Barringer watched as she walked away.

Not feeling in a celebratory mood, Bryson stepped outside to get some air. Being the oldest, everyone assumed he would be the first to have children, especially their parents. After his divorce, he didn't even want to remarry – let alone have children. He was convinced that marriage wasn't for everyone. Neither were children…

"What's up, man?" Garrison asked, stepping out onto the porch. "You good?"

"Yeah. I'm good…just came out here to get some air."

"Listen, Bryson…Viv and I will host the family next month. I don't want to put you through that, man. You don't talk much about it, but I can only imagine how difficult it must've been to go through the divorce and all."

Bryson frowned. It *was* difficult to talk about. In fact, he hadn't spoken to anyone about it. All they knew was that it had taken a toll on him. But he kept on working, pretending he was over the affair and divorce when the reality was, those events that threw his life off track, still churned inside of his heart. Still angered him. After all, he did love Felicia. And he was the model husband for her – a provider, a lover, her confidant. Everything. But she apparently needed more than what he could give.

"I wish you would talk about it."

Bryson slid his hands inside of his pockets then turned around to look at his brother. He knew what the *it* was that Garrison was referring to. "There's nothing to talk about, Gary. It's over and done with. I have no problems having the dinners at my home." Bryson took his keys from his right pocket. "Tell Barringer I'm out."

With that, he walked to his car, jumped in, then

drove away. He lived ten minutes away from Barringer, in a four-bedroom, two-level brick home. With a two-car garage and an in-ground swimming pool out back – his backyard completely private with an eight-feet brick wall around the perimeter.

And it all meant nothing…

He'd debated selling the house because he couldn't stand that he'd once shared this home with someone who had betrayed him. Had been unfaithful to him. He had replaced all the furniture, rugs, anything Felicia picked out, or anything that reminded him of her was tossed in the trash. But that still didn't rid him of her presence.

He pulled up in the driveway, sitting there looking at the house. Some days he didn't even want to go in. He remembered weeks after the divorce, he stayed at a hotel to avoid the house. It had been easier that way. He shook his head and opened the car door.

I have to get rid of this house, he thought to himself, before getting out of the car and heading to the door.

CHAPTER 9

He'd been staring at her for a good five minutes. Intently. Purposely. He wanted to brand her face into his memory before he peeled back the layers to find out what made Kalina Cooper tick. To help her, he needed to know her. He watched her burgundy lips move as she silently read emails. She was focused on her work, something he admired being a business owner himself. "So is this your full-time job?" he finally asked. They were both sitting on the same side of the table, as he had requested, facing the windows and the front entrance of the café, their backs to the counter. Laptops side-by-side. Legs a scoot away from touching.

"Yes. This is what I do," Kalina responded.

Bryson nodded. According to what he read about her and *The Cooper Files* on her website's *About Me* page, Kalina had taken the idea of starting a blog, used it in conjunction with her college studies and *The Cooper Files* was born. She even had over one-hundred thousand followers on her company's Facebook page.

"Do you play golf?" she asked without even looking up at him, biting her tongue to keep from laughing.

"No. Why do you ask?"

She shrugged. "No reason. You asked me a

question so I thought I'd ask you one. By the way, I just sent you an email," she told him while she was still typing, not missing a beat, her fingers moving impressively around the keyboard while her eyes remained on the computer screen.

"Okay," he said, refreshing his inbox. "Got it." He clicked to open the email she'd forwarded to him:

Question: I've been dating this guy for a year. He says he loves me, but my friends tell me that they've seen him flirting with other girls when I'm not around. So my question is, how can you tell when a man really loves you and not just saying it?

After reading the email, Bryson turned to his right to look at Kalina.

"What?" she asked, feeling his eyes on her.

"Why'd you send me this one?"

"Because you're a man."

"I *am* a man, Kalina. How observant of you," he joked. "I'm actually surprised you know that, especially since you don't look at me much."

Kalina rolled her eyes. She'd gotten two hours of sleep last night and all she wanted to do was get through these emails, not chit chat with Bryson. "I don't have to look at you to know you're a man," she decided to say, even when she knew a response wasn't necessary. And he was right – she didn't look at him much. It would be hard to focus on work if her brain was constantly flooded with images of his face – his stately nose, dark eyes, a bone structure that made him overbearingly masculine and a skin complexion that tempted her want to try one of her aunt's new chocolate-filled pastries. It was bad enough he wore some enchanting cologne that had intoxicated her from the moment he sat down and his hands, those large hands, looked as strong as everything else about him.

"Do you want me to send you a different question instead?" she asked.

"No. This one is fine. I just thought you would want to answer these kinds of questions."

"If you don't want to do it, I will," she told him. "I've answered this question a million times before."

"So tell me what your response would be."

She looked at him, holding his gaze for the first time, seeing something akin to a smirk on his face. Her eyes rolled down to his lips, then back up to his eyes again. Withholding a smile, she asked, "You like to talk, don't you?"

He grinned. "I just find what you do very interesting."

"Why?"

He shrugged his broad shoulders. "I just do."

"Okay, well, my answer is, you can tell if a man likes you because he will bend over backwards to make sure you're happy. He will support you, take care of you, be there for you, be faithful to you and he will not make you feel insecure. Of course I'm only speaking from things I've seen. Things I've learned."

"Things you've learned…"

"Yes."

"So you've never had a man do these things for

you?"

"No." Focusing on the task at hand, she said, "Let me know when you're ready for me to read over your response."

For a moment, Bryson sat there, pondering the question, thinking about all the ways he had loved and devoted his life to making his ex-wife happy. He began typing:

> You'll know if his love his real by his actions, not by mere words. Anyone can tell you they love you. A stranger off the street could walk up to you right now and say they love you, but would you believe them? Obviously not. Why? Because other than the fact that you don't know the person, they haven't demonstrated anything to prove they actually love you. My advice to you is to take some time to sit down and think about what love means to you then ask yourself if that's what you're getting from your boyfriend.

"Okay, boss," Bryson said. "Can you check this one, please?"

"Sure. Give me a sec," she said, finishing her email. Then she leaned over, glanced at his computer screen and read his answer.

Bryson eyes brushed across her hair, as he inhaled the fruity scent coming from it. It must've been the shampoo that had her luscious strands smelling like something he could eat for dessert.

"It's good, but I need you to go a little deeper."

"Deeper?"

"Yes. Deeper. Have you ever been in love, Bryson?"

Bryson thought about his ex-wife again. She was

the only woman he'd ever loved. Before her, he was a bachelor and was very content with that lifestyle. But when he married Felicia, he didn't know he had the capability to feel so much love in his heart. Then she broke it – his heart and his trust.

"Well, have you?" Kalina asked, turning to him again, seeing something painful in the depths of his eyes.

"Yes."

"Then dig deeper," she said, pushing her chair away from the table. She stood up and said, "I'll be right back."

She quickly hurried off to the bathroom, having had two cups of coffee now. When she came out of the stall, she saw Edith standing near the sink.

"So, how's it going?" she asked all girlishly, not something you would expect from a sixty-year-old.

Pumping soap into her hands, Kalina replied, "It's going okay, I guess. It's actually not as bad as I thought it would be. The only downside is, he loves to talk."

Edith grinned. Yeah, he did love to talk. She knew that all too well.

"All right, well, I hope you guys get a lot of work done. Let me get back out here. I'll chat with you before closing."

"Okay, Edith."

Kalina dried her hands, walked back to the table and sat down. "How are you doing?"

"I think I got it this time," he responded. He turned his computer screen her way. "Let me know if that's deep enough for you."

Kalina leaned near him to see his computer

screen again:

> You'll know if a man really love you by what he does and not what he says. Would he forego his own satisfaction to make you happy? Does he do things for you without waiting for you to ask? Does he ask about your day, tells you how beautiful you are? Does he make sacrifices for you? Do you know that, without a shadow of a doubt, your man would give his life for you? If you cannot answer 'yes' to every one of these questions, then your man may just simply like you, but he does not love you. I've never been an advocate for listening to what other people had to say about things that concerned another person's relationship, but sometimes, we have to face the reality that, maybe they're right.

"Good. I like it," Kalina told him. "Just make sure you spell-check it."

"Spell-check?" He read over his email again, realizing his mistake. "Oh…I left the 's' off the word *love* in the first sentence."

"Yep," Kalina said.

Bryson quickly made the correction then asked, "But other than that, you like it?"

"Yes."

"What do you like about it?"

"I like the questions. Those are very good questions, and they'll make her come to her own conclusion. That's typically how I like to respond to questions…they need to be answered in a way which allows the person to formulate their own opinion. We're only giving them something to work with."

"Okay. Got it."

"Good. I'm going to send you ten more emails. Is that okay?" she asked, looking at him, their gazes holding yet again. "What?"

"You seem a lot nicer today for some reason."

She chuckled a bit. "Just in a better mood, I guess. Actually, I seriously don't know how I'm in a better mood after only getting two hours of sleep last night."

Bryson frowned. He had no emotional connection to Kalina, but the fact that she wasn't sleeping bothered him. He'd had his own issues with sleep deprivation a few years back. It was almost to the point where he had to be hospitalized due to a spike in his high blood pressure. It was under control now, and he remembered how the doctor had pointed to his lack of sleep as a cause of it. "Did you say two hours?"

She yawned. "Yes. Two hours."

"That's not good. Not good at all."

"It's fine. I'm used to it."

"You shouldn't be…lack of sleep can lead to some serious health problems, Kalina."

"And how would you know that?"

"Because I've been there before. I almost had to be hospitalized."

"Well, I had a physical back in January and my doctor gave me a clean bill of health. I'm fine."

Kalina proceeded with sending emails to Bryson, then she returned to answering her own emails before hearing her phone vibrate on the table. When she saw it was someone calling from the assisted living facility, she immediately grabbed the phone and answered frantically, "Is everything okay?"

Bryson looked at her the moment he heard the panic in her voice, and while she held the phone, he saw her hands tremble.

"Yes, everything's fine, Ms. Cooper. We just wanted to inform you that your mother's walker has arrived."

"Oh," she said, releasing a sigh of relief but that didn't lessen the hard thumps of her heart. The last time she got a call from the facility, her mother had fallen and hit her head. Now every time they called, it sent her into a state of panic. "Thank...thank you for letting me know."

"You're welcome."

Kalina closed her eyes and inhaled deeply, releasing a slow, steady breath. "Let me know what it costs, and I'll pay for it on Saturday."

"Um...let's see...it was sixty-eight dollars."

Kalina made a note of it. "Perfect. I'll bring a check on Saturday. Thanks for calling."

"All right, Ms. Cooper. Enjoy the rest of your evening."

"You, too." Kalina set her phone on the table again, staring absently at her computer screen.

Bryson turned to look at her. He noticed her hands were arched over her keyboard like she was about to type, but she didn't type a thing. Her hands were still trembling. "Are you okay?" he asked.

Had she heard him? She just sat there, still in a daze.

"Kalina."

She looked at him this time. "Yes?"

"Are you okay?"

"Yes," she said, in a fake, cheery tone. "I'm fine."

"Then why are your hands trembling?"

She looked at her hands and said, "No reason.

Um…are…are you done with the questions I sent you?"

He took a moment to gaze at her before he answered her question. She wasn't fine. Something disturbed her to the point of distracting her from doing her job. He'd only spent a few hours with her and he knew she wasn't a woman who was easily distracted. She was a woman on a mission. A woman who worked to fulfill her purpose of helping people, and the ironic thing about that was, *she* needed help more than anyone. Deciding to let it go for now, he answered her, "I haven't completed them all. Let me get back to work."

Kalina took a few more deep breaths before she was able to start working again.

The moment she began typing, Bryson glanced at her. There was definitely something going on with her and, for some reason, he felt like he needed to know. Who exactly was Kalina Cooper?

CHAPTER 10

"So how are things going at the café with Bryson?" Lizette asked bright and early in the morning when she showed up for work.

Kalina shrugged. "It's going. Yesterday was the first day we worked together, and he seems pretty knowledgeable about relationships."

"Really?"

"Yes. So far, so good."

"Soo…is he married?"

"I don't know."

"Well, was he wearing a ring?"

"No."

"Aha! So you checked?"

Kalina failed to hide a smirk. "No, I didn't check."

"Then how do you know he wasn't wearing a ring?"

"Easy. He has these massively, muscular, strong-looking hands…none like I've ever seen before. You can't miss them."

"So he's not married…"

"I doubt it. I'm sure he would be at home in the evenings if he was, instead of hanging out with me at a café." Kalina didn't know anything about Bryson other than what she'd learned from her aunt.

It seemed weird to be working side-by-side with someone she barely knew.

"Yeah, you're probably right. I'm just surprised he's doing this for free."

"Me, too. He seems to be very—" Kalina stopped mid-sentence when she saw an email in her inbox from Bryson. Why was he emailing her so early in the day? Why was he emailing her at all? He'd already sent answers to the questions she'd assigned to him last night. Curious, she clicked on the email:

From: Bryson Blackstone
To: Kalina Cooper
Subject: You

Have you ever been in love, Kalina?

--

B. Blackstone

———

She couldn't hide the frown in her forehead if she wanted to. Why was he asking her that?

"He seems to be very what, Kalina?" Lizette asked.

"Huh?" Kalina said, looking at Lizette. The frown of confusion remained, along with her rapid heartbeats.

"You were saying something about Bryson."

"Oh, um…never mind," Kalina told Lizette, returning her attention to Bryson's email. Deciding to respond with a simple answer, she replied:

From: Kalina Cooper
To: Bryson Blackstone
Subject: Re: You

No.

--

Kalina Cooper
Editor | CEO
The Cooper Files

———

The disturbance in her forehead smoothed out, and she was back in business mode. "Hey, Lizette, I think we should do an article on what true love is. There seems to be a good number of readers, well women particularly, asking for clues and signs that their significant other truly loves them."

"All right. When are you looking to post it?"

"As soon as possible if it'll reduce the amount of emails in my inbox."

"I hear ya. I'll draft something up today and we can review it in the morning."

"Thanks, Lizzie. Now let me get to work. I'm meeting Isaiah for lunch today."

"Isaiah? You looking for another house?"

"No. Not going through that process again anytime soon. I promised Isaiah I would take him to lunch as a good gesture for all of his hard work in finding this house for me, so it's today or never."

"Didn't you tell me Isaiah had a thing for you?"

"He did, but he knows this is just business. Besides, if I ever did decide to date, the man has to be older than I am. Isaiah is twenty-seven."

"So. He's a grown, single man."

"Your point?"

"He's a grown, single man," Lizette repeated, then laughed.

Kalina laughed too. "Well, women mature earlier than men so I wouldn't go younger. Definitely older."

"How much older...like, what's your cutoff age?"

Kalina grinned. "I don't know, Lizzie. I haven't given it any thought."

"Okay, let me help you out...when you say older, are you talking like Idris Elba older or Denzel Washington older?"

"It would help if I knew how old they were."

"Idris is in his early forties and Denzel is sixty."

Kalina frowned. "Denzel is sixty?"

Lizette laughed. "Never mind. Let me let you get back to work."

Kalina grinned. "Good idea."

* * *

Bryson leaned back in his chair after reading Kalina's one-word response. She answered 'no' and didn't give any further details. She'd never been in love...

It seemed odd for her to have a profession, specializing in helping people with their relationship issues when she had never been in love herself. How could she accurately answer questions about love when she'd never experienced it – the good and bad of it?

Still, she seemed to be pretty good at it. He'd watched her work yesterday and she must've answered ten emails in a matter of minutes. And he couldn't help but recall the way her fingers moved around the keyboard as she typed. He also remembered how her hands were trembling when she had received that phone call.

He'd been tempted to reply back to her email, ask her a follow-up question, but he didn't want to make her uncomfortable. They didn't know each other but were going to be working together for the next month or so, and since he was who he was – the man who took charge and control of his own life – he would change that. He wanted to know her – not just the shell of information she'd made available on her website or even the little he learned about her from Edith. He wanted to get to know her from his own viewpoint and he would, starting this evening.

"Mr. Blackstone," his assistant said, tapping on the door of his office.

"Come in, Rose."

Opening the door, she said, "I found the realtor everyone has been raving about in these parts. His name is Isaiah Russell." She placed a yellow Post-it note on his desk calendar. "Would you like for me to schedule an appointment with him?"

"No. I'll take care of it, Rose. Thank you."

"You're welcome, Sir," she said, leaving his office.

Bryson picked up the note, pressed the speakerphone button on is desk phone and dialed Isaiah's number. When he didn't get an answer, he left a voicemail:

Hi, Mr. Russell, this is Bryson Blackstone calling. I need to sell my house and buy a new one and I need this turned around pretty quickly. I hear you're the go-to guy for this. You can reach me at 910-555-8849. I look forward to your phone call.

Bryson pressed the speakerphone button again to disconnect the call. He glanced at his watch. He was meeting Everson for lunch and didn't want to be late, especially since his management-analyst brother could hardly squeeze any time out of his jammed-packed schedule to do lunch. He logged out of his computer, took his car keys from the top drawer of his desk, then headed out the door.

CHAPTER 11

"Man, I'm starving," Everson said after he'd chugged down a full glass of water without coming up for air.

"Starving or thirsty?" Bryson grinned.

"I skipped breakfast this morning…had an early meeting with a client."

"Bet you won't do that again."

"Yeah…I've learned my lesson. Even if I have to grab one of June's protein bars the next time, I'm going to eat something."

Bryson chuckled. "A protein bar? You think that'll hold you until lunch?"

"Hey, it's better than nothing."

They ordered quickly when the waitress came by then Everson said, "So that was some dinner last night."

"Yeah…I had to bail."

"Why?"

"I couldn't handle any more of the shenanigans."

"Seemed everything was fine until you got into that little back-and-forth with Candy."

Bryson shook his head. "She's been angry at me since I threatened her boyfriend…"

Everson frowned. "What boyfriend? I didn't know she was seeing anyone."

"She's not now…at least not him anyway. You

remember that guy she was talking to named Quinton?"

"Oh, yeah. The bald head dude that could never make eye contact with any of us."

"Yeah, that's him. I saw this fool at some restaurant with another woman. So I approached him when he left the place, told him he better not contact Candice again, and he didn't. But Candice called him and asked why he was distant, all of a sudden, and he told her I threatened him and that he didn't want to see her anymore. He didn't tell her I caught him kissing another woman. He told her I *threatened* him. Ever since, she's had an attitude."

"Why don't you just tell her you saw Quinton with another woman?"

"Because I don't want to hurt her. I keep telling myself she's still in her twenties. Still growing and maturing. She'll get over it one day."

"Let's hope so." Everson looked around the restaurant for a moment, wondering where the waitress was with the food. "I can't believe Garrison and Vivienne are having a baby. That's crazy."

"It is. I know I won't hear the last of it when mother returns. She's been on my case about getting remarried. She's expecting grandchildren from all of us, you know."

"Well, she's certainly not getting any from me and June any time soon. I want to be married for at least three years before I start trying to bring a new life into the world."

"I don't even think I want children anymore. A new wife either," Bryson said.

"You're still not with it, huh?"

"Not at all. Not after I was lied to. I wasted six years of my life with Felicia and I was nothing but faithful to her."

"But you can't pre-judge every woman based on what Felicia did to you."

"True, so I guess you can say, it's my preference. I have no desire to marry again. Mother should get enough grandkids from all of you to meet her needs. She won't even notice I don't have any children."

Everson shook his head. He realized his brother was speaking from anger, but after keeping the same stance for two years – being anti-marriage and anti-children – Everson knew he had to say something. Bryson had always wanted children. That didn't need to change just because his marriage didn't work out. "It won't be that easy, Bryce, and if you want children, you shouldn't let a bad experience keep you away from that. Dad started his own business and had four sons and a daughter to leave it to. Even though Barringer, Garrison and Candice are the only ones who chose to work there, you could've chosen to work there and so could I because Dad established it for *us*. He was thinking long term. Who are you going to leave your business to? When Bryson Blackstone is of retirement age, what happens to Blackstone Tree Service?"

Bryson leaned back in his chair and thought about everything Everson was telling him. His brother was right, of course, but starting over again, meeting a woman worthy of marrying and one who wanted to have children would require a lot of time.

Besides, he didn't like the idea of starting over. He was very laid back and old school – not lazy by any means, but also not as enthusiastic as his brothers. The truth of the matter was, they'd never been through a divorce. They didn't know what it was like to be misled by a woman – to have her lie to your face, cheat on you and then try to turn it all around to make it seem like her infidelity was *your* fault. Later, he found out Felicia didn't even want children…

When the food arrived, the men didn't waste any time diving in, especially Everson since he'd been starving himself for most of the day. Bryson had tossed a French fry into his mouth when he looked up and saw Kalina walking in with a man in tow. And she was dressed up – had on a turquoise blouse and a knee-length, white skirt. She also wore heels – nude, five-inch stilettos that showed off the muscle definition behind her legs. Her hair wasn't wild and wind-tossed as it normally was whenever he saw her. It was combed, appeared silky straight, falling down to the middle point of her back. He watched her smile when the man had whispered something to her. Then she swept her hair behind her ear, revealing a pair of gold hoop earrings and the fact that she'd painted her fingernails the same color as her blouse.

Talk about a transformation…

Was this even the same woman, or was this her drop-dead, gorgeous twin? *This* Kalina was definitely different from *work* Kalina. *Café* Kalina. While *café* Kalina was beautiful, she didn't make any effort to enhance that beauty and since she had today, Bryson could only assume she was on a date. And here he was thinking she had no time for a personal life. That all of her time was devoted to work. That she was single. Maybe Edith didn't know everything about her niece.

His eyes followed her to the table as he watched the tall, light-skinned man she was with pull out a chair for her. After she was seated comfortably, the man sat down at the seat across from her, looked at her and smiled.

Everson took another bite of his cheesesteak sub when he looked up and noticed that something, or someone, had taken Bryson's attention away from his food. Bryson was looking at a table near the back of the restaurant, staring at something and seemingly in a trance. Had the man even blinked? And why was he not eating?

Everson turned to look in the same direction as Bryson had been looking. He wanted to see what it was that had his brother's undivided attention. Then Everson saw a familiar face. "Hey, it's Kalina," he said.

That took him out of his trance. Bryson hid a frown and looked at his brother. "You know her?"

Everson nodded since he had tossed the last bite of his sandwich in his mouth. With a mouth full, he went on to say, "She's one of June's friends. They met at an Alzheimer's walk three years ago and have been friends ever since."

"They met at an Alzheimer's walk?"

"Yeah. June's mother had Alzheimer's, and I'm almost certain Kalina's mother has it too. I can't remember if her mother is still alive or not, though, but June's mother died like four years ago."

"Oh," Bryson said. That's all he could say at the moment since he didn't know Kalina.

"How do you know her?" Everson inquired, wiping his mouth with a brown napkin.

"Who?"

"Kalina."

"Oh...um...I see her at Edith's Café pretty often," he said, not wanting to go into details about working with Kalina. "So her mother has Alzheimer's?"

"Yeah, and now that I think about it, her mother *is* still alive. Kalina was over at the house, about four months ago, in tears, telling June how her mother had fallen and hurt herself. She mentioned she was in one of those assisted living facilities or something."

"Oh." *So Kalina knows Everson and June*, Bryson thought to himself. He wondered why Kalina never mentioned that.

Everson finished his glass of water. "Well, I hate to eat and run, but I have a one-thirty appointment on the other side of town."

"All right, Everson. I got the check."

"Thanks, Bryce," Everson said, standing up. "Hey, think about what I told you, man. It's not too late to start over." He gave Bryson a pat on the shoulder before he walked away.

Bryson couldn't wait until the waitress returned with his Visa card so he could walk over to Kalina's table. He'd been dying to know who this guy was she'd been chatting it up with, laughing and carrying on. Was he her man? She made it seem like she had no life, like she wasn't interested in anything relationship related. And when he emailed her to ask if she had ever been in love, she had said *no*. But here she was, having lunch with some dude, and from the looks of things, she was enjoying his company.

Bryson took a long swig of water. He didn't know why the sight of seeing her with another man bothered him so much. After all, she wasn't *his* woman. She was free to have breakfast, lunch or dinner with whomever she chose.

Once he had his card back, he stood up, tucked his wallet into the back, right pocket of his pants and headed towards her table. "Hi, Kalina."

Kalina quickly looked up towards the direction of the smooth, deep voice she recognized and saw Bryson standing tall at her side. The sight of him there caught her by surprise. A little ruffled at first, she mellowed out and said, "Hi, Bryson. You having lunch?"

"No. I already had lunch. I was heading out when I saw you over here…thought I'd come over and say hi."

"Cool…glad you did. Oh, by the way, this my realtor, Isaiah Russell. Isaiah, this is my friend, Bryson Blackstone."

Bryson looked confused for a moment and said, "Wait…you're Isaiah Russell?"

"In the flesh," Isaiah said.

"Well isn't this a coincidence. I just left a voicemail for you. You came highly recommended and I need the best."

"He's definitely the best," Kalina added in.

Bryson felt his eye twitch at her statement, even more so when Isaiah glanced at her and smiled as if he was giving her an appreciative, nonverbal thank-you.

Returning his attention to Bryson, Isaiah asked, "Are you buying or selling?"

"Both. I need to sell my house and buy another one right away."

"Okay. I'll give you a call. Once I get a price range, I can send you some options to look at."

"Anything with a list price up to eight-hundred and fifty thousand dollars will work, but it must have four bedrooms."

Four bedrooms? Why a single man needed four bedrooms was beyond Kalina. Then again, she was single and had three bedrooms. *Maybe he just likes his space.*

Isaiah took a card and a pen from the inner pocket of his suit jacket, flipped it over, then began writing notes about what Bryson wanted. "Okay, got it." He took another card from his pocket and handed it to Bryson. "Look for a phone call from me tomorrow."

Bryson took the card and said, "Sounds good. Let me give you my business card as well." He took out his wallet, slid out a business card and handed it to Isaiah.

"Thanks, man. I'll be in touch," Isaiah said.

"Hope you two enjoy the rest of your lunch. Have a good one." Bryson glanced at Kalina before turning to walk away. He was tempted to tell Kalina that he would see her later this evening, but he didn't know what kind of relationship she had with Isaiah, so he quietly exited the restaurant. He would find out all he needed to know later.

CHAPTER 12

Kalina watched Bryson walk into the café empty-handed. Where was his laptop? He strolled in nonchalantly, his eyes fixed on her after he'd briefly spoken to Edith.

"Hi," he said, pulling out the chair across from her and not beside her as they'd sat yesterday. He was the one who requested, no insisted, that they sit side-by-side. For some reason, he chose to sit across from her this evening.

"Hi. Where's your laptop?" she asked, looking at him.

Bryson sat there, holding her gaze before his eyes traveled down to her pink-tinted lips that matched the hint of color on her cheeks. She hadn't changed clothes. She wore the same outfit as when he saw her earlier at lunch. And her hair was still long and straight, falling down to her breasts.

"Bryson?"

"Yes?" he responded, his eyes connecting with hers again.

With raised brows, she said, "Your laptop?"

"I didn't bring it," he said, interlocking his fingers.

Kalina frowned. "What do you mean you didn't bring it?"

"I think it's important for us to spend this

evening getting to know each other, Kalina."

"You know who I am...well you know enough, anyway. I'm a girl who needs help answering emails."

"And you'll get that help. As a matter of fact, I want you to send me fifty emails tonight and I promise I'll have them all answered by tomorrow evening. But right now, precisely at this moment, I need to know who you are."

"And just what do you want to know?"

"Well, where are you from?"

Kalina felt her body temperature shoot up a few degrees. This isn't what she signed up for. He was supposed to be working, not interviewing her. "Fayetteville, North Carolina."

"Is that where your parents live?"

Kalina inhaled a deep breath. He wanted to talk about her family – a subject she liked to stay away from. Her family hadn't been a *family* in a long time, but, to appease him, she answered, "The man who used to call himself my father, still lives there."

"Care to elaborate?"

"No. I don't."

"Okay, then. What about your mother? Is she there, too?"

"Got some coffee for you two," Edith interrupted, setting two cups on the table. "Enjoy."

"Thanks Edith." Kalina and Bryson said in unison, catching the other's gaze.

Kalina took a sip of coffee. Afterwards, she said, "I don't want to talk about my parents. Ask me something else, and I'm not talking about personal things."

"How else will I get to know you if I don't get personal?"

Kalina shrugged. *That's not my problem, now is it?*

Bryson quietly sipped on his coffee while he came up with another topic of conversation. "So, how do you know Isaiah Russell?" He'd been dying to know this since he saw them having lunch together.

"Isaiah was my realtor," Kalina answered. "I went to him a couple of years ago, told him I needed a three-bedroom home with a finished loft over the garage and less, than a week later, he found my house."

Bryson nodded. "Must be some man to land a date with you."

Kalina smirked. "He's decent, but us having lunch together wasn't a date. I promised him lunch after he found my house and I had completely forgotten about it until recently, and after all the stars aligned with the moon, we were able to make it happen today."

"Oh. I see."

Bryson took a sip of coffee. He still wanted to know about her mother and he planned on finding out here and now. Everson had told him a little, but he wanted to hear the story from Kalina, and he knew he had to be strategic about it. So using the little information he already knew, he asked, "Do you know a woman named June Blackstone?"

"Yes. As a matter of fact, I do. She's a good friend of mine."

"You know her husband?"

"Yes. I know Everson."

"He's my brother."

"Really?"

"Yes. You know what I find odd?" Bryson asked, narrowing his gaze.

"What's that?"

"That you didn't even mention you knew some Blackstones when you met me."

"That's not odd. I just didn't see the relevancy."

"Blackstone is a rare surname."

"And?"

"And there are not many of us."

"I know what *rare* means, Bryson."

"So when I told you my name, it didn't cross your mind to ask me if I was related to June or Everson?"

"No, it didn't cross my mind. I have a lot on my mind these days, Bryson…like these emails I should be replying to instead of answering your questions." Kalina quickly typed a response to an email, clicked send, then looked up at him again.

"How do you know June?"

Ugh. Make it stop. "I met her three years ago at a walk we did together."

"A walk?"

"Yes…an Alzheimer's walk we did to help raise awareness for the disease."

"And why is it that you chose to do an Alzheimer's walk?"

The way he asked the question gave Kalina an indication that he already knew the answer. Still, she wasn't going to talk about her mother with him. She took a sip of coffee and said, "Because I wanted to."

Bryson reclined in his chair. "So it has nothing to do with your mother having the disease and living in an assisted living facility?" There, he said it. He didn't want to say it that way, but he knew Kalina would keep alluding him if he hadn't.

Kalina frowned. This guy had some nerve. "Don't talk about my mother," she snapped. "Don't ever mention anything about my mother. You don't know me, and just because you answer a few emails doesn't make you an expert on people, it doesn't make you my friend and it *does not* give you the right to talk about my mother."

Kalina slammed her laptop closed, stuffed it inside of her bag and left the café without even saying goodbye to her aunt. She was that upset.

As soon as she exited, Edith came from behind the counter and, sitting in the chair Kalina had gotten out of, she asked, "Goodness, Bryson. What on earth did you say to make her storm out of here like that?"

Bryson released a heavy sigh. "I was trying to get to know her...particularly trying to get her to open up about her mother."

"Why were you talking about her mother?"

"Because I know she's in a facility, Edith, and I simply wanted to talk about it."

Edith shook her head. "That's a painful subject for her to discuss, Bryson. It's difficult for me to talk about Madeline at times and it's especially hard for Kalina. She won't even talk to me about what it's doing to her."

"Exactly. So why am I trying, starting from

scratch, walking blindly into this situation and I don't know all the facts? I'm still new to her. Why should she trust me?" Bryson leaned back in his chair and shook his head. "I *need* to know her past. I need to know why she's putting up a wall and hiding behind this premise of helping other people to forget the troubles in her own life."

Edith sighed. She didn't want to tell Bryson everything about Kalina. She wanted him to find out some things on his own, but that didn't look too promising. "Okay…um…her mother, Madeline, who's also my sister, *is* in an assisted living facility. She was diagnosed with early onset Alzheimer's disease at age forty-eight. Madeline doesn't know who Kalina is anymore. She doesn't know who I am, either." Edith shook her head. "The thing is, I know she doesn't have long to live. Kalina knows it too, but she's in denial and she doesn't like to talk about it. She goes to visit her mother every Saturday and stays for as long as she can tolerate without completely falling apart and having a breakdown like she used to do years ago when she would visit. We both try to be there to support Madeline, but it's hard, you know, when the person doesn't even recognize you anymore. Doesn't even know your name."

"Kalina's father…where is he while all of this is going on?"

Edith shook her head. "He left Madeline and Kalina shortly after the diagnosis."

"He did what?" Bryson asked in disbelief.

"He left her, or them, I should say…said he couldn't watch Madeline die a slow death. So he packed up his stuff and left. When I found out what had happened, I moved them both in with me. Kalina was only thirteen at the time."

Bryson rubbed his hand across his mustache. "Unbelievable." Now, things were starting to make sense. They say a person was a product of their environment and Kalina was definitely a product of hers. No wonder she'd never been in love. She didn't believe in it. It must have been devastating for her to watch her father up and leave her mother while she was going through such a tumultuous time in her life.

"Bryson, I know it's a lot to ask, but I believe if you take the time to really talk to her and get to know her, she'll eventually talk to you about all of this. For now, why don't you tread softly…continue to assist her with the emails and slowly let her open up to you? A person can only keep things inside for so long. When she gets comfortable with you, she'll eventually talk about it."

Bryson gave Edith an inquisitive glance. "Edith, I need you to level with me. What's the real reason why you want me to help Kalina? I know you didn't just wake up one day and decide to ask me to do this."

"No, I didn't," Edith said. "I figured you had the time when I noticed you coming in the café more frequently during the last month or so. And almost every one of those days, I saw you staring at Kalina. Since you were staring at her so hard, I assumed you had some interest in her, but with her negative view of men, I also knew you didn't stand a chance unless I interfered. Trust me, other men have tried to talk to Kalina and she fanned them all away like flies."

"Why didn't you interfere on their behalf?"

"Because I didn't like them. I know you. You're a decent, sophisticated, hardworking man, Bryson. I don't know any details about your divorce and, honestly, it's none of my business, but if I could choose any man on this earth to be with Kalina, it would be you. That's why I came up with the bet. You *must* like her because you're still helping her out. And, as I recall, you *did* inquire about who she was."

Yes, he had inquired about her. It was when Edith told him that Kalina was her niece. "So this was all a set up?"

"Not necessarily. It was a way for you to get to know her. And she really does need the help, Bryson, and I'm not just talking about with the emails."

Bryson stood up and said, "Okay. I'll focus on helping her with the emails. If she opens up to me about other things in her life, fine, but I'm not going to press her for any more information."

Edith smiled. "Thank you, Bryson. I really appreciate this."

"Yeah, no problem," he said, heading out the door. In his car, he sat there for a moment and thought about what Edith had said:

I don't know any details about your divorce and, honestly, it's none of my business, but if I could choose any man on this earth to be with Kalina, it would be you.

He shook his head. Yes, he had been staring at

Kalina. Yes, he was impressed by her emails and yes, she was a beautiful woman. But the last thing he wanted to do was get entangled with a woman who didn't believe love existed, and he wouldn't. He *would* help her with the emails for a month and that would be the end of it. His life after divorcing Felicia had been free of headaches. He planned to keep it that way.

CHAPTER 13

Kalina headed upstairs to her bedroom. She stripped off her clothes and jumped in the shower, letting the warm water calm her down. She ran her fingers through her hair as water rained down on her. Talking about her mother was a sensitive subject in itself and she couldn't help but wonder why Bryson almost insisted on doing so.

After she towel-dried her hair and slipped into a comfortable, cotton pajama set, she called the assisted living facility to check on her mother. After the nurse assured her Madeline was fine, Kalina sat on the bed, removed her laptop from the bag and placed it on her lap. Since she wasn't able to get any work done this evening, she was even further behind. All thanks to Bryson…

She blew an angry breath and shook her head. Her inbox had grown by another three hundred emails. How on earth would she ever catch up if all she did was fall behind? After scanning the new emails that had come in, she saw that Bryson had sent a message with a subject line of *please read*. What did he want? More answer to his intrusive questions?

From: Bryson Blackstone
To: Kalina Cooper
Subject: Please Read

Kalina, the evening didn't go the way I expected it to. I simply wanted to know a little more about you, but I can see how insensitive I was to your feelings. I'm sorry I upset you.

I do owe you some emails, so please go ahead and send as many as you want my way. I'll turn them around as fast as I can. Hope to hear from you soon.

--

B. Blackstone

———

If she didn't need the help, she would ignore him altogether, but she needed his help. She needed all the help she could get. So, she began sifting through emails, starting with the oldest first, sending them to him one by one until she'd sent close to a hundred. Then she began reading and answering emails, the norm for her during bedtime.

When 3:00 a.m. rolled around, she was so exhausted, she amazed herself that she could still read an email, understand the question and reply back with an answer. In four, short hours, she had to be up again. Lizette would be there at eight on the dot to get started tweaking the blog. So, deciding she'd had enough for the night, well morning, she folded her laptop closed and rested.

CHAPTER 14

In the morning, Kalina sat straight up in the bed when she heard the chimes of her doorbell. She glanced at the clock, seeing a bright, red 8:13 a.m. "Oh my gosh. Lizette!"

This wasn't the first time Lizette had stood outside, waiting for Kalina to answer the door and it probably wouldn't be the last. Kalina threw on a robe and rushed to the front door. She opened it and said, "I'm so sorry, Lizette. I was up late again and lost track of time."

"No need to explain, Kalina. It's fine," Lizette said, stepping into the living room.

"It's not fine. I need to be more professional."

"No, what you need is more than two hours of sleep every night."

"A girl can only dream…"

Lizette giggled. "I'm going to head on up and get started."

"All right. I'll be up there in a few." Kalina hurried back to her bedroom, took a quick five-minute shower before slipping into a blue, jean skirt and a yellow tank top. She grabbed her laptop and rushed upstairs to the 'headquarters' to start the workday.

At her desk now, she opened her laptop but didn't pay any attention to it. She stared out of the window for a while, thinking about how freeing it was to run her own business. At the same time, it came with a lot of stress. There had been times when she thought about giving it all up and doing something less stressful, but during those times, she'd think about her mother and the high healthcare cost associated with her living in a facility. How would she be able to afford her mother's care if she quit?

So, through a long yawn, she opened her inbox and saw a bunch of emails from Bryson. She'd sent him eighty-nine emails to answer and it appeared he'd done them all. The last email was sent a little after two in the morning. *Impressive*. She began reading his responses and sending them on to the recipient after she approved his answers.

"Hey, Kalina...I have the *true love* blog post ready," Lizette said. "I'm sending it to you as we speak."

"Perfect. Thank you."

"Welcome."

Kalina scrolled up to the top of her inbox to find the email from Lizette when she saw one from Bryson – an email he'd sent a few minutes ago. She clicked on it:

From: Bryson Blackstone
To: Kalina Cooper
Subject: Emails

Can you call me? Cell is 910-555-8849.

--

B. Blackstone

———

Call him? Why did he want her to call him? His emails from last night had been acceptable. There was nothing to discuss about them and, even if she had found a problem, she would simply email him back and ask him to make some revisions. She shook her head. *I don't have time for this today...*

From: Kalina Cooper
To: Bryson Blackstone
Subject: Re: Emails

I'm very busy today. What is this about and can it wait?

--

Kalina Cooper
Editor | CEO
The Cooper Files

———

After sending the response to him, Kalina clicked on Lizette's email to read the blog post. She'd written a healthy size article, almost a full page.

"I see you really got into this article, huh, Lizette?"

Smiling, Lizette said, "I did, and it took a lot of research, too. But I enjoyed writing that one."

Kalina would spend the next hour or so going through it – sifting through the post for spelling errors and grammatical mistakes, not that Lizette made many. She'd add to it where she felt more details were needed and take away parts that contained too many details. It was all a part of the revision process. Kalina took pride in having content-rich material on her blog and this was one way to ensure that she did.

CHAPTER 15

Bryson sat behind his desk, reviewing his employee's work schedules for next week. He had his cell phone next to his computer, just in case Kalina decided to call, not that he thought she would.

When his phone rang, he quickly snatched it up, without even looking at the display and said, "Hello."

"Mr. Blackstone. Hey, it's Isaiah Russell."

"Oh," Bryson said, deflated. He was hoping it was Kalina instead.

"Did I catch you at a bad time?" Isaiah asked.

"No. No. You're good."

"Cool. I was wondering if you had a chance to look at the listings I sent to you late last night."

"I did, and I would like to see all three."

"Okay, what does your schedule look like today?"

Bryson glanced at his watch. "I can get out of here at noon today. How about I meet you at one o'clock?"

"That works for me," Isaiah responded. "Meet me at the house on Saint Ives Place. We'll take a look at that one then head to the others."

"Sounds like a plan."

"All right. Later."

Bryson checked his email when he ended the call with Isaiah. There weren't any emails from Kalina. He sighed. For some, unexplainable, nagging reason, he got the feeling Kalina wasn't going to show up this evening at the café and that bothered him. He couldn't let her dictate this working relationship. He wasn't a pushover and he didn't want to be perceived as such. Kalina may not have liked him, but she would respect him.

With his phone still in his palm, he dialed the café. He'd get Kalina's number one way or another.

"Edith's Café. How can I help you?"

"Hi Edith. It's Bryson."

"Oh, hi there. How's it going? You hear from Kalina today?"

"Yes. I emailed my phone number to her and told her to call me. She replied back that she was too busy which leads me to the reason why I'm calling you."

"Which is?"

"I need her number."

"Oh, ah…Bryson, Kalina is very strict with her cell phone number."

"I understand that, but I need to talk to her."

Edith hesitated again. If Kalina found out she'd given Bryson her number, she wouldn't hear the last of it.

"I won't tell her how I got the number," Bryson said as if reading Edith's thoughts.

Edith sighed again. "Okay, Bryson. I'm going to trust you on this one. You got a pen?"

"Yep."

"It's 910-555-2703."

"Got it. Thanks Edith."

"Don't make me regret giving you her number."

Bryson grinned. "I won't...see you a little later today, hopefully."

"Okay. Bye."

Armed with Kalina's number now, Bryson wasted no time punching the digits into his cell phone. He listened to the rings, four of them, and when he thought the voicemail would pick up, he heard:

"Hello."

Ah, the sweet sound of her voice over the phone... "Hi Kalina. It's—"

"Bryson?" she asked, immediately recognizing his voice.

"Yes, it's Bry—"

"How did you get this number?" she interrupted to ask. She was very careful not to give him her number. Even when she sent emails to him, she deleted her number from her email signature.

"I have my ways. Listen, I wanted to talk to you because I didn't like the way you left the café yesterday. I'm sorry I upset you."

"You've already apologized for that."

"Yes, and you didn't respond to my email, so I wanted to talk to you...wanted to make sure you received my apology and now I know that you have."

"Okay. Was there something else?"

"Yes. Did you get the other emails?"

Kalina tapped a pen against her desk calendar. "Yes. I've reviewed them and sent them off."

"How were they?"

"They were fine. All of them."

"Good. I'm not that busy today if you would like to send more emails my way."

"No. I'm not going to do that, Bryson."

"Why not?"

"Because you're busy running your own company. It wouldn't be fair for me to infringe on your time. I'm already not paying you anything."

How had she known he was running his own company? He hadn't told her, so Edith must have filled her in. He wondered what else Edith told her about him. "Doesn't matter," he responded. "Send me more emails, okay."

"Why?"

"Because I want to help you, and I'm pretty good at this, if I say so myself."

Kalina's eyes sparkled. He actually wanted to help. She'd completely forgotten how angry she was when she left the café yesterday and how irritated she was that he'd somehow managed to get her number. He genuinely wanted to help her and she appreciated that. "I'll send you a few."

"And we're still meeting at the café this evening, correct?"

"Yes. I'll be there. Oh, and do me a favor?"

"What's that?" he asked.

"Bring your laptop this time, please."

Bryson chuckled. "Will do."

"All right. I'll see you later."

"Yep. Later."

When Kalina set the phone on her desk, Lizette

asked, "What was that about?"

"Bryson wanted me to send him more emails...said he wanted to help me. And I don't know how he got my number..."

"Well, that's nice of him to help out. I know you appreciate it."

"I do," Kalina said. She glanced outside again and said, "It's starting to rain now."

"Uh oh...you know what that means."

"Yes. More emails." Kalina grunted and scrubbed her hands down her face. "I better go ahead and send Bryson more of these emails before he changes his mind."

"Yeah. Good idea."

CHAPTER 16

"So, how was your day?" Bryson asked as soon as Kalina was sitting comfortably next to him at the café and had opened her laptop, setting it on the table in front of her. She wasn't dressed up today and her hair was pulled back into a lazy ponytail. No earrings. No make-up. No bangin' outfit. She was plain, rocking a jean skirt and a yellow shirt.

"It was good. I must've answered two hundred emails, but then, two hundred more came in so it almost feels like I didn't do anything." She grinned. "Oh, and thank you for taking on more during the day. I appreciate it."

"You're welcome."

"And just so you know, I'm not sending you anymore during the day. We can work at the café."

"If you say so," he said, withholding a smile.

Kalina looked at him. "Yes. I do say so." She saw those slender lips of his curve into a full smile. Her eyes landed on his mustache, down to his chiseled chin and back up to his eyes again.

"Yes?" he asked when their gazes held.

"What?" Kalina said.

"You have a question or something?" he asked, mildly amused.

"No."

"Then why were you staring at me so intently."

She smiled and returned her eyes back to the laptop. "No reason. Um...let me send you more emails."

Edith walked over to the table and asked, "Are we drinking coffee this evening?"

"Please," Bryson responded. "I'll take a regular with two packs of sugar."

"And I'll take a dark roast," Kalina told her.

"Okay. Coming right up."

Kalina continued sending Bryson emails and when she'd sent about thirty his way, she picked up her cell and dialed the assisted living facility. When someone answered, she said, "Hi. This is Kalina Cooper. I'm calling to check on my mother...Madeline Cooper."

"Let me find her nurse for you. Just a sec."

Kalina held the phone to her ear with her shoulder so she could continue working.

Bryson glanced over at her. The woman had a lot on her plate and was struggling to keep up with it all. She probably would never admit to it, but she *was* struggling.

"Kalina," she heard a voice on the phone say.

"Yes, I'm here."

"Hey, it's Joan."

"Hi, Joan. I hope you're doing well this evening."

"I'm doing fine and so is your mom. She slept for most of the day. By the way...I was wondering if the doctor discussed with you about switching her to an all-liquid diet."

Kalina stopped typing, held the phone to her ear with her left hand again and said, "Yes. He mentioned it a month ago, but I haven't heard anything since. I think he was waiting until it was absolutely necessary."

"Looks like we've reached that point. Beginning tomorrow, we're going to start spoon-feeding her some Ensure. She'll still be getting all the nutrients and vitamins she needs every day, but it'll be in liquid form."

Kalina closed her eyes. A liquid diet to her meant her mom was nearing death – something she didn't want to think about but thought about every day since her mother had been in the facility. In a way, she felt like her mother had died a long time ago because of the awful, dreadful illness that took her mind away.

Bryson looked at her. Her eyes were closed as she held the phone to her ear. She looked like she'd gotten some bad news and he wondered if her mother was okay.

"Kalina, are you still there?" Joan asked.

Kalina, fighting back tears, exhaled a long breath before opening her eyes again. She swallowed hard and said, "Yes. I'm here, Joan. I will talk with you more about it on Saturday when I'm there."

"Okay, sweetie. See you later."

"All right. Bye."

Kalina placed the cell on the table next to her laptop and rubbed her eyes. "Excuse me. I'll be right back," she said standing up.

"Okay," Bryson responded.

Kalina walked behind the counter to find her aunt and said, "Edith, I called the facility to check on mama and they said they were switching her to an all-liquid diet now," Kalina said with tears in her eyes.

"Yes, we knew they would do it soon. Madeline hasn't been eating much and she needs her nutrition."

"I know," Kalina said, pinching the corner of her eyes while forcing tears in.

Edith walked towards her with open arms and hugged her tight. "You know it's best for her right now."

"Yes. I know…it just seems like…like this is it."

Edith unwrapped her arms from around her niece and said, "Sweetheart, Madeline has been dealing with this disease for a long time. The doctor has already warned us that she was in the final stages of it."

"I know. You're right," Kalina said, even though it was hard to accept.

"Relax. Breathe. Think positive thoughts, okay."

Kalina nodded. "I'll try, Edith."

"All right, honey. I'll be over there with your coffee in a minute."

Kalina left from behind the counter and walked back over to the table, joining Bryson.

"Everything okay?" he asked, seeing sadness in her eyes.

She nodded and continued with the emails.

Edith had brought over their coffee and when Bryson took a sip of his, he glanced at Kalina. She was staring blankly at the computer screen again. Her hands were in typing position but her fingers didn't move. She didn't blink. She only stared.

"So I realize I haven't told you anything about

myself," he said, taking her out of her trance.

She turned to look at him. "You don't have to. It's not like we're going to be around each other for an extended period of time anyway."

"Doesn't matter. We're going to be working together on a daily basis so you should at least know the basics."

"Such as?"

"Well, I'm thirty-eight. Like you, I'm also an entrepreneur. I own Blackstone Tree Service."

"You own a *tree* service?" Kalina asked. Edith had already told her this, but she didn't believe it.

"Yes. Why did you ask it that way…like you don't believe me?"

"You don't look like the outdoorsy type…you look more white-collar."

"Well, I am more white-collar now. I spend most of my days at the office. However, when I started the business eight years ago, I was out in the field all the time. I still go out from time-to-time if we're understaffed or after storms when demand is high."

"Interesting," Kalina said. "How do you like working for yourself?"

"It's wonderful…the American Dream, right?"

"I suppose."

Bryson clicked on send, successfully answering another email. "I have three brothers and one sister. You already know Everson."

"Yes," she said, typing again. "I know Everson and June."

Bryson waited a moment to see if she would expound on how she knew them, but she hadn't wanted to talk much about it yesterday and she didn't seem too eager to talk about it today either. So he continued, "I've been divorced for two years."

Kalina stopped typing, turning to look at him. "Really?"

"Yes. We were married for six years and she cheated on me."

With eyebrows raised, Kalina asked, "She cheated on you?"

"Yes. Apparently, the affair had been going on for a few months before I found out about it."

Shifting her body towards him and using the backrest of her chair to rest her arms, she said, "That must've been devastating."

Bryson smiled uncomfortably. It was devastating, but he'd done a good job hiding that fact. "The crazy thing is, I never wanted to marry. I was content with being single. Then, one day, I felt the sudden longing for a family…a wife, children, a dog…the whole nine and I met her around the same time. We dated for a short while then we got married."

"Do you regret it?"

"Hmm…um…yes and no. At times, I feel like, if I would've listened to my intuition and avoided marriage in the first place, I would've saved myself the trouble. On the flip side, I'm glad I got to experience it because now, I know what love is not…guess you can say I took it as a learning experience."

"So that's why you're so good at answering these questions."

He smirked. "Yes, that would be why."

Kalina took a sip of coffee. "What about children?"

"We didn't have children, and now I'm glad we didn't. That would've complicated the divorce."

Kalina nodded. "Yes…very much so."

"You told me you've never been in love," Bryson said.

"I haven't."

"Not ever?"

She grinned. "No. Why is that so hard for you to believe?"

"Well, you're smart, beautiful…there must've been some men after you."

"There was, but I shut them down. I didn't have time to date. I started college right after high school, and in college I started the blog. I spent all of my time working. Plus, I—"

"You what?" he asked when she paused, trying to keep her engaged in conversation.

"Never mind," she responded. She hesitated to talk to him about her personal life, but why? After all, he had been sharing personal things with her.

Bryson frowned a bit, removing the irritation from his forehead before she could see it.

For the next fifteen minutes, they both worked quietly. Out of nowhere, Kalina said, "I don't have good role model when it comes to love and relationships."

Finally, Bryson thought, feeling a wave of relief that she was opening up to him. "What do you mean?"

"My father, if you can even call him that, left my mom and I."

"That's terrible," Bryson said.

"Yeah, what's even *more* terrible is why he left."

"Don't tell me there was another woman."

"No, well not in the beginning, anyway. Um…he left when my mother was diagnosed with early onset Alzheimer's disease."

"Wow. I'm truly sorry to hear that, Kalina."

"Thanks," she said, flashing a lazy smile. "I was thirteen at the time. I knew something was wrong with my mother, but I didn't know what it was. She was forgetting things she should've known, things she'd been doing routinely for years. Finally, the diagnosis came and my father said he couldn't watch her deteriorate into nothing. Said he couldn't watch the woman he loved lose her mind."

Bryson shook his head.

Kalina sighed heavily. "All I could think about was, if he really loved her, wouldn't he have stayed and did everything in his power to take care of her instead of running away? How is that love?"

Bryson quietly thought on what she asked.

Kalina continued, "So from that point forward, I always considered love to be something tangible…something you can pick up and throw away at any given time, at least when it comes to relationships between two people who say they're in love. So no, I've never been in love. I love my mother and I love my aunt Edith, but I've never loved anyone romantically. Why fall in love when it comes with no guarantees and is almost certain to end in heartbreak?"

"Seems your father has given you a negative view of what love is."

Kalina shook her head. "No. He painted a very clear picture of what love is. You want me to break it down for you?"

"Yes, break it down for me."

"Love is being with a person for years, saying vows before God to this person and leaving them at the very moment they need you. Boom. There you have it."

"That's not what love is, Kalina."

"That's what it is to me. Perception is reality, right?"

"Um…not in all cases."

"Well, in this case, it definitely is to me."

Bryson opened his mouth to respond, but nothing came out.

"What?" Kalina asked when she saw his hesitancy to speak.

"Nothing."

"What is it? We're in the middle of a conversation. You can't just stop talking."

Bryson chuckled. "I'm trying to check myself today, Kalina. I don't want another repeat of last night."

"I'm not going anywhere tonight…have too much work to do. Now continue. What were you going to say?"

"I was going to ask a question."

"Then ask me."

"How are you able to answer these questions from your readers when your perception of love is so flawed?"

"My perception is not flawed. It's *my* perception. With that being said, my views do not prevent me from answering these questions about love because I've studied human behavior…majored in it. Also, I do a lot of research."

"That's all fine and good, but until you've experience love firsthand—"

"And have my heart broken? No thanks. I watched my mother weep, not cry, but weep and wail for days when my father left. That's when I decided I would never put myself in that predicament, and I haven't."

Bryson grimaced. He typed another email before asking, "So how is she doing?" He'd asked the question before he realized it. Edith had warned him about bringing up Kalina's mother in conversation. And he even knew not to mention anything about her again, especially after watching Kalina bolt out of the café last night. Still, the question had rolled off his tongue as easily as the coffee slid down his throat.

"Who?" Kalina asked.

"Oh, never mind. Sorry."

"Are you asking about my mother, Bryson?"

He looked at her. "I was, but, like I said…never mind."

Kalina finished typing an email then said, "I don't like to talk about her, but since I've discussed her already, um…she's not doing all that well. She's lost a lot of weight."

"And she's in assisted living?"

"Yes," Kalina said as she worked. "I go to see her every Saturday. Of course she doesn't know who I am. She never recognizes me. And you want to know what the messed up part is."

"What's that?"

"She always asks for Stanley."

"Your father?"

"Yes. Amazingly, she asks for him by name. The man who left her heartbroken is the *one* name she remembers. I swear I want to scream every time I hear her say that man's name."

"So I take it you don't have a good relationship with your father."

"Good? I don't have a relationship with him period, nor do I want one."

"When was the last time you spoke to him?"

"I haven't seen or spoken to him since he left."

"He hasn't tried to contact you?"

"No. All I know is he remarried and is living happily ever after in Fayetteville. Hope his new wife knows what a loser he is…guess she'll find out if she falls ill."

Bryson frowned. It was hard for him to imagine a man who would do something like that – a man who would pack up, leave his wife and his child and not even bother to make contact.

Kalina yawned, stretching her hands high above her head. "Gosh, I'm so tired."

"Why don't you leave a little earlier tonight so you can get some rest?"

She giggled. "Aw, you're cute. You think I actually sleep when I get home? I'm usually up until two or three in the morning, working."

Bryson hid a frown. She had told him before that she didn't get much sleep. He recalled her saying that, one night, she'd only slept for a mere two hours. "That's not good for you," Bryson cautioned.

"Seems you're stressed out enough as it is."

"Stressed?" she said, laughing it off. "Who said I was stressed?"

"You don't have to say it, Kalina. I can sense it."

"How?"

"You don't remember our first ever interaction with each other, at this café while you were talking to Edith about a reader's question you'd been stumped on?"

"Yes. I remember. It was just last week."

"Correct, and you nearly bit my head off when I said something to you."

"Oh, you had that coming, Bryson." Kalina laughed. "You were being nosy, too…"

"Nosy?" he said, amused.

"Yes. Nosy."

"How can you call it *nosy* when you were having a *loud*, *public* conversation?"

She grinned. "Well, it was a conversation you didn't need to be in."

"Well, I was in it, and now look at me…helping you with these emails and all. So something good came out of it, right?"

Smiling, she said, "Yes. I suppose you're right."

"So go ahead and take off."

"I can't. I'm a workaholic. I have to work until I'm satisfied that I've done a good job, then I'll stop."

"And how many emails do you typically answer when you get home?"

"It depends…ranges anywhere from seventy-five to a hundred and fifty."

"Okay. Send those to me."

Kalina shook her head. "No. I told you I wasn't going to do that to you again."

"I don't mind it. Plus, I would rather you get some sleep."

"Stop it. I'll be fine."

He didn't like it, but what could he do? He couldn't make her go home and sleep.

Kalina clicked on another email and said, "Hey, Bryson, I should let you answer this one. This reader said she met a guy at the grocery store and he told her that what they had was love at first sight. So she wants to know if love at first sight is possible."

"That's an easy one," Bryson said. "Absolutely not."

"What?" Kalina said, her mouth still open in shock. "I thought for sure you'd say yes."

"Nah...I don't buy the love at first sight thing, reason being, you can't love someone when you don't know that person. If you see someone and think you're in love, nine times out of ten, you're just highly attracted to the person and may even want to get to know them better, but it's definitely not love."

"I'm impressed. Let me forward this email to you so you can take this woman to school."

Bryson laughed. "You like that, huh."

"Definitely. Well said, Mr. Blackstone. Well said."

At closing, Kalina and Bryson walked with Edith to her car. Then Bryson proceeded to walk with

Kalina to her car, parked near his. He'd had a strong urge to hold her hand and fought the magnetism pulling him to do so.

"So you're going to bed when you get home, right?" he asked her. In a way, he was telling her.

"Probably not." Kalina glanced up at him, thinking how much taller he looked standing in front of her versus sitting next to her. She also thought something else – that Bryson was perhaps the most handsome man she'd ever seen in her life. That was probably because she never paid any attention to a man before Bryson came along. She'd usually dismiss a man faster than she could type. But she couldn't dismiss Bryson. They were working together. He had her email address. Her cell phone number.

"Do I need to take your laptop home with me, Kalina?"

"No," she said barely looking at him. "I think I will take your advice and go to bed a little early…probably around midnight or so."

"Midnight is better than three in the morning."

"Definitely." Kalina unlocked the door to her car. She was thoroughly surprised when Bryson stepped around her to pull on the handle, opening the door for her.

"Thank you," she said, unable to stop smiling. She got inside of her car and sat down comfortably on the driver's seat, placing her laptop bag and purse in the passenger seat.

Bryson remained standing between the opened car door and Kalina. "Hey, so do you usually eat dinner before you come to the café?"

"Yes. I'll grab something at home, or swing by a fast food restaurant and get something."

"Well, how about I take you to a proper dinner tomorrow night?"

"Dinner?" she said frowning. "Like a date?"

"Yeah. A dinner date, similar to the lunch date you went on with Isaiah."

"Hmm," Kalina said. She didn't want to do dinner with Bryson. She wanted their relationship to be work-related and nothing more. She couldn't handle anything more. "I…I can't do dinner. I have to work and—"

"Just a couple of hours," he said. "And, as always, you can send me a batch of emails, equivalent to the amount you could've processed in those two hours."

"Um…I don't know. Let me think about it."

"Okay, but don't think too hard."

"All right," Kalina said, strapping on her seat belt. "See you tomorrow, Bryson."

"Have a good night, Kalina," Bryson said, pushing the door closed. He watched her drive away before he got inside his car, heading for his large, four-bedroom, lonely house.

CHAPTER 17

She'd showered, put on a big T-shirt and now, with her laptop resting on her thighs, she began the task of answering emails again. Then Bryson crossed her mind…

She frowned. Why was he occupying precious time in her brain that could've been spent on work? She tried to shake it off, but couldn't help but think about their conversation earlier this evening. He'd told her he owned a tree service, so she decided to Google the name of his business to see if he had a website. He did. She scanned through the various services he offered – trimming, removal, maintenance and fertilization. His business was accredited by the Better Business Bureau and had nothing but good reviews on Google and Yelp.

Not bad, Kalina thought. She took pride in her work. She was sure he did as well. She had much respect for anyone who believed in their dreams enough to make them a reality. And then there was the guy behind the successful business – Bryson Blackstone. He didn't seem as bad as she assumed he might be in the beginning. And, to be a divorced man, he was good at giving relationship advice.

When she saw a new email from him hit her inbox, she smiled and said, "What do you want now, Bryson Blackstone?"

She clicked on the email to open it:

From: Bryson Blackstone
To: Kalina Cooper
Subject: sweet dreams

Go to bed, Kalina.

--

B. Blackstone

————

She grinned. "You go to bed Bryson," she said out loud before deciding to respond back.

From: Kalina Cooper
To: Bryson Blackstone
Subject: Re: sweet dreams

Call me.

--

Kalina Cooper
Editor | CEO
The Cooper Files

————

Kalina cringed when she clicked send. She actually told *him* to call *her*. What was she thinking? Not even a minute later her cell phone was buzzing on her nightstand. She felt flutters in her stomach at the thought of talking to him again.

"Thirty more minutes and I'll be in bed," she said, right out of the gate.

From the tone of her voice, Bryson could tell she

was smiling.

"What are you still doing up?" she asked him.

"I'm in bed," Bryson said. "I was about to close this laptop, but I wanted to send you a quick email to make sure you were going to bed at midnight like you said you would."

"Aw…so I'm the last person you thought about before you rested your head. I want you to know that it's an honor and a privilege…" she said, withholding laughter.

"You're silly…you know that?"

Kalina giggled.

Bryson did, too. He liked this playful side of her.

"Actually, I'm in bed right now with my laptop resting on my thighs, as usual."

Laptop resting on her thighs…

Bryson forced the visual away from his mind. He was attracted to her physically, but he was never the kind of man to let a woman's physical beauty cloud his judgment. He was more interested in the inner workings of a woman's mind. Her heart. His goal was to find out those things that weighed heavily on Kalina, to get her to open up to him. It would be a difficult task, but he'd made some progress tonight. He'd gotten her to freely talk to him. Now, he wanted to push the envelope even further.

"Hello?" Kalina looked at her phone to make sure it was still connected, then held it back to her ear.

"I'm here," Bryson said, "And I have a question for you."

She yawned silently then asked, "What's your question?"

"Did you smile when you saw my email?"

"What?"

"My question was pretty straightforward, Kalina. Did you smile when you saw my email in your inbox a few minutes ago?"

Goodness. His voice was as intoxicating over the phone as it was in person. "I did."

"Why?" he asked.

"Why did I smile?"

"Yes. Why did you smile?"

"Because I thought it was funny...telling me to go to bed like you just *knew* I wouldn't without your coaching."

"Yeah, that's because you wouldn't."

Kalina laughed. "Probably not."

"See, that's what I'm talking about."

She giggled more. Turning the tables on him, she asked, "So, did you smile when you saw my email?"

"I did," he answered quickly.

"Why?"

"Because I know it's not like you to ask a man to call you...shows you're getting comfortable with me and, eventually, you'll learn to trust me."

"Hmm..." she said. How could he draw that conclusion from a simple email?

"You don't think you can learn to trust me?"

"Um..." Kalina drawled out. Her smile had since faded. She'd never trusted a man before and she didn't plan to now. Didn't matter how nice he was or how attracted she was to him.

"Well, I'm going to *make* you trust me."

"No need to waste your time, Bryson. I've never

trusted a man."

"There's a first time for everything, Kalina. You probably never thought you'd be on the phone with a man, close to midnight, having a conversation, but here we are."

Yeah, here we are. What are you doing, Kalina? Almost a week ago, she would cringe at the thought of working with and conversing with Bryson. Now, she was relaxed. He had a way with words and she was hoping he was as sincere as he came across.

"You're quiet all of a sudden," Bryson said.

"I was thinking."

"About what?"

About why I feel comfortable enough with you to let my guard down. "Nothing. Um, I think I'm going to go ahead and put this laptop down."

"You do that. Have a good night, Kalina."

"You too, Bryson."

Kalina folded her laptop closed, connected her cell phone to the charger and turned off the lamp on her nightstand. Resting her head on the pillow, she thought about Bryson again. She wanted to know more about him and the reason he was being so generous with offering his help. He could very easily have said no, that he didn't have time to devote to helping her out. So why was he doing it? Was he interested in her? She'd made it clear that she didn't want, and wasn't looking for, a relationship. But she couldn't deny there was something about him that made her wonder.

CHAPTER 18

A Week Later

She couldn't get into her zone with work today. She'd been working hard all week – her and Bryson – answering a ton of emails together and sharing stories about their lives. The more time she spent with him, the more she liked him.

Last night, he'd been talkative, as usual, but Kalina noticed something else – he'd been staring at her often. She'd be typing an email or taking a sip of coffee and when she glanced up, he'd be staring intently. And every night, he walked with her to her car, opened the door and watched her leave before he would take off.

Kalina stretched her arms up high in the air. "Oh, I'm so not ready for this today," she said, yawning. Lizette had already started working. Meanwhile, Kalina was in the kitchen pouring herself a cup of coffee. Since she wasn't ready to work just yet, she decided to call a friend she hadn't spoken to in some time – June Blackstone.

She dialed June's number and took a sip of coffee while waiting for her to answer.

"Hey, girl!" June said all excited. "Long time no speak."

"I know. I've been hustlin' these emails, girlfriend."

June laughed. "You are so crazy. So what's been going on? How have you been?"

"Good. Staying busy and all. What about yourself?"

"Been traveling a lot with Everson and having a ball. How's your mother doing?"

"She's hanging in there…they switched her over to a liquid diet. Oh, and they ordered a walker for her since it's difficult for her to get her balance now."

"Oh, okay. Sounds like they're taking care of her."

"They are. I'm going to see her tomorrow."

"Cool. So what else have you been up to?"

"Um…not much," Kalina said. She wanted to ask June about Bryson, but didn't want her to get the wrong idea. Would she get the wrong idea? *Only one way to find out.* "Hey, I wanted to ask you something, June."

"What's up?"

"First, let me preference this by saying, please do not mention anything to Everson about this, but what's the deal with Bryson?"

June drew in an excited breath and said, "Bryson? You like Bryson?"

Yes. "No, I'm just asking about him. What's his story?"

"Wait, how do you know Bryson?"

"He frequents my aunt's café and now he's sort of working with me."

"Oh. Okay. Well, Bryson is Bryson. What you see is what you get. He's divorced. He was married for six years, but his wife cheated on him or something like that. He's been divorced for two years now and he swears he'll never marry again."

"Hmm…okay," Kalina said. June had told her some of the same things Bryson had. He didn't mention the latter though – that he would never marry again. "Is that all?"

"Yeah, pretty much. He's not as outgoing as his brothers. He's more laid-back, quiet—"

"Quiet?" Kalina said, snapping her head back. "Around me, he talks more than a telemarketer."

June giggled. "Well, he's quiet at our family gatherings. I don't know how he was when he and Felicia were together. I wasn't around then. Everson told me he was more of himself, whatever that means. Oh, and he owns his own business. He's usually working, and I have my own theory about that."

"About what?"

"The amount of time he spends working. He's usually at his office all day, even after closing, well into the night. I swear sometimes, I think he spends the night there."

He spends the night at his office? Now Kalina knew why he jumped at the chance to help her with work. He wanted something to occupy his down time. If he could flood his time with work, he wouldn't have any time to think about his failed marriage and what Felicia had done to him. In essence, he needed the time with her at the café as much as she needed his help.

"The brothers actually get together to play cards on Friday nights," June said. "They order pizza and wings, hang out and have a good time. You should come by and keep me company."

"Um…I don't know—"

"Oh, come on. I have a bottle of red Moscato with our names written all over it."

Kalina smiled. She could use a night of unwinding, and it had been a while since she and June hung out. "Okay."

"Yes! Can't wait to catch up with you."

"Same here."

"All right. See you later."

"About what time?"

"Six or so."

"I'll be there." Kalina slid her phone in the right front pocket of her slacks, carefully ascending the stairs with a cup of coffee. She finally sat down at her desk, opened her laptop and got to work, answering emails.

"Hey, Kalina, I'm sending you an email from Harland Jewelers," Lizette said. "Looks like they're inquiring about placing an ad on the blog."

"Okay. Thanks, Lizette."

"No problem."

Kalina reviewed the email quickly as she did with all ad requests and saw that Harland Jewelers were interested in a four-month ad rental on *The Cooper Files* blog. She replied back with a fee of two-thousand dollars, since her rate was five-hundred dollars per month.

"It's so nice outside today," Lizette said.

"It is…the perfect summer day."

"I can see myself right now, stretched out on a beach somewhere with a Corona."

"A Corona, Lizette?" Kalina laughed. "You

don't even like beer."

"With the week I had, maybe I should start liking beer."

"Girl, tell me about it. Why does it seem that this week has been so tiring?"

"You too? I thought it was just me."

"No, I feel it too," Kalina told her. "I didn't even want to come up here. I would much rather jump back into bed. Ugh." Kalina rubbed her eyes.

"Hey, what are you doing for lunch today?"

"I'm working through lunch…probably just going to grab something from the kitchen. Why?"

"I wanted to invite you to come with me. I'm meeting some old college buddies for lunch."

"Thanks for the invite, but I have to work through lunch, especially since I'm clocking out right at five today."

"Okay."

"And why don't you have a nice long lunch and take the rest of the day off?" Kalina told her.

"Cool. Thanks!"

"You're welcome."

Kalina responded to another email, took a sip of coffee and pondered over the next email in her inbox:

A year ago, I broke it off with my ex because he was too needy and clingy. He wanted more than I could give. He recently messaged me on Facebook and told me that he was a changed man and he wanted another chance with me. I'm still single, but I'm sure I do not want to try to attempt this relationship again. How can I turn him down easy?

Kalina typed her reply:

There's no need to beat around the bush in a situation like this. Just be honest and kindly let him know that you do not wish to give the relationship another try. If it will help, try to discuss the reasons why you two ended in the first place. Most likely, if you get back together, those reasons will be the same reasons you end up breaking up again.

She sent the email then stared outside again. Bryson had told her that he couldn't meet her at the café this evening, but he didn't say why. Now she knew it was because of the card game he had with his brothers. Would he be surprised to see her there?

CHAPTER 19

"Hey, girl," June said, throwing her arms around Kalina. "It's so good to see you."

"You as well…looking good as always."

"Oh, please, honey," June said. "Look at you…got the hair looking gorgeous and that outfit is too cute."

"Aw, thank you, June." Kalina had decided to give extra consideration to her appearance this evening. She'd flat ironed her hair, applied a hint of makeup to her face and brown lipstick to her lips. She wore a dressy, low-cut white blouse with a faux pearl necklace and a pair of khaki shorts that fell at the midpoint of her thighs. A pair of nude sandals completed the outfit.

"Girl, we cannot let two months pass before we see each other again."

"I know. Life just gets so hectic."

"Tell me about it. I eat hectic for breakfast," June joked.

The women laughed, then June said, "Well, come on in."

Kalina looked over to the kitchen where she saw Bryson, Everson and four other men sitting around the table.

Everson looked up after throwing his cards down and saw Kalina walking towards the couch. He threw a hand up and said, "Hey, Kalina."

"Hi," Kalina responded.

Bryson's head turned so fast, he almost snapped his neck. He watched Kalina sit on the couch and saw her lips curve to a cordial smile when their eyes connected. *What was she doing here?*

Everson glanced at Bryson, watching him ogle Kalina. He had yet to turn away. In fact, Everson remembered how Bryson had been staring at Kalina this exact same way when they saw her during lunch a few weeks back. Bryson had told Everson that he saw Kalina frequently at a café, but maybe he needed to be introduced to the woman since he couldn't seem to keep his eyes off her.

Deciding to do his brother a favor, Everson said, "Hey, Kalina…come here for a second."

"Kalina's *my* company, Everson," June said.

"It'll just take a second, June," Everson told her.

Kalina stood up and headed to the kitchen. "Once she was standing next to Everson, she asked, "What's up?"

"My, my, my…what do we have here?" Rexford said evenly, staring at Kalina.

Bryson shot him a cold glare before turning his attention back to Kalina.

Everson said, "Hey…wanted to introduce you to my people since this is the first time you're here at the same time they are. These gentlemen are my brothers – Barringer, Garrison and Bryson. Rexford and Colton are my cousins."

"Nice to meet you," Barringer and Garrison said together.

Rexford, the player of the family, said, "Nice to

meet you, beautiful," then flashed a smile before glancing down at her hand to see if there was a ring on her finger.

Kalina smiled.

"Nice to meet you, Kalina," Colton said.

"You as well," Kalina responded. "Nice to meet all of you." She looked at the group collectively, seeing similar features in the brothers, even their cousins. This was one handsome group of men. Seemed good genes ran in the Blackstone family, but it was only one of them that caught her eye – Bryson. She wondered why he didn't speak to her. He was staring, but he hadn't said a word.

A playful smile touched Bryson's lips when he saw the confusion on her face, then he said, "It's not nice to meet you, Kalina. It's *very* nice to meet you." He reached for her right hand and when he grasped it, he brought her hand up to his mouth and pressed his lips against the backside of it.

Kalina's cheeks turned red. Seemed he was good at making her blush. And had her heart rate picked up? Pulse quickened?

Bryson released her hand and asked, "Why don't you leave your number so we can get to know each other better?"

Playing along, Kalina responded, "No thanks. I'm taken."

"Oooo," his brothers and cousins all hummed together.

"Well, if you're not taken by me, then, baby, you ain't taken," Bryson told her.

"My man," Rexford said all rowdy and animated, reaching across the table to slap hands with Bryson.

The shock on Everson's face was priceless. Who was this man and what happened to Bryson? The Bryson he knew would never approach a woman like that.

Bryson watched the befuddled look on his brother's faces, but when he saw Everson's mouth fall open he knew he had to put an end to the charades. "I'm just playing around guys. I know Kalina already." Bryson laughed.

"Shrew," Barringer said. "I thought you had lost your mind for a minute."

Kalina laughed and patted Bryson on his broad shoulder, letting her hand rest there. "You shouldn't do your brothers like that, Bryson. Poor Everson looked so uncomfortable."

"I was. Man!" Everson said. "I was like…is he really trying to put his mack down right here in front of everybody?"

The group laughed together.

"So you know Bryson already?" Everson asked Kalina.

"Yes. He's been kind enough to assist me on some projects I'm working on," Kalina told him.

"And I need to speak with you about that later, hopefully before you leave," Bryson said.

"Okay. I'll let you guys get back to your game. Nice to have met you Barringer, Garrison, Rexford and Colton, is it?"

"You got it," Colton said.

"What about me?" Bryson asked.

Kalina's bottom lip twitched. "I'll deal with you later, Bryson."

Bryson chuckled, watching Kalina walk away.

His eyes rolled down her glistening legs then back up to her hair that was done neatly, hanging down her back.

"She's pretty. Nice woman, too," Barringer said.

"She is, isn't she?" Bryson agreed.

"Sure is," Rexford said. "I need some chocolate in my life. Mmm, mmm, mmm. What's her deal, Bryce? She seeing anybody?"

"You interested?" Garrison asked Rexford.

"No he's not interested," Bryson answered, unable to hide the frown growing in his forehead. "She's not like the women you go after, Rex. She's different."

"Whoa…sounds like Kalina might be more than just a workmate," Colton added. "I think you better stand down, Rex."

"Kalina and I work together. That's all," Bryson said.

"So why are you being all possessive if you only *work* with her?" Rexford asked.

"Because she's a decent woman who I care about," Bryson said honestly. "Besides, Rex, don't you have enough women fighting over you already?"

The men chuckled.

"If you like her, Bryson, you should probably let her know," Garrison suggested. "I haven't seen you date anyone since Felicia and—"

"There you go bringing her up again," Bryson said. "Why are y'all so fascinated with Felicia?"

"It's not a fascination with her," Everson said. "It's confusion surrounding your divorce. We *did* know Felicia for over six years. We were all at the wedding and now—"

"Everything doesn't need to be laid out in the open, especially issues regarding my personal life, now are we playing cards or what, fellas?" Bryson asked.

Everson picked up the deck of cards, shuffled them and said, "Your deal," placing the stack on the table in front of Bryson.

* * *

"So how's your mom?" June asked Kalina after she placed a bowl of popcorn on the table. Then she poured them both a glass of wine.

"Honestly, she's not doing so well. It's like everything the doctor told us would happen is happening. She's having difficulty speaking now. She can't do simple tasks we take for granted."

June nodded, remembering how her mother was during the final stages of Alzheimer's. "I know how it is, Kalina. I lived it."

"I need to ask you something and, forgive me if this sounds a little insensitive, but how did you prepare yourself for...you know...your mother's death?"

"Well, I had to be real with myself. I knew it was going to happen, and I didn't want to hold out hope that science would miraculously come up with a miracle cure and save her life in the nick of time. I just saw things for what they were. She was going to die and there was nothing I could do about it. Still, when she died, it was still hard on me. I don't think the pain will ever go away, but I find solace in knowing that she's not hurting anymore and that, while she was living, I was there for her."

Kalina took a sip of wine. "I try to see my mom at least once a week. I feel guilty that I don't go more often than but I think if I did, I would lose my mind. I can barely keep it together now."

"Well, at least you're there for her."

"Yeah, unlike my father."

June shook her head. "I still can't believe he left her like that. My father wouldn't leave my mother's side. He stayed by her until the end."

"Well, she was lucky to have a man like him."

"Yes, she really was." June took a sip of wine. "Speaking of having a man, what's up with you and my brother-in-law?"

A smile grew on Kalina's face. "Nothing. We work together."

"Doing what?"

"He helps me out with the blog. We usually meet at my aunt's café in the evenings and—"

"Wait…you're serious."

Kalina grinned. "Yes, I'm serious."

"You mean to tell me that Bryson Blackstone—"

"Shh…don't let him hear you. I don't want him to think I'm talking about him."

"Well, you *are* talking about him." June laughed. "You like him, don't you?"

"We have a good working relationship. In that aspect, yes, I like him."

"And there's nothing else? No sparks? No chemistry?"

"No, ma'am," Kalina said after taking a sip of wine. No chemistry…who was she fooling? The two of them had more chemistry than a nuclear power plant. "He told me about his divorce and I told him about my wish to never fall in love. We have an understanding."

"Oh, stop it, Kalina."

"I'm serious. My father showed me how selfish and conniving men are."

"Not all men. Do you think Bryson is conniving?"

"No, but that still doesn't change my stance on the view of men in general."

June shook her head.

Kalina grabbed a fist full of popcorn. She could hear the men getting rowdy and moving about in the kitchen. Moments later, Bryson sauntered into the family room where she and June were sitting. He was wearing a pair of dark jeans and a pullover black shirt that hugged his shoulders, abs and chest. What a man! He was built like a mountain – tall and ruggedly strong. Firm. He was as handsome as men came. He had a can of Coke hidden in his hand.

"You guys done already?" June asked him.

"No, just taking a break. I came in here to see if I can borrow Kalina for a second."

June looked at Kalina and smiled. "Of course you can, that's if Kalina doesn't mind being borrowed."

Kalina couldn't wipe the grin off her face when she saw June wink at her. She stood up and followed Bryson outside into the darkness, stopping when they were standing next to his Mercedes. Bryson turned around, leaned up against the car then looked at her. Stared at her. He shamelessly rolled his eyes down the length of her legs, to her toes, then back up to her face. The lights from the street bounced off her brown skin, giving it an even softer look. He swallowed hard and tried to keep is breaths even. He didn't want her to see what she was doing to him. He'd been tempted to reach out, stroke her hair, touch her face – force some kind of physical contact with her, but to stop himself, he stuffed his hands in the pockets of his jeans.

"You didn't tell me you would be here tonight," Bryson said.

She hid a smirk and crossed her arms. "Was I supposed to?"

"No. No at all. It was a nice surprise though, because while I love my brothers and my family, all I could think about was you, sitting there in the café alone and I was so close…so close to getting up from the table, telling my brothers I had to go so I could be with you."

Kalina nibbled on her bottom lip. It was nice to know he'd been thinking about her. She inhaled a breath and asked, "So why did you need to borrow me?"

"Because you have yet to respond to my dinner invitation and it's been two weeks."

"Has it really been two weeks?"

"Yes, it has, and I've been patiently waiting for an answer."

"Well, I thought by avoiding the question, you would've gotten a hint, but I'll just tell you outright…I think we should stick to being—"

"Being what, Kalina? What are we, exactly?"

"We're business associates."

His chuckled echoed in the night air. "Business associates?"

"Yes. We work together. We're not coworkers and we're not exactly what you would call friends."

"Wow. We're not friends either?" he asked. "Because when you introduced me to Mr. Russell, you introduced me as your friend."

"Only because I didn't know what to call you at the time."

His smile remained. Of course they were friends. He knew it, as well as she did, and if she thought he would dismiss the idea of dinner, she was sorely mistaken. "We've been seeing each other every evening for the past two weeks and you don't want to have dinner with me. So I suppose coffee seems more *innocent* to you?"

"No. Us working in front of our laptops with coffee is innocent. It's business. Nothing more. Nothing less."

"Man…you're a tough nut to crack." *But I will crack you…*

Kalina grinned. "Why do you even want to have dinner with me?"

"Because you work so hard, I thought I'd step in and force you to see that you deserve a break every now and then. For goodness sakes, woman…give those poor fingers a break," he said, and in a bold move, he reached for her hand.

"That's what I was doing tonight…taking a break and hanging out with June."

"And now it's my turn," Bryson said.

His turn…

"Yo, Bryce, are you done, or did you want to

play a lil' while longer?" Garrison shouted from the porch.

"I'm not done just yet...give me a minute," Bryson replied. Returning his attention back to Kalina he said, "The joys of having siblings."

She grinned. Still holding his hand, she responded, "We can go out to dinner next Friday. How does that sound?"

"That's a whole week away."

"Very good, Bryson," she said, amused.

"Nah, I'm not waiting that long to take you to dinner. We'll go tomorrow night."

"I can't go tomorrow night. I visit my mother on Saturdays and—"

"And I'm sure you would like to relax with a glass of wine and a juicy steak afterwards."

That does sound tempting.

"Come on, Kalina. Don't make me drop to my knees. It's not time for me to propose just yet."

"I beg your pardon?"

"I'm joking," he told her. "Have dinner with me, tomorrow night."

"Okay," she said finally, just to appease him.

"Good. I'll swing by and pick you up at six."

Kalina frowned. "Pick me up?"

"Yes. Is that a problem?"

"I was thinking I'd meet you there, you know, in case I feel uncomfortable and need to make a run for it."

Bryson laughed. "You'll be fine. I won't make you feel uncomfortable, Kalina." He kissed the back of her hand for the second time tonight before releasing it. Backing away from her, he asked, "Can you text your address to me?"

"Yes. I'll do that," she said without even hesitating.

Shortly after he'd went back inside, Kalina told June she was heading home. She needed to get her rest in preparation for visiting her mother, and then for dinner with Bryson afterwards. She didn't know how she would have enough energy for both, even with the right amount of sleep.

CHAPTER 20

Visiting her mother today wasn't as tiring as usual. Madeline had slept for most of the time she was there. When she woke up around one in the afternoon, the nurse showed Kalina how to spoon-feed her, so Kalina gave it a try. The entire time she fed her, Madeline stared back at her. Kalina would smile and continue feeding her. She would give anything for some indication from her mother – a sign that she recognized her and appreciated her for being here. It would mean the world to her for her mother to know that her only child stood by her side no matter what.

* * *

Kalina came walking outside when she saw Bryson pull up. She quickly opened the door and hopped in the passenger seat. "Hi," she said, looking at him, noticing the smile on his face. She had on a red romper, showing off her legs, and some Bohemian style sandals that exposed all of her toes.

After Bryson had checked her out, even noticing the red lipstick on her lips that matched her outfit, he said, "You know, I was going to get out and actually ring your doorbell, walk you to the car and open the passenger door like a gentleman."

"Oh, no need for the gentlemanlike hodgepodge," Kalina said nervously.

He glanced at her. "What...are you talking about?"

"Just saying...no need to be all formal. It's not like this is a date or anything. Just dinner between...friends."

Dinner between friends? Not with that smokin' hot outfit. "Yes. Dinner between friends," Bryson said, beginning the drive to the restaurant. "There's a steakhouse on the Riverwalk in downtown."

"The Riverwalk?" she said, frowning.

"Yes. Is there a problem?"

"Um...no."

"Kalina, what's wrong?"

"I'm just surprised you're taking me to the Riverwalk on a Saturday night. It's usually packed with couples. The last time I was down there, I saw this guy kissing this woman and they were really into it...like they'd forgotten they were in public. Yuck."

Bryson smirked. "There's nothing wrong with a little P.D.A."

"A little what?"

He frowned and glanced at her before he returned his attention back to the road. She didn't know that P.D.A. was the acronym for public displays of affection? Then again, how could she? The woman had probably never been kissed.

Once he'd found a park, they strolled down the Riverwalk together. The place was a romantic retreat for couples and there were plenty of them out there, holding hands, kissing, hugged up and sharing a meal. The smell of food was as intoxicating as the romance that stirred about in the air.

At the restaurant, Bryson opened the door for her and soon after, the hostess showed them to a table near the windows, giving them a spectacular view of the nightlife in downtown as well as the water and the lights off in the distance. Beautiful.

"I know I suggested steak," Bryson said, "But there's plenty more on the menu if steak is not what you want."

"It's fine. I haven't had steak in a while," Kalina said, browsing through the menu now. "Which steak do you like the best?"

"I usually get the ribeye with sautéed Parmesan shrimp, and for sides, the garlic mashed potatoes and mixed vegetables."

"I'll get the same, minus the shrimp," Kalina said, lowering the menu to the table.

"You don't eat shrimp?"

"I do, but I'm in the mood for steak tonight."

"And what kind of wine shall I order?" Bryson asked.

"Something sweet."

"Like you," he said, gazing at her, watching her smile uncomfortably. "I'll check to see if they have some Kalina Cooper on the menu because, if they do, I know what I'm ordering."

Her cheeks reddened as she smiled and looked out of the window to take the heat of his stare away from her face.

When the waitress came by, he ordered their

meals, requested a bottle of Moscato and when he was alone with Kalina again, he asked, "So how was your day?"

"It was okay," she said, fiddling with her thumbs. Gosh, this was uncomfortable. Why did she ever agree to dinner with him? It felt so different – felt like he was an actual date instead of the man who helped her with work. The setting was a huge contrast to being with him in the café, and it didn't help matters that he was looking incredible – wearing a button-up, gray T-shirt and a pair of black slacks with black, leather shoes. And had he gotten a haircut for the occasion, too?

"You look beautiful tonight, Kalina."

She beamed. Okay, so maybe this wasn't so bad. All she had to do was talk to him the same way she would if they were having coffee together. After all, she must've felt comfortable enough to do this if she agreed to come to dinner with him. It was her first time having dinner alone with a man, but Bryson, she knew, wasn't just any man. "Thank you," she finally said.

"You're welcome."

She brought her hands together underneath the table and interlocked her fingers. "So as you know, I'm an only child," she told him, watching him nod. "I was wondering how it was for you, growing up in such a large family?"

"It wasn't as bad as you might think. I was the oldest, so I got to boss everybody else around."

Kalina laughed. "Of course you did."

"No, I'm kidding. I wasn't bossy at all. And as for having a big family, it's nice knowing you have people there to support you, and that they have your back. Honestly, you can meet and forms bonds and close friendships with some of the nicest people around, but no one will have your back like family."

"Well, I didn't have much family, and my father didn't have my back. He didn't have my mother's back either."

"But you have your aunt. She's there for you, right?"

"She is. I don't know where I would be without her...probably would've been raised in a foster home or something."

"Well, it's a good thing she was able to help out."

"It is. Lately, I've been trying to stay away from her and give her some breathing room without always bombarding her with my feelings. I mean, after all, my mother is her sister. She's just as stressed out as I am."

"No doubt," Bryson said. Edith had told him that Kalina was holding a lot of feelings inside and not talking about them. It was another reason why she wanted him to be there for her.

"So besides Edith, you don't have anyone else to confide in?"

"I talk to June since she knows what I'm going through. Sometimes, I talk to my friend Lizette, but I can't share everything with her since she works for me and I have to see her every day. I don't want our conversations to center on me and my issues."

"You know that's not healthy for you."

"It's fine."

"No, it's not fine," he said, straight-faced.

"If I haven't had a nervous breakdown yet, chances are I won't have one," she said, lightheartedly, trying to steer the conversation away from becoming too serious, but when she looked at him, she realized it was too late. What she said bothered him.

They sat quietly for a few moments, not saying anything to each other. She stared out the window. He stared at her.

"I've been meaning to ask," Bryson said, ending the awkward period of silence that separated them. "Why haven't you hired someone to help you with the emails?"

"Are you tired of doing it already?" she asked. "You only agreed to do it for a month. Two more weeks then you're done."

He gave her a hard, penetrating look. "I'm not tired of the emails, Kalina. I'm curious. You have a successful company. I'm sure you do well for yourself, so why not hire someone?"

"Well, I really can't afford to hire anyone right now."

"Why not?"

Did he not just hear me? "Because I can't afford it." *I did just say that, didn't I?*

"Why can't Lizette help you?"

"Lizette has specific job duties. She writes blog posts, does the maintenance on the site and a little marketing. Those responsibilities keep her occupied."

"So you can't afford to hire someone, even on a part-time basis?"

"No, especially…" She hesitated, then

continued, "I take care of my mother's medical expenses. It's not cheap for her to stay in assisted living, you know."

"If you don't mind me asking, how much do you typically spend a month for her care?"

"About four thousand dollars."

"Four thousand a month?"

"That's what I said when I found out how much it would cost. But I sucked it up and began working as hard as I could to fund her healthcare, especially since she wasn't eligible for any government health benefits."

"What do you mean she's not eligible? She's the definition of eligible."

"That's what I thought, too, but they don't cover her stay in a facility. I guess they look at it like, it's not necessary for her to be there, which is really absurd."

"So if you moved your mother in to live with you—"

"She still wouldn't be eligible for benefits, because they would consider *my* income which is greater than their threshold."

"That's ridiculous."

"That's the way it is. There's nothing I can do but keep working."

The food arrived just in time. Kalina didn't want to talk about her mother any longer and Bryson hadn't wanted her to either. He could see the pain in her eyes and hear it in her voice. Although she tried to hide it, she couldn't hide it from him.

After Kalina tasted the mashed potatoes, she said, "I hold a lot of things in, but I think you do, too." She was thinking about what she'd learned from June when she made the statement – that Bryson didn't want to marry again because of what Felicia had done to him.

"Why do you think that?"

"Because I noticed when you speak about your ex-wife, you don't call her by her name, almost like you are afraid of bringing up memories of her."

Bryson took a sip of water. "When I closed that chapter of my life, I didn't plan on rereading it, rewriting it or reopening it. And believe me, once I'm done with someone, whether it be business or personal, I'm done. There is no coming back…no in between. I don't operate like that."

"So I guess my next question is irrelevant."

"No, not necessarily. Just ask it and I shall answer."

"Would you marry again?"

"Why? You interested?" he asked smoothly.

Kalina could feel her cheeks turning red again.

Bryson laughed out loud, dabbed his mouth with a napkin and said, "You should see your face right now."

She hid her face behind her hands and got herself together. Lowering her hands, she said, "I wanted to know because, if I were in your shoes, it would be difficult for me to trust another person. I'd be afraid the same thing would happen all over again."

"Well, to answer your question, no, I do not wish to ever marry again."

"Why not?"

"Because I have the power to avoid disappointment and I'm going to use it."

Kalina nodded. "So you should understand why I chose the single life."

Bryson shook his head. "No, I don't understand that. From what you've told me, you've never been in love...never been in a relationship. You denied yourself of an experience before you could even get to experience it."

"I don't see it that way. I see it as a way of protecting myself from disappointment. Sound familiar?"

"No," Bryson responded. "That's different from my stance against remarrying."

"How? How is it different?"

"Because I've loved before."

"Oh, so I should fall in love, let the guy break my heart, then declare that I'll never love again. Um...no thank you."

All Bryson could do was shake his head.

Kalina added, "Plus, if I had to deal with a man like my father, I'd rather die alone."

The ringing of her cell phone impeded their conversation. Kalina dug around in her purse, searching for her phone and when she found it, her heart instantly sank deeper into her chest. It was the facility, but why were they calling on a Saturday night?

"Are you okay?" Bryson asked when he saw the shift in her demeanor. He'd seen it twice before.

"It's assisted living," she told him. She answered the call. "Hello?"

"Hi, Ms. Cooper. We're calling to let you know that your mother has fallen and is being examined by a doctor as we speak."

Kalina swallowed hard and asked, "Well, is she…is she conscious?"

"She is, but—"

"Is she trying to talk or anything?"

Bryson watched Kalina's hands shake as she tried to find out the status of her mother. When he saw a lone tear roll down her face, he reached across the table and covered her trembling hand with his hands.

"She's making some noises, but it's incoherent."

"Okay," she sniffled. "I'll be there as fast as I can." Kalina ended the call and got up from the table in a hurry.

"Kalina, where are you going?" Bryson asked quickly.

"I'm going to go find a taxi."

"Kalina."

"Stay. Enjoy the rest of your evening. I have to go. I'm sorry," she said, hurrying to the outside entrance where she took out her cell phone and began searching for taxicab companies while walking along the Riverwalk, alone.

Bryson took enough money from his wallet to cover the bill and tip before quickly exiting the restaurant, turning to the right and to the left, trying to figure out which direction Kalina had went on the Riverwalk.

Deciding to head the same direction as they'd come in, he quickly walked to get to the parking lot, relieved when he saw her standing in the middle of the lot with her cell phone next to her ear. Was she really calling a taxi?

"Kalina," he said, walking up to her. "What are

you doing?"

"I'm trying to get a taxi to take me to my mom," she said tearfully.

"No. I'll take you."

She shook her head. "I can't ask you to do that, Bryson."

Bryson took her cell phone from her hand and ended the call before sliding her phone inside the front pocket of his pants. "You're not asking. I'm offering. I will take you over there, Kalina."

"No," she said, tears still streaming down her face like an impromptu waterfall. "Can you please give me my phone?"

Placing both hands on the sides of her face and using his thumbs to brush tears away like wipers on a windshield, Bryson said, "Kalina, let me help you. I want to."

She shook her head in defiance.

"Kalina, sweetheart, let me help you."

Through trembling lips, she managed to say, "Okay."

Bryson guided her to his car, opened the passenger door to help her get in and then he quickly jumped in the driver seat. He asked her for the name of the facility. Once he told her, he knew exactly where it was, so he began the fifteen minute drive to get there.

Kalina's cell phone rang from Bryson's pocket. He took it out, looked at the display and said, "It's your aunt."

She took the phone from his grasp and answered with a shaky voice, "Edith, are you there already?"

"Yes, but they're taking her to the hospital as we

speak, so meet me there."

"Okay. Bye."

She ended the call then said to Bryson, "They're taking her to the hospital now."

"The hospital is a few blocks away from the facility, if I remember correctly."

Kalina nodded. "It is."

Bryson glanced over at her, watching her hands tremble as they rested in her lap. "It's going to be all right, Kalina." He reached for her hands, covered them with his hand to prevent them from shaking. "It's going to be okay."

CHAPTER 21

At the hospital now, Bryson pulled up in the fire lane. "Go ahead and find your mom. I'm going to go park."

"No, Bryson," she said looking at him. "You've done enough by bringing me here. I don't expect you to stay."

"I want to stay."

"No," she said softer than a whisper and with the saddest expression he'd ever seen on a woman. "Go home. I'll be fine."

He exhaled a worried breath. If he didn't stay he'd only be at home, worrying about her. "Are you sure?" he asked, concerned.

She sniffled. "Yes. She pulled the handle to get out of the car. "Thanks for the ride."

"You're welcome, Kalina," he said downcast. He wanted to be there with her but he could understand that this was a private family matter and he wasn't...family. Before she could get out of the car, he reached for her arm and once he had her attention, he said, "If you need me for anything, I don't care how big or small, I want you to call me, okay?"

"Okay."

Bryson watched Kalina walk to the front entrance of the hospital, the automatic, sliding glass doors inviting her inside. The sinking feeling of fear and worry that something bad was going to happen to her was all the confirmation he needed to confirm what he knew was already true – he'd let Kalina into a place he promised he'd never allow a woman to touch – his heart. After learning her, knowing her story and getting to know her as a person, he felt a closeness he hadn't felt to a woman in a long time.

He shifted the car in gear but was reluctant to drive away. Kalina told him she would be fine, but he wasn't so sure about that. Judging by her reaction in the restaurant and the way her body trembled in fear on the ride to the hospital, she wasn't okay. She was far from it. She needed help and if she didn't get it, she would end up with some stress-related illness. He was sure of it.

Bryson slowly drove away from the hospital. Everything inside of him was telling him to go back. His only solace was that Kalina wasn't alone. Her aunt was with her. If something happened, at least she had some support.

* * *

"What happened to her, Edith?" Kalina asked, tears wetting her face again.

"Oh, Kalina," Edith said, throwing her arms around her niece. "I haven't been able to talk to the nurse yet. All I know is that she fell somehow. I don't know if she hit her head or what?"

"When the nurse called me, she said mom was uttering some sounds but they couldn't make out what she was saying."

"Sweetie, we're going to hope for the best right now."

"Okay," Kalina said, her hands steadily trembling.

When Edith saw how badly she was shaking, she walked Kalina over to a chair and sat next to her. "Kalina, calm down, sweetie. Please."

"I am calm."

"No. You're shaking."

"I know. This is a normal reaction right?" She dabbed her eyes. "My mother is dying and there's nothing I can do about it. I'm so tired of living in a constant state of fear. It's killing me Edith. It's really killing me." Kalina leaned against her aunt's shoulder when she felt Edith's arm around her.

"I know, Kalina. I know," Edith said, sniffling. "I try to be strong for you, Kalina, but I know it's not enough. But we have to rely on each other, sweetie. We're all we have."

"I know."

A nurse stepped into the waiting room and said, "Ms. Edith?"

"Yes," Edith said, standing up.

Kalina stood up, too.

The nurse continued, "We've done a thorough examination on Madeline. She didn't hit her head, which is very good news. She did, however, fracture her hip, so she's in surgery as we speak."

"Surgery?" Kalina said.

"How long will she be in surgery?" Edith inquired when she saw the panic on Kalina's face.

"Anywhere from two to four hours."

"Okay," Edith said.

"And she's doing well in surgery?" Kalina asked.

"Yes. So far, so good. We'll be sure to keep you up-to-date and let you know when she's in recovery."

"Thank you," Edith replied.

"You're certainly welcome."

Kalina and Edith returned to their seats, both quiet for a moment, soaking in all the nurse had said. Madeline was in surgery. All they could do now was pray she came out of it successfully.

CHAPTER 22

It had been a long, stressful night…

Sunday morning, Kalina sat straight up in the chair, stretching, remembering where she was and what happened last night. Her mother had successfully come out of surgery and, for a brief moment, she and Edith were able to see Madeline as she rested quietly. Peacefully.

Kalina rubbed her eyes. Seemed every muscle in her body ached and, as she tried to stand up, her joints crackled and popped. Sleeping in the chair locked her body up tight. Standing up now, she stretched her arms, watching Edith walk in her direction with two cups of coffee on a carrying tray and two pastries.

"Good morning, sweetie. I figured you'd want coffee this morning."

"Thanks, Edith."

"And I got you this cream cheese croissant."

Kalina took it, sat down again and sipped on the coffee before taking a bite of the pastry. "Did they say how long mom was going to be in here?"

"About a week is what the nurse said."

"An entire week?"

"Yes, but look at it this way…at least she'll be getting the care she needs."

"You're right." Kalina folded the plastic wrapper

back over the croissant. She'd taken a bite, but didn't want any more of it. She was too nervous to eat.

The nurse greeted Kalina and Edith, then told them that they could visit with Madeline. They wasted no time going to her room, and when they opened the door, they saw her lying there, sleeping. Still, they sat down and watched her, waiting for her to open her eyes, make some noises – something.

A few knocks had them looking in the direction of the door, watching it open as a woman walked in with a bouquet of flowers. They thanked her after she'd placed the vase on the countertop, then she quickly exited.

"Aw, these are nice," Kalina said. "I wonder if they're from the facility."

Edith stood up, walked over to the counter, removing the small card from it. The note read:

Get well soon. – Bryson

Edith smiled. How thoughtful of him to do such a kind gesture. But then, another thought crossed her mind – how did Bryson know Madeline was in the hospital?

"Who's it from, Edith?"

"It's from Bryson. Did you tell him your mom was here?"

"I did. I was with him last night. He's the one who drove me here."

"You were with him last night?" Edith inquired.

"Yes. He talked me into having dinner with him. I got the phone call about mom while we were eating and he insisted on bringing me here, even though I wanted to get a taxi."

"Well, that was nice of him," Edith responded.

Kalina heard her phone vibrating in her purse. She took it out and saw Bryson's name on the display. "Looks like we talked him up," she said. She stepped out of the room to take his call.

"Hi, Bryson."

"Kalina, how's everything going?"

"It's going as well as it can be, I guess."

"How's your mother?"

Kalina pulled in a breath and said, "She had to have surgery last night. She fractured her hip when she fell. The good thing is, she didn't hit her head."

"And how did the surgery go?"

"It went well. She's resting now. The doctor says she's going to be here for about a week."

"Okay, um—" He wanted to do something to show his support, but he didn't want to come across as being intrusive.

"Oh, thanks for the flowers, by the way. They're beautiful. I'm sure mom will love them."

"You're welcome. Hey, can I bring you and Edith some lunch or anything?"

"No. You've done enough already, Bryson, and thank you so much for bringing me here last night. I'm sorry about dinner, though."

"That's okay, Kalina. Getting you to the hospital was more important. Anyway, I'll let you get back to your mom."

"Okay."

"I'll try to call you again before the day is over."

"All right."

Kalina placed her phone back inside the pocket of the red romper she still had on from last night before returning to her mother's room. She walked over to the bed and studied her, softly stroking her hair. Madeline was only fifty-seven years old, but she looked much older. Her looks began fading years ago.

"I love you, mom," Kalina whispered. She remembered when they would take turns brushing each other's hair, painting their fingernails together and watching movies. Madeline wasn't only her mother – she was also a friend – someone Kalina could count on. Confide in. If she was having trouble in school, she didn't hesitate to talk about it with her mother.

Kalina glanced back at Edith and just that quick look jogged another memory – something that was buried deep inside of her mind but was coming to the forefront now. She remembered coming home from school one day – she must've been ten years old – and hearing Madeline and Edith arguing about something. They were both yelling, furious and her mother had tears in her eyes. Peeping around the door with her backpack still on her back, she just watched. Edith ended the argument by yelling, "You can have both of them. I don't care." After that she left, slamming the door behind her.

Blinking quickly to bring herself back to reality, Kalina stood up from the bed and sat down next to Edith again. "It's so strange to me that, with all this research and all this money being thrown at funding the research, no one knows why people get Alzheimer's disease. Doesn't that seem odd to you,

Edith?"

Edith nodded. "Well, it's not just Alzheimer's disease…they still don't know where cancer comes from or multiple sclerosis…and the list goes on."

Kalina shook her head. "A lot of people think it's a conspiracy, you know."

"How so?"

"Well, if there was a cure for diseases like Alzheimer's, cancer and multiple sclerosis, it would cripple the health care industry. Think about all the money drug companies would lose if there was a cure for most of these diseases and people didn't have to worry about buying all this outrageously priced medication any longer. Think about how empty hospitals would be…their revenue would decrease dramatically, not to mention the amount of jobs that would be lost."

"I don't know, Kalina. I have to think that if there was a cure, it would've been announced and given to people."

Kalina buried her face in her hands. "You're probably right." She stood up and said, "I'm going to go for a walk."

"Okay, sweetie."

Kalina took the elevator to the ground floor then walked outside, the sun hitting her from all angles. She wondered how it would feel to be normal for a change – to not live in a constant state of panic. Would she ever know that feeling?

CHAPTER 23

Bryson sat at the dinner table at Barringer and Calista's house again. Even though their relationship seemed strained, Barringer and Calista had somehow managed to make a feast together – smothered pork chops, macaroni and cheese, a Greek salad, corn, biscuits and fried chicken. And everything tasted as good as it smelled.

Bryson glanced around the table. Candice, Calista and June were asking Vivienne if she'd thought of any baby names, especially since she recently found out she was having a boy. She told them that Garrison tossed around the idea of naming his son after him and, so far, she was on board with the idea.

Barringer, Everson and Garrison were discussing something sports related, but Bryson didn't know what they were talking about, nor was he trying to know. His mind was elsewhere.

He had tried to call Kalina a few times Sunday evening, but didn't get an answer. He called her again this morning. Still, no answer. Since Monday nights were family dinner night, he'd been here with the family, too worried to eat. How could he eat and be merry when the woman he cared so much about was suffering? He needed to know what was going on and he needed to know now.

"Ain't that right, Bryce?" Barringer asked, looking at Bryson.

Bryson stared back into the faces of his inquisitive brothers as they waited for him to respond. Only problem was, he didn't know what to respond to, especially since he hadn't been paying any attention. Bryson brushed them off, took out is cell phone and decided to send Kalina a text message:

Hey...been trying to reach you. If I don't hear from you within the next ten minutes, I'm going to come looking for you.

He sighed heavily and took a sip of water as his foot bounced underneath the table.

"Hey, Bryson, are you seriously considering selling your house?" Garrison asked.

"You're selling your house?" Barringer asked in disbelief, so much so that he asked the question much louder than he'd expected to. Now, everyone at the table were zeroed in on Bryson, waiting for his response.

Bryson could only shake his head. Somehow, his brothers found out everything about him and each other. That came with being a Blackstone and being well-known in the community. "Yes, I'm thinking about selling my house," Bryson responded. "As a matter of fact, I've already been looking at other properties."

"But why are you selling after you spent so much money upgrading your place?" Barringer asked. "Man, you are not going to find anything better than the house you already have. It's immaculate."

"You're right…the house is immaculate. It's my dream home, but it's also a house that's full of bad memories, and I don't wish to wake up to those every day of my life," Bryson responded.

"Oh," Barringer said. Now, he knew this move was divorce-related. Felicia-related.

Bryson didn't talk much about his divorce. He'd told Kalina that Felicia had cheated on him, but he hadn't spelled it out for his brothers. He assumed there was enough speculation surrounding the divorce. Could they not piece together what happened? Still, inquiring minds wanted to know and since Felicia moved to the west coast, they weren't going to get any answers from her.

Ignoring the stares of his family, Bryson checked his phone. There was no reply from Kalina, and he was growing anxious and even more worried. And he was experiencing another emotion – irritation. Why did it always feel like the family wanted to drill him at these family dinners?

"Just be careful not to make a hasty decision because of something that happened in the past," Garrison added. "I mean, I still don't know what happened between you and Felicia."

"I'm sure you all know, but that's neither here nor there," Bryson said. "I don't come to these dinners to discuss my private life with you guys."

Candice rolled her eyes. "Oh, so I suppose you come to hear everybody else discuss their private life while you have nothing to add, as usual."

"Candice, you really should practice thinking

before you speak," Bryson said evenly.

Candice grinned. "You're one to talk."

"Candice, chill," Everson said. "You don't have to make trouble every time we get together for dinner."

"*I'm* not the troublemaker in this family. Far from it."

Ignoring them, Bryson checked his phone again. Five minutes had passed and still, he hadn't heard anything from Kalina.

"Let me get this straight," Garrison said. "You're selling your house because it reminds you of Felicia?"

"In some ways, it does remind me of her, but I'm selling the house because I want to start over."

"Have you seen anything you like yet?" Everson asked.

"Not yet. I looked at three houses last week and this week, I have four lined up so far."

Everson nodded. "Well, if you need a second opinion on some of them let me know."

"Thanks, Everson."

"No problem."

Bryson stood up. "Sorry to eat and run, but I have somewhere to be."

"But you didn't touch anything on your plate," Calista said. "Can I wrap it up for you?"

"Sure," Bryson said, even though he really didn't care one way or the other. He just wanted to get to Kalina.

Calista walked to the kitchen, came back with a sheet of aluminum foil then wrapped up his plate, handing it to him.

"Thanks, Calista."

"You're welcome."

"All right, bro…later." Barringer said.

"Later," Bryson said before quickly exiting.

When he was sure that Bryson was gone, Barringer whispered to Garrison and Everson, "Anybody else notice he's been acting strange lately?"

CHAPTER 24

Bryson stood at Kalina's front door, pushing the doorbell. It was a little after eight o'clock and her car was parked in the driveway. That didn't mean she was home. She could've been with Edith, but still, he wanted to find out.

He pushed the doorbell again and waited, releasing a worried sigh while mumbling, "Where are you, Kalina?"

When he heard commotion at the front door, he stood in anticipation, eager to lay eyes on her.

Kalina opened the door and asked, "Bryson, what are you doing here?"

He studied her for a moment, looking her up and down. Her hair was a mess like she'd just gotten out of bed from a hard sleep. She had on a white T-shirt and a pair of gray leggings.

"I'm sorry, did I wake you?"

"Yes, you did. What's going on?"

"Nothing…wanted to come by to check on you since I haven't been able to reach you by phone. I've been trying to call since Sunday afternoon, and I've sent texts—"

"I know. I…I don't want you to worry about me, Bryson. It's not your job."

"Then whose job is it, Kalina?"

"What?"

"I asked you whose job is it?" he said, taking steps forward until he was standing in the foyer. "Who's going to make sure you're okay? That you're not over here crying your pretty eyes out and thinking that everything is hopeless? That nothing matters? That you've been dealt a hand full of bad cards and there's nothing left for you to do but fold? Who's going to help you when you stop talking about your *true* feelings to Edith because you don't want her to worry excessively about you? Who's going to be there when you finally break down and totally lose it?"

Tears dropped from her eyes. "It can't be you. You don't understand, Bryson."

"But I do understand," he said, closing the door behind himself. "Kalina, I know what it feels like to lose someone I love and, while I know your mother is still alive, I know she's not the same person you remember. It must be a pretty messed-up feeling to love someone and that person doesn't even know you. It must be awful to watch someone you love die little by little over the years."

More tears fell from Kalina's eyes.

Bryson inhaled a deep breath when he saw them. Edith was right – Kalina needed help. She needed all the help she could get, and that's what he was willing to give. He walked up to her, standing in the space that should've been hers and wrapped his arms around her. Her head laid against his chest as she cried all she wanted to. A person could only hold in pain for so long. Pretty soon, it would manifest itself somehow. For Kalina, that time was now.

"It's okay, Kalina. It's perfectly fine to cry. You need to get it all out." He strummed his hands up and down her back. "Come on...let's sit down."

She followed his lead, taking slow steps towards the couch then sat down. He sat down next to her, taking her into his arms again, listening to her cry. It bothered him. He never could stand to see a woman in tears, especially one he cared about. Her whimpers crept into his heart, but he knew she needed this release, so he let her do it. He let her cry.

Minutes later, when she'd stopped crying, he said, "Kalina?"

"Yeah?" she said faintly.

"You all right?"

Instead of answering him with a direct answer, she said, "When I was thirteen, my mom gave me a small, porcelain jewelry box. It was white and decorated with pretty pink flowers and long, green stems. It was trimmed in some sort of metal, bronze maybe...and, when you opened it, it played a song she used to sing to me whenever she would put me to bed...*You Are My Sunshine*...do you know that song?"

"I do. My father used to sing it to my sister when she was a baby."

"Well, my mom kept that jewelry box on her vanity, and before she gave it to me, I used to go into her room to play with it. I can't tell you how shocked I was that she gave it to me. I was beyond excited, so much so that I took it to school one day to show my friends and it slipped out of my hands and fell to the sidewalk, shattering to pieces. I was heartbroken. I couldn't believe I did that. It was the *one* thing my mother gave me that had actually meant something to her, and I broke it. And to make matters worse, that was the same year she was diagnosed with Alzheimer's, and then I understood why she'd given me the jewelry box…she wanted me to have memories of her…good memories. Happy times. But I broke it. She gave it to me and I broke it." Kalina cried again, her tears wetting his T-shirt. "I broke it," she cried.

Bryson tried to console her the best way he could. He cradled her neck with one hand and rubbed her back with the other. He began rocking her gently and telling her over and over again that things would be okay. No matter how bleak a situation appeared to be, there was always a way out.

Soon, her body-quaking wails became less intense until she wasn't moving at all. Her sniffles dried up. Her breathing evened out. Her body lay heavy against his. That's when he knew she had fallen asleep.

With little effort, he lifted her from the couch and carried her down the hallway in search of her bedroom. The first bedroom he came to was neat – looked to be a guest bedroom. Further down the hallway, he passed a bathroom on the right, then a little further, he came to another bedroom. There. This was more like it. This had to be her room. There was an unmade, queen-size bed centered in the room. Clothes were scattered about on the floor. Empty water bottles littered the nightstand next to the bed which gave him a clue on which side she preferred to sleep. Her opened laptop was on the other side of the bed.

Bryson lowered her to the bed then pulled the covers up over her. "Get some rest," he said softly, even though she was completely out.

Afterwards, he gave her disorganized room one last look before leaving here there to rest. He walked back to the living room, sat on the couch and rubbed his eyes, feeling a bit overwhelmed. He hoped he was doing enough to help her. Then he thought of his own personal crisis involving his divorce from Felicia. For a few weeks he had known she was having an affair. He watched the changes in her, saw her having dinner with the man – the man who was their accountant. He even had to listen to her deny the affair when he already knew otherwise. Once she couldn't lie about it any longer, she had apologized and told him she wanted their marriage to work. She said she was willing to go to counseling and start over. She begged him for another chance, citing how everyone makes mistakes and how this had been a mistake she'd made – one she wouldn't make again. A few days later, she was with the accountant again.

It was a difficult time in his life. Divorcing the woman he thought he would spend the rest of his life with had proven to be the hardest thing he had ever done, especially when the family loved her so much. And since he offered no explanation why he had divorced her, he left everyone to their own assumptions.

He glanced at his watch. It was close to ten. He had to open his office in the morning before 8:00

a.m. He preferred getting there around 7:30 a.m. so he could get organized before his men came to clock-in. Tonight, he knew Kalina needed him more.

He stood up and walked to the kitchen. It was more of a mess than her bedroom. Dishes were piled up in the sink and the island was covered with things that should've been put away – coffee, sugar, bread, cereal boxes, oatmeal and potato chips. When would she have time to clean? All her time was tied up in her company – making sure she kept the blog up and running and that her business was a success. From their conversation over dinner, he got the impression that her drive behind it wasn't because she wanted to become rich and famous. Her motivation for working was so she had the funds to take care of her mother's medical bills.

Rolling up his sleeves, Bryson began rinsing dishes before loading them all in the dishwasher. He cleared the countertops and the island. Afterwards, he wiped them down with some antibacterial surface cleaner he'd found in the cabinet underneath the sink. Afterward, he swept and mopped the floor, restoring her kitchen to a condition in which Kalina probably hadn't seen it in quite some time.

He took a bottle of water from the refrigerator and walked to her room with it, leaving it on the nightstand. He watched her for a moment as she slept. She was quiet, sleeping as soundly as a newborn.

Deciding to tidy up her room a bit, he picked up all the clothes on the floor and threw them in a hamper he found in her walk-in closet. He picked up her shoes and placed them with the rest of the organized shoes in her closet. Scooping up all the empty water bottles from her nightstand, he took them to the kitchen, dropping them in the recycle bin he found there.

Finally, he took her laptop from the bed and after turning off the lights, he closed the door. He sat on the couch with her computer comfortably on his lap and, on discovering her laptop wasn't password protected, he opened her inbox and decided to answer as many emails as he could. Her inbox contained a little over four-hundred unread emails. What a daunting task for a young woman with her issues.

At any rate, he got to work, answering and replying to emails, one after the other. He knew she preferred to check over his email responses, but lately, she hadn't been checking them. She was comfortable with his responses so he was certain she would be okay with his replies.

Bryson rubbed his eyes and looked at his watch – 1:37 a.m. He'd gotten her inbox down to three-hundred emails and now, he couldn't keep his eyes open. He placed her laptop on the coffee table before reclining on the sofa. He'd much rather have his bed, but he wouldn't leave Kalina alone. He would stay the night, just in case she woke up and needed to talk.

CHAPTER 25

The knocks at the door took Bryson out of his sleep. He opened his eyes, took in his surroundings, remembering where he was – at Kalina's house. He glanced at his watch. It was a few minutes after eight. So he knew it must've been Lizette at the door.

Bryson opened the door and watched a frown form in the woman's forehead. No doubt she was confused to see him answering Kalina's door.

"Um, who are you?" Lizette asked.

"I'm Bryson."

"Oh...*you're* Bryson, the coffee shop guy," she said, looking him up and down.

Bryson grinned. "Yes, that would be me. And you work with Kalina, correct?"

"Yes. I'm Lizette."

"Nice to meet you, Lizette."

"Hey, speaking of Kalina, where is she exactly?"

"She's still sleeping. Why don't you come in and set up wherever you guys work. I'm sure she'll be up in a lil' while."

"Alrighty," Lizette said, walking in with her bag. She headed up the stairs to the loft.

Bryson walked to the kitchen, took a canister of Folgers from the pantry and brewed a fresh pot of coffee. Deciding to cook breakfast for Kalina, he fried some eggs and bacon, gathered it into a plate and left it in the microwave. He walked to her bedroom, tapped on the door and when he didn't get an answer, he turned the knob, pushed it open and saw her lying there, in a different position from when he'd last checked on her. This time, she was facing the nightstand. He also noticed she'd drank some of the water he left for her.

Stepping further into the room, he said, "Kalina."

"Huh?" she said, with her eyes still closed.

"Are you okay?" he asked, deciding not to go any closer. He didn't want her to feel uncomfortable in any way.

Kalina opened her eyes, looking up at the tall man standing in her bedroom. She remembered crying in his arms last night. Remembered him telling her everything was going to be okay. When she'd gotten up to use the bathroom last night, she noticed her room had been cleaned up. Clothes and shoes weren't scattered about on the floor. In fact, she noticed that her shoes were placed neatly in the closet. The empty water bottles that were on her nightstand were gone and replaced by only one bottle of fresh water. She knew he'd left it there, just like she knew he'd cleaned up her room. And he stayed the night…

After her early morning bathroom trip, she walked to the living room and saw him lying there, his lengthy body stretched out on the expanse of the sofa. Her laptop was on the table.

"Kalina?"

The sound of his voice, saying her name, forced her out of a daydream. "Yes?" she said, softly.

"Are you okay?"

"Yes. I'm okay."

"All right. Ah…it's almost 8:30. Lizette arrived about thirty minutes ago so she's already upstairs. Also, I also left you some breakfast in the microwave. I'm going to get going now, but I will check in on you later, so please answer your phone for me, sweetheart."

"Okay. I will."

Kalina sat up in the bed, stretching. When she got up, she took a shower – a long, hot one. After getting dressed, she walked to the kitchen and for a second, she thought she was in the wrong house. It had been cleaned from top to bottom. She shook her head.

Bryson…

He'd made coffee, too and walking over to the microwave, she pressed a button to open it, revealing a plate of eggs and bacon he'd cooked for her. She smiled. She'd never had a man do anything like this for her before. She never had a man, period. So why was Bryson doing this? Was he *that* concerned about her? Why would he go above and beyond to help her like this? It was still a bit of a mystery to her, but she had to admit that she liked the perks of having him as a…friend.

Pushing the microwave door closed, she pressed the number one to heat up her food for a minute, then after pouring a cup of coffee, she sat at the island and ate breakfast. She figured she'd call Edith, too. She was sure Edith was still at the hospital.

"Hey, there Kalina. I hope you got some rest."

"I did. How's mom?"

"She still hasn't opened her eyes. Her vitals are good, according to the nurse, but it's a waiting game now."

"Okay. I'll be back up there around six."

"All right, honey. See you then."

After she'd finished eating, Kalina looked around the kitchen again. She couldn't remember the last time it had been so organized and tidy. Bryson must've thought she was a slob judging by the way it looked before.

She took her plate to the sink and after taking her laptop from the living room table, she headed upstairs to get to work.

"Well, well, well...don't we looked well-rested and refreshed this morning," Lizette said.

"I do, because I sure don't feel refreshed. It's been a rough weekend for me. That's for sure."

"Does that mean Bryson spent the weekend or what?" she asked with a smirk.

"Get your mind out of the gutter, Lizzie."

"What am I supposed to think? You got the man answering your door and all..."

"My mother fell over the weekend and broke her hip. She's in the hospital right now."

"Oh my gosh, Kalina. Why are you working? Go be with your mother."

"I will, later, but I have to get some work done right now."

"Kalina—"

"I have to work, Lizzie, but trust me...I'm okay. Bryson stopped by to check on me last night and I...I sort of broke down and he was there for me." A small smile touched Kalina's lips. *He was there for me.*

She opened her laptop and was surprised to see the numbers of new emails in her inbox. Just last night, there were over four-hundred. Now, there were a little over three hundred. Had Bryson been answering emails on her behalf?

She clicked on the 'sent' folder and sure enough, she saw emails that had been answered late last night and on until early this morning – the last of which was sent at 2:38 a.m.

* * *

Bryson blinked quickly when he felt his eyes closing. Three cups of coffee later, he was still exhausted from last night, but even still, he was glad to help Kalina. He found himself thinking about her often today, envisioning her lying in bed, tears stained into her beautiful face. Everything about her was beautiful – well except for her tears. And her life. Her life as in turmoil. He couldn't imagine what she was going through with the strong possibility of losing her mother. He had a good relationship with his parents. All the siblings did. To think about them dying was heartbreaking. He had a feeling that Kalina's heart was already broken.

He took his cell phone from his shirt pocket and dialed Edith.

"Bryson?"

"Hi, Edith."

"Hey, Bryson. Is everything okay with Kalina? I

spoke to her this morning."

Bryson leaned back in his chair. "Yes, Kalina's fine. I was calling you to find out how Madeline is doing?"

"Oh," Edith said surprised he was inquiring about her sister. "She's okay. The nurses have been in and out all day checking on her. They said her vitals were good and—"

"Edith, give me your gut feeling. I don't mean to come across insensitive by any means, but if it's not looking too good for her, I need to start preparing Kalina now. So please, just tell me straight up."

Edith swallowed hard and sighed. "It's not looking good at all, and my gut feeling is..." she stopped talking to take breath and to dab her eyes. With a shaky voice, she continued, "My gut feeling is that she's not going to make it out of this hospital. I think Kalina knows it, too, but she's not ready to face that reality yet."

Bryson leaned forward, propped his elbows on the desk and shook his head.

"Listen, Bryson...I know I told you to be an outlet for Kalina, but I think it's time to let her be."

Bryson frowned. "No. I can't do that."

"Why not?"

"Because I'm...I'm invested now. I can't walk away from her and pretend like I don't care about her because I do, Edith."

"I know you do, Bryson, but—"

"Do you know I was with her last night? Did she tell you?"

"No. She didn't mention it."

"I stopped by her house last night because she

wasn't answering my phone calls. And she just broke down and cried herself to sleep in my arms. She needs me and I can't walk away now. I won't walk away."

Edith nodded. "Okay, Bryson."

CHAPTER 26

"You give the best hugs," Edith said to Kalina.

"So do you, Edith."

Edith returned to her seat.

Kalina sat down beside her as they sat in her mother's room. Madeline was still sleeping. Still connected to a monitor and intravenous fluid. "Have you been here all day?"

"Yes, I have."

"Who's running the café?"

"No one. I closed up shop for the day."

"Well, I'm staying with mom tonight and tomorrow so you can get a break and get back to the café."

"Oh, no, honey. I'll be fine," Edith said. "Besides, you need to work."

"I brought my laptop with me. I can work right here while I'm sitting with mom."

"Well, we'll both stay."

They both looked shocked when they heard mumbling noises from Madeline. They rushed over to the bed and saw Madeline open her eyes.

"Mom?" Kalina said, holding her mother's frail hand. Tears of happiness welled up in her eyes. "Mom, can you hear me?"

Madeline continued mumbling.

"I'm going to get a nurse," Edith said, leaving

the room to walk down to the nurse's station.

Kalina kissed her mother on the cheek and stroked her hair. "Mom, it's me. It's Kalina."

Madeline's eyes closed again.

"Mom," Kalina said, wanting desperately to see her mother's eyes again. "Mom?"

When Edith was back in the room with the nurse, Madeline's eyes remained closed.

"She just closed her eyes," Kalina said. "But she was mumbling before."

The nurse nodded. "Okay."

"Why is she mumbling?" Kalina inquired. "She usually attempts to say clusters of words. Why isn't she doing that? Did the fall do something to her?"

"It could have, Ms. Cooper, but your mother has late-stage Alzheimer's. Losing the ability to communicate comes with the final stage."

The final stage...

With tears resting on her eyelids, Kalina said, "So she's never going to talk again?"

"It's highly unlikely at this point," the nurse said.

Tears effortlessly rolled down Kalina's face. She walked away from her mother's bed and returned to the chair.

Edith remained talking to the nurse, but Kalina was too distraught to listen any longer. She knew what the nurse was saying in not so many words...her mother was dying and it would only be a matter of time now.

When the nurse left the room, Edith sat down next to Kalina. She swallowed hard and said, "Kalina...um..." Tears fell from her eyes. "I think it's time for us to face the reality that your mom is not going to leave this hospital."

"Don't say that, Edith," Kalina cried. "Don't say that."

"I don't want to say it. She's my sister and I love her, but it's time to face reality."

Kalina shook her head. "No."

"Kalina—"

"No, Edith. I will not give up on her. I can't give up." Kalina exited the room in tears. With her vision blurred, she made her way to the cafeteria where she sat down at a table in the corner and dabbed her eyes with a napkin. She took out her laptop, hoping that by working, she'd forget her aunt's words, but even after sending fifteen emails, the tears kept flowing – almost like they were uncontrollable. And she didn't bother wiping them away anymore. So what a few people had walked by staring at her like she was a crazy person? She didn't care. She was in pain.

"Your aunt told me I would probably find you here."

Kalina looked up when she heard Bryson's voice. How long had he been standing there?

Bryson sat across from her, not saying anything for a while. He observed her, watching tears fall, one after the other each one feeling like a stab to his heart. In a calm, caring voice, he said, "I think you need to talk to someone…a professional."

"No, I don't."

"You do, Kalina."

"Then I won't. I've been dealing with this for years on my own—"

"And that's the problem," he said, interrupting

her. "You need to talk to someone."

Kalina slammed her laptop closed. "And tell them what, Bryson? That my mother is dying? What would be the point? It's not like a therapist can make my mother any better."

"The therapist would be for the purpose of helping you, Kalina…helping you to cope with all that's going on."

Kalina covered her face with her hands, still in tears and exasperated. She flipped her laptop open again and began working.

Bryson sighed. "I brought you some dinner."

"I'm not hungry."

"You need to eat, Kalina."

"I'm…not…hungry, and I don't need you here with me, Bryson. I'd rather be alone."

"I'm sure you would like to be, but I'm not going anywhere."

Frustrated, she asked, "Why can't you leave me alone?"

"Because I care about you, and I don't want anything bad to happen to you."

Kalina swiped tears from her face.

"Kalina, look at me, please."

She looked up at him, into his worried eyes. "Please eat. You need to eat, sweetheart. Please."

Kalina closed the laptop and placed it in the chair beside her. She would rather have been alone, but then she thought about all the things Bryson had done for her the night before. And he didn't have to bring dinner to the hospital, taking time out of his day – his life – to help her. But he did. The least she could do was show her appreciation for it. She pulled the Styrofoam tray in front of her and opened it to see that he'd brought her some rotisserie chicken, peas and mashed potatoes. She took the plastic spoon from the package, tasting the mashed potatoes first.

"You like it?"

Kalina nodded. "Where's your food?"

"I ate already."

"Oh."

Kalina ate quietly, feeling Bryson's eyes on her. Her tears had since dried up. "Thank you for bringing dinner."

"You're welcome."

"And thank you for cleaning up my bedroom and the kitchen. I know you thought you were in the middle of a war zone when you stepped into my house."

"No, I just know you."

"Oh gosh…you think I'm a slob."

"No, not at all, Kalina. I know what you've been going through. If I was under as much stress as you, I'd be too preoccupied with other things to worry about chores."

Kalina continued eating, taking a bite of chicken.

"So are you staying here tonight?" he asked.

"I want to. Edith wants me to leave, though. I don't think she wants me to be here when it happens…when mom dies."

"Kalina, you shouldn't be—"

"I know I shouldn't be thinking about that, but I've thought about it every day for years and now, I feel her slipping away. It's such a helpless feeling to love someone so much, yet not be able to do a thing to help them."

"Kalina, I've seen all that you've done for your mother. You take care of her medical bills and you work nonstop to make sure you have the funds to do so. You visited her frequently, even when she doesn't know who you are, and yet she can do nothing in return for you. That in itself says a lot about you...about your character."

"I just wish she knew I was there. That Edith was there. She's going to die thinking that she was alone because the only person she halfway remembers is Stanley."

"And you said he's never tried to contact you or Edith to find out how your mom was doing over the years?"

"Not once, Bryson. He's been completely absent this whole time, but why should he care about us when he was a new life. It's just...it's not right."

"No, it's not right."

Kalina dabbed her mouth. "I don't understand why he couldn't work through it with her. That's what true love is supposed to be, right? If the tables were reversed, she would not have left him like he left her. I know she wouldn't have."

"All I can tell you is that people grieve in different ways. Now, I personally find that what your father did was very cowardly. He should've stayed, helped her, supported her and not left that burden on you and Edith, but he didn't. He has to answer to God for that."

Kalina suspired. "Yeah."

"In the meantime, I'm worried about you."

"And, like I told you last night, it's not your job

to worry about me. You have your own problems and issues, I'm sure."

"I do, but you're at the top of that list."

Kalina didn't want to smile, but a lazy, brief one peered through. "How is it that nearly a month ago I had no idea who you were and now, we're friends?"

"I guess sometimes, when you meet people, it's not by chance. It was because you were supposed to meet them, and I truly feel I met you for that purpose…to help you."

"Well, I think it's sweet, but I don't want you to get sucked up into my drama. You've done enough for me already."

"I could do more, and I *will* do more. I'm here for you, Kalina. Someone has to teach you that not all men are not like your father."

You've already taught me that. Kalina closed the lid on her food tray.

"So are you going to stay the night?" Bryson asked again since she didn't give him a definite answer when he asked her earlier.

"Yes. I'll leave early in the morning so I can let Lizette in to work."

"Then I'll stay with you for a little while and keep you and Edith company."

Instead of trying to talk him out of it, she placed her hands on one of his hands and said, "Thank you."

Her touch ignited something in him. It was the first time she'd ever really touched him intentionally. And from that one touch, he knew she deeply appreciated all the things he was doing to help her.

CHAPTER 27

In the morning, Kalina gave her mother a kiss on the cheek, hugged Edith and headed home to shower. After filling Lizette in on her mother's condition, she opened her laptop. Scanning through the emails first, she saw that Bryson had spent the night answering more emails. She smiled, then decided to thank him.

From: Kalina Cooper
To: Bryson Blackstone
Subject: thanks

Just opened my laptop and realized you had been up working last night. Thank you, Bryson. I'll find some way to repay you. I promise.

--

Kalina Cooper
Editor | CEO
The Cooper Files

———

After sending the email, she got an idea for a new post and poll on the blog. "Hey, Lizette…"

"Hey, what's up?"

Kalina swiveled her chair around and said, "You know what I've been going through with my father and all, and I want to put this out there on the blog…not my story per se, but something related to it. Can you come up with a post about marriage and sticking around when the other party gets sick? I'm thinking we can title it, *In Sickness and Health,* with two question marks behind the title, then on the right sidebar, I want a new poll asking readers if they left someone or know of someone else who left a spouse because they were sick."

"Hmm…" Lizette tapped her nails on the desk.

"You have a suggestion?"

"Yes I do, actually. I think it will resonate more with readers if they knew your story, Kalina."

"My story?"

"Yes. And quite honestly, I think it's time you found out why your father left your mother the way he did."

Kalina shook her head. "I know why he left her. He's a coward."

"Kalina…"

"Well, that's the reason. What other reason could there be?"

Lizette shrugged. "I don't know. That's why you need to go to Fayetteville and pay your father a visit."

"What?"

"Talk to him, face-to-face, then tell your story."

Kalina thought about it for a few minutes. "I don't know if I can do that."

"It will be good for the blog, Kalina. Just think about it before you make a decision."

"Okay."

Kalina turned back to her computer, then saw an

email reply from Bryson. She clicked on it:

From: Bryson Blackstone
To: Kalina Cooper
Subject: Re: thanks

I'm not looking for repayment, but I could use your advice on the houses I'm looking at today. If you can't make it, I completely understand. Just thought I'd put it out there in case you needed to do something to clear your head for a while.

--

B. Blackstone

———

She could use an outing to take her mind off of things, especially considering what Lizette was proposing. Her father leaving like he did had been a thorn in her side for a long time. Maybe it was time to face him. But since she was under enough pressure as it was from her mother being hospitalized, she wasn't sure how much more she could take.

CHAPTER 28

"So you never emailed me back," Bryson said, as soon as Kalina answered the phone. It was a little after five, so he knew Lizette had already left for the day.

"Sorry. I got distracted with some ideas Lizette and I were tossing around for the blog."

"So I take it you can't come with me."

"Would you be disappointed if I didn't?"

"Yeah, actually I would," he said honestly. "But I understand if you can't make it."

"Do you want me to meet you, or—?"

"So you *are* coming with me?" Bryson asked.

"Yes. I can leave right now."

"Wonderful. Get your purse and come on outside. I'm already parked in front of your house."

"You are?" Kalina said standing, peeping out of the window, watching his Mercedes slow to a stop in front of her house.

"Yes…just pulled up. You want to ride with me?"

She laughed. "You're a piece of work, Bryson."

"What? Just thought I'd come by in case you said yes. If you said no, I would've driven off and not even had mentioned I was here."

She giggled more. "Yeah…sure. I get the feeling you would've coaxed me into coming with you anyway."

"Probably."

"Yeah. That's what I thought. Anyway, I'll be right out."

"Okay."

Kalina jogged downstairs with her phone, walked to her bedroom to grab her purse and, after she'd locked the front door behind her, she got in the passenger side of Bryson's car.

"Good evening," he said, looking over at her with a pair of dark sunglasses hiding his eyes.

"Good evening," Kalina told him and before she could stop herself, she leaned close to him, then pressed her lips against the side of his face.

Bryson closed his eyes behind his shades, feeling an ache in his abdomen. Her lips touching him had nearly rendered him unconscious.

"So where are we off to?" Kalina asked.

Bryson glanced at her. "Did you just kiss me or did I imagine that?"

Kalina giggled. "I kissed you, now where are we going?"

Bryson smirked. He hadn't seen her this chipper in a while. He knew it was probably something she was forcing herself to do, but still, he appreciated her taking the time to do this with him. "There's a house not too far from here…the GPS says it's about two miles."

When they arrived, he parked behind Isaiah's car.

They both got out of the car, then Bryson walked up to the front door with Kalina beside him.

"Hey, man. Good to see you again," Isaiah said.

"Hi, Kalina. Good to see you again, too."

"You as well, Isaiah."

He stared at her for a moment.

Bryson noticed Isaiah staring Kalina down so he decided to break the man's trance by bringing his hands to a clap and saying, "So Isaiah, tell me what we got here."

"Oh, ah…this is a four bedroom, four bath, two-level home. The kitchen is equipped with stainless steel appliances and granite countertops. All the bedrooms are upstairs. Go ahead and look around."

Walking to the kitchen, Kalina said, "Wow. This is nice."

"Yeah, it's not bad. The kitchen I have now is a lot bigger than this, though."

"That's what you should've done," Kalina said. "You should've taken me by your house so I can have something to compare your likes to."

Had she really never been to his house? He didn't realize that until now. "I'll take you by there later," he said.

She followed Bryson upstairs while Isaiah remained standing in the kitchen. Bryson wasn't too impressed with the size of the bedrooms, especially the master. His current master bedroom could hold a king size bed, a sitting area and two large dressers. This bedroom could only fit a king-size bed and nothing more.

"What do you think, Bryson?" Kalina asked, sinking her index finger in his front pocket and tugging at his pants.

"What are you doing?" he asked with a grin on his face.

"Getting your attention. What do you think about the house?"

"I'm not feeling it. Let me go tell Isaiah to mark this one off the list."

"Okay," she said, following him.

She stood outside, admiring the landscaping of the house while Bryson spoke with Isaiah on the inside. When the men finally stepped out, Isaiah locked up place and returned the key to the lockbox while Bryson told Kalina a little about the house they were going to see next. He said it was about fifteen miles away. The two headed for Bryson's car when Isaiah said, "Hey, Kalina."

She turned around and said, "Hey. What's up?"

"Can I speak to you for a minute?"

"Sure."

Isaiah headed for his car, so she followed him there. "What's up?"

"I didn't think you were seeing anyone or interested in seeing anyone because you turned me down cold, but now I see you with Mr. Blackstone like y'all are a couple."

Kalina smiled wide and said, "I'm not seeing anyone, Isaiah."

"Oh, come on…you're out here house hunting with the man. Why else would he want you to look at houses with him?"

She shrugged her shoulders. "Because he wants a woman's viewpoint."

"Or maybe he wants a woman. You."

"If it makes you feel any better, I told him the same thing I told you, Isaiah. My heart will never belong to anyone. If I don't give it out, I don't have to worry about someone breaking it, now do I?" She smiled and walked away.

Bryson sat curious. What did Isaiah have to talk to her about? When he saw them together in the restaurant, she said he was her realtor and she'd promised him lunch. Now, Isaiah wanted to speak to her in private for some reason. And why was she smiling so hard?

"Is everything okay?" Bryson asked when Kalina was in the car with him again.

"Yeah, it's fine. Isaiah was just being Isaiah."

Just being Isaiah...

Bryson was glad he wore his sunglasses so she couldn't see the jealousy in his eyes. What did she mean he was *just being Isaiah*? Were they friends? Did she kick it with him on a regular basis? Did she confide in him about her mother the same way she did with him? Leave kisses across his jaw? The thought of it irritated him.

Bryson cranked up the car. "Did he say something about the house, or...?"

"No. He thought you and I were a couple."

"And?"

Kalina smirked and looked at him. "What do you mean, *and?*"

"What if we were a couple? He'd be jealous?"

"Possibly."

"Why would he be jealous?"

"Because he wanted to date me a while ago and I told him no...told him I wasn't interested in a relationship, so when he saw me with you, he was curious."

"I see. You two seem to hit it off pretty well. I

mean, you were practically glowing with that beautiful smile on your face."

"I wasn't smiling all that hard, Bryson."

"If you say so."

While he continued the drive to the second house they would see today, Kalina took her cell phone from her purse and dialed Edith.

Bryson glanced at her then looked back at the road.

"Hey, Edith. How is she doing?"

"She woke up like she did yesterday and went back to sleep immediately afterwards."

"Okay. Keep me posted if anything changes."

"Will do, sweetie."

"All right. Bye."

Kalina put her phone back inside of her purse and zipped it up.

"Everything okay?" Bryson asked.

"Yes. Edith said my mom woke up and went back to sleep. It's like she can't stay awake for long periods of time."

Bryson nodded. "I can only imagine how tired she must be."

"Yeah, and the pain medication is keeping her relaxed, too."

Bryson slowed to a stop behind Isaiah as they parked on the street in front of the house. Getting out of the car, they followed Isaiah to the door.

"What do you think about the outside of this place?" Kalina asked Bryson. The house was large – a two-story, red brick home that came with a three-car garage.

"It's okay," Bryson responded, unenthused.

When they walked in, Kalina was blown away by the grand foyer, the spiral staircase, the fireplace and the massive floor-to-ceiling windows. The house was something out of a dream. That's why she couldn't understand why Bryson didn't seem impressed.

She followed him upstairs. The four bedrooms were all good sizes, and Bryson didn't have any complaints about the master. It came with an ensuite, walk-in closet, a sitting area as well as a balcony with a private sitting area. And the kitchen…the kitchen was a cook's dream. There was plenty of storage, granite countertops, of course, and the pantry was huge. Then there was the nice size laundry room, the outside deck that could easily be converted into a sunroom and a backyard that looked more like a city park. As a matter of fact, the sellers must've had kids because there was already a swing set equipped with two swings and a slide. In one of the trees was the cutest treehouse.

"It's beautiful back here," Kalina said.

Bryson slid his hands in his pockets. Had he heard her? He was too busy imagining what life would be like with a few kids running around, playing in the yard. He wanted children, but dreams of having any fell to the wayside when…

"Bryson?"

Bryson turned to look at her. "Yes?"

"What do you think?"

"I think it's nice, but it would be more suitable for someone with a family, or better yet, someone who wanted a family."

"Oh."

"We can go. I'll tell Isaiah to mark this one off the list."

"All right," Kalina said, walking behind him. All of a sudden, he seemed upset. And he implied that he didn't want a family, something she had found hard to believe. He was the perfect man for a family, but maybe the divorce made him have second thoughts.

CHAPTER 29

Bryson had stopped for Chinese takeout before arriving back home. When they pulled up in the driveway, Kalina marveled at how beautiful his home was. The house was incredible on the outside – multi-colored bricks enriched by coffee-brown trim, two-car garage and the landscaping was impeccable, well what little she could see of it.

"Goodness, Bryson. You have a lovely home," she told him as they stepped into the garage entrance that lead to the kitchen.

"Thanks."

He showed her to a table, placing her takeout container there. He sat down, too.

"May I ask why you're selling?"

"You can ask anything you want…doesn't mean you're going to get an answer."

"Are you in a bad mood?" she asked.

"I'm kidding," he told her. "I'm selling because I don't want to be reminded of Felicia."

"Your ex-wife? That's her name? Felicia?"

"Yes. Felicia. I don't want to reflect on or remember things that happened here."

"So not only are you the victim of a cheating spouse, but now, you're making yourself a victim in your own home."

Bryson took a spoonful of fried rice to his

mouth, then mumbled, "I'm not making myself a victim—"

"In a way you are. You're letting her win. I haven't seen all of your home, but it looks magnificent. I'm not surprised you turned down every house you've seen so far. Nothing can compare to this house, and I think you know that already."

He nodded. "Barringer told me the same thing."

"Then stop trying to sell it."

"No. This is what's best for me right now, and don't try to tell me otherwise Ms. Bachelor's Degree in Behavioral Science." He grinned.

So did she. Palms up, she said, "Okay. I'm done."

When she finished eating noodles, she excused herself from the table then stepped outside to call Edith again. Nothing had changed with her mother's condition. Edith had basically told her the same thing she told her earlier.

Kalina sat on the top step that lead up to the front porch and sighed.

Once Bryson saw that she wasn't returning, he got up from the table and came outside to where she was sitting. He sat next to her.

"You okay?"

She nodded.

Bryson threw an arm around her. "Since you're here already, would you like to see the rest of the house?"

"Sure." Kalina stood up and Bryson followed her lead.

Back inside, she followed him around the lower

level, telling her about all the upgrades he had done to the place – the floors, new lighting, surround sound, painting – he'd done a lot to make his home his dream home. Now he was ready to throw it all away.

Upstairs, he showed her the bedrooms there, well, all except for the master. He hadn't used the room since before the divorce. He couldn't bring himself to sleep there anymore.

"I take it this is the master?"

"Yes. I don't go in there," he said and kept walking, heading for the stairs.

"You don't?

"No."

"Why not?"

"Because I don't." He turned around, watching as she touched the doorknob. "Kalina, don't go in there."

"Why, Bryson?"

"Because I don't want you too, okay?"

"You know what…I'm going to head home. You're in a bad mood."

"I'm not in a bad mood. I just—" He sighed heavily.

Kalina walked pass him and jogged downstairs, stepping outside onto the front porch again. Taking out her cell, she searched for the number to a taxi service when she felt Bryson's arms around her, his chest pressed against her back.

"I'm sorry," he said softly.

"Bryson—"

"Don't go, Kalina. Please."

She turned to face him and said, "I think I

should."

"Okay, let me explain…I…I don't use that room because I don't want to be reminded of her…of making love to her and thinking about her making love to someone else while pretending I was everything she wanted. I don't want those memories."

Kalina sighed. "Okay. I understand and I apologize. I didn't mean to upset you. With that being said, I still think I should go."

Bryson placed his hands against her face. "I need you to stay."

"Why?"

"Because I don't…I don't want to be alone tonight, Kalina."

Kalina encased her arms around his muscular frame, squeezing him. "Okay. I'll stay."

"Thank you," he said. "Can we just go back inside and talk for a while?"

"Lead the way," she told him.

She followed him into a sitting room, listening as he released a heavy sigh when he sat next to her on the couch.

"You look tired, Bryson."

"I am tired."

"I know you are. You were up late doing work for me."

"And I didn't mind it one bit…I just wanted to help you."

"Why is that?" she asked, turning to face him and propping a leg up on the couch. Bryson paid attention to her foot since it was up on the couch now. He was tempted to reach out, play with her toes, but refused. She'd probably slap him and run out the door.

He shrugged. "Because I want to be there for you. I told you I would."

"Why, though? It's not like we knew each other before. You were just some random coffee shop dude."

"And what am I now?"

"You're a good man...the only man I've ever considered a friend."

"I don't know about that...you seemed comfortable with Isaiah."

"No...I promise you I've only had lunch with him once. And if I didn't promise him a lunch, I would not have been with him that day."

"So he doesn't know you as well as I do?"

"No. The only person who knows me more than you is my aunt. And Lizette. And June. So, count yourself lucky."

"Why?"

"Because I usually don't feel comfortable talking to people about my feelings, especially a man."

Bryson hid a smirk. He felt privileged to be able to be in a position where she felt comfortable. Whether she would admit it or not, that meant she trusted him. After she said she would never trust a man, she trusted him.

She trusted him...

She wouldn't mind at all if he just so happened to pull her foot in his lap and massage it, so he did. He held her foot in his large hands, feeling her jerk at the sensation of his hands on her body, but she didn't snatch her foot away from his grasp. She looked at him, held his gaze for a moment as if she wanted to say something, but she didn't say a word, especially after he firmed his grip on her foot and rubbed it.

Forcing herself to breathe, she said, "Oh my gosh that feels so good." She watched him smile.

"Lay back, close your eyes and put your other foot up in my lap."

She did as he asked. Bryson went to work on her feet, digging into the arch with his thumbs, listening to her moan. He concentrated on her toes, massaging them one-by-one.

"Ah…oh, Bryson, your hands are like magic."

He grinned. "When you go to get your pedicures, they don't massage your feet?"

"No, and even if they did, it wouldn't be as good as this. This is…mmm," she pushed out a long exhale through her lips, closed her eyes and licked her lips. This was the life.

Bryson smirked. While he had her in the zone, he figured he'd use it to his advantage. "Hey, so my family meets on Monday evenings for dinner. I volunteered to be the host this month, and I would like it, very much, if you could accompany me."

Kalina's eyes popped open. "Accompany you?"

"Yes."

"Who's going to be there?"

"My family…my brothers and their wives. Well Everson and June won't be there. They're out of town. My sister Candice will be there, and my parents."

"Your parents?"

"Yes."

"You...you want me to meet your parents?"

"Well, they will be there so, yes. And I want you to cook dinner with me, Kalina."

"Wait...first you ask me to accompany you to dinner and now you're asking me to cook with you."

"Sorry, let me explain. So the person who hosts the family dinner is responsible for *cooking* the family dinner. Nothing can be store bought."

"Oh...I get it. So you want me to help you cook."

"If you want."

Kalina closed her eyes again and yawned, enjoying her foot rub. "I'll help you cook, Bryson. I would love to help...you...ahh..."

He grinned. "Good." He took her other foot and began rubbing, hearing her moan softly, watching her fold her bottom lip underneath her teeth and alternate between releasing moans up to the ceiling.

When she grew quiet, he realized she'd fallen asleep. She was sleeping soundly. Peacefully. It had been a long day for her. She was busy working, looking at houses with him and now, she was out.

He lifted her legs so he could stand up from the couch, then lowered them again. He stood there for a moment, loving how nice it was to have her there. He wasn't busy thinking about bad memories. Her presence there felt right – felt like she belonged there. And even though he knew Kalina had no intentions on being involved in a relationship, he enjoyed the challenge of making her see that he was a good man. That there was no need to judge all men by the actions of one man.

Upstairs, Bryson took a thin blanket from a closet in the hallway then jogged back downstairs to where she was sleeping. He spread the blanket over her, watching her rest again, admiring this beautiful woman lying on his sofa with a relaxed, peaceful face. She was a damaged soul, but in his eyes, she was *his* damaged soul and he would do whatever it took to make her realize how much he cared for her.

CHAPTER 30

"I still think you should've waken me up last night," she said as they stood at her front door, seven o'clock in the morning.

"It's fine, Kalina. You needed to sleep."

She unlocked the door then returned her attention to him, angling her head up to stare into his eyes. "Will you stop saying that, Bryson? It's not fine. You have a job to do, too."

"I do, but you happen to be more important to me than work."

Kalina smiled, but it appeared more like a blush. When she saw Bryson inching closer to her, her heartbeats increased, pounding against her chest with fierce thumps. She swallowed hard when she felt his hand rest at the nape of her neck. She glanced at his lips seconds before feeling them touch hers. She was too stunned to think about this being her first kiss and how Bryson was making a move on her. She lost herself in the moment of being in his embrace, lips-to-lips with a man who cared about her.

Like he knew she'd never been touched before the foot massage he gave her last night, Bryson also knew she'd never been kissed. He felt her lips tremble. He felt her give up all control to him, something he didn't mind. But, he would've liked some indication that she was okay with his lips taking over hers. Touching hers. Consuming hers. He got that signal when he heard her moans become louder and felt her arms constrict around him. He'd been waiting a long time for this moment and it was everything he dreamed it would he.

Kalina, pulled away from him when it all became too much – when she felt like her heart was going to jump out of her chest. Her breathing felt forced. Goose bumps ran down her body and made her shiver. The man wasn't even touching her at the moment and she was shivering...

She licked her lips, then said, "Um, I'm going to get to work now. Thanks for driving me home." Before he could say anything in return, she'd opened the door, stepped inside, closed it and leaned against the back of the door, breathing and panting like she'd just ran a mile.

Kalina, what are you doing?

Why did she allow him to kiss her when she had never let a man do that before? What was so special about Bryson Blackstone that made her weak – made her want to forget all the reasons why she never wanted a relationship? Made her want to be as close to him as he obviously wanted to be with her? The answer scared her, because history – her personal, family history – taught her that a man will love a woman as long as she never fell ill. As long as everything was okay in the relationship. As soon as a problem arose, the man was out the door. She wouldn't let that happen to her. It didn't matter how nice Bryson was, or how much he said she was a *priority* to him or even all the time and effort he'd put into helping her – she wouldn't allow a man to do to her what Stanley did to her mother.

* * *

Bryson was feeling extra good today, especially after spending the bulk of yesterday with Kalina. She had takeout at his place and, after he gave her an intoxicating foot massage, she fell asleep on the sofa. He couldn't help but take the time to admire her, to think about how beautiful she was and how little she really knew about men. He hoped to teach her.

For the first time since taking steps to sell his home, he was having second thoughts. Kalina loved his house and since he'd created some new memories there with a woman he was falling in love with, he wanted to keep it. Being there with her last night felt right. It was perfect, and they'd shared a kiss this morning, even though she pulled away from him and practically ran inside of her house, closing the door in his face. He found it amusing. Why would she allow him to kiss her, especially if she disliked men so much? He smiled at the thought of being the man – the only one – to have been able to break down her barriers. With a little more time, he'd have her all to himself, or would he? Kalina made it clear she'd never wanted a relationship. She had some deeply rooted trust issues and they wouldn't go away just because he kissed her.

Walking to his desk, he picked up his cell phone and called Edith. He'd been meaning to do so yesterday, but was occupied with work, house-hunting and anything that involved Kalina Cooper.

"Hello."

"Hi, Edith. It's Bryson."

"Hi. How are you this morning?"

"I'm good. Are you at the hospital this morning?"

"No. I'm at the café right now, but I'm going to head up there later. How are you doing with work and helping Kalina out and all of that?"

"Everything's good. I have a question for you, though," he said.

"Okay."

"Do you remember the conversation we had about a month ago, about Kalina? It was when you told me that if you had to choose a man for Kalina, it would be me."

"Oh, yes. I remember that, and again I want to stress… I wasn't trying to set you up with her. I know my Kalina doesn't want to date, fall in love or any of that, and since I knew you didn't want that either, I thought you'd be the perfect person to help her."

Bryson continuously paced the floor near his desk. "Gosh, Edith, I didn't think I wanted that again, but with Kalina, I feel things I never wanted to feel again."

"What are you saying? You're falling for her?"

"Yes, but—"

"But I was under the impression you didn't want a relationship, Bryson."

Bryson frowned. "I don't, but for her, I'd make an exception. I like her a lot, but I don't want to fall in love with a woman who doesn't want love…who doesn't want me."

"But you already love her."

"And that's the problem," Bryson admitted. "I'm struggling with what to do at this point."

"Well, I believe Kalina wants to fall in love. She's just afraid. If you can show her that she can trust you, I think you'll be okay."

He'd already shown her that she could trust him, and if that wasn't enough, there was no need to further put his heart on the line. He had to stop himself from loving her. "Ah…I have to go, but I'll talk to you soon, Edith."

Bryson dropped his phone on the desk and shook his head. He was making a mistake with Kalina – one that he couldn't afford to make. There was no sense in falling for an emotionally unavailable woman. Kalina had enough problems, and like her, he didn't want to get hurt either. But it seemed to be too late for him. His heart was already involved and now, he was at her mercy.

CHAPTER 31

She wondered why he hadn't called…

Since he snuck a kiss this morning, Kalina hadn't heard from Bryson. She was sure he would've called to discuss the dinner menu and what they would be cooking tonight for his family, but he hadn't. Had he forgotten that he'd invited her over to help him cook and stay for dinner with his family? She was excited to see his brothers again, meet their wives and meet Bryson's parents. She glanced at the clock. It was already after two in the afternoon.

"Guess I'll have to call you, Bryson Blackstone," she said in a low monotone.

"Hey, Lizette, I'm going to step outside for a minute. Be right back."

"Okay, girl," Lizette said, steadily typing.

Kalina quickly jogged downstairs and after she stepped outside of the front door, she dialed Bryson's number, surprised he'd answered so quickly with, "Hello."

"Hey…it's Kalina."

Silence. Bryson closed his eyes with the phone pressed to his left ear. *I can't do this to myself.*

"Hello? Are you there?" Kalina asked.

"Yes, I'm here. What's up?"

She frowned. "Is something wrong, Bryson?"

"No…just busy today," he said, feeling awful for lying.

"Oh, well call me back when you get some time."

"No, you're on the phone now. What's up, Kalina?"

Something wasn't right. It was coming through loud and clear in his voice. Anyway, Kalina said, "I was calling to see what was up with this dinner thing."

"Oh, um…about that…" He drew in a deep breath then said, "I was thinking that maybe it's not such a good idea."

Kalina frowned again. "What do you mean?"

"I don't think it's fair of me to ask for your time when you're already going through so much. So I got this…you go and take care of your mother."

Kalina's frown deepened. She opened her mouth to say something, but no words came out. Why did it seem like he was blowing her off? "Okay…if that's what you want."

I want you, is what he wanted to say. Instead, he said, "Yes. Take care of your mother. I'll talk to you later. Bye."

"Bye," Kalina said, listening to the dial tone since he had already hung up the phone.

She shook her head. Before, he was excited about her coming over, spending the evening with his family. Now, he was acting weird, canceling at the last minute and quickly ending the call. And why did the call seem so final – like he hadn't really planned on talking to her again?

She was certainly disheartened by the

cancellation. She walked back inside and sat at her desk. For a moment, she thought about calling him back, but if he didn't want her to come to dinner, she surely wouldn't beg. She inhaled a long breath and forced herself back into work mode. "Hey, Lizette...remember the discussion we had about my father and the blog post about loving someone who's ill?"

"Yeah. Are you going to talk to your father, finally?"

"Yes. I'm leaving tomorrow at noon, so you can work at home Tuesday and Wednesday."

"Cool. So did you talk to him and arrange to meet somewhere, or—"

"No. I'm going to show up at his house. I have his address. I don't have any other information."

"Wait...so you're going to spring this on him?"

"I am. I don't want to give him any warning that I'm coming. That way, he can't prepare a bunch of lies to tell me. He will not get a chance to prepare for this."

"Wow, Kalina. I'm all for you going to see him, I mean, it was my idea, but are you sure you want to do a pop-up visit?"

"He's already ruined my life. What's the worst that could happen? Anyway, I'm leaving tomorrow...going online to book a hotel now."

"All right, boss lady," Lizette said. "I hope you get the answers you've been looking for."

"Honestly, I don't know what to expect. I just know I need to go."

CHAPTER 32

Bryson had been in the kitchen cooking since four in the afternoon when he heard the doorbell. He had called his sister to come over to help him prepare the food, and since he needed to talk to her, he figured this would be the perfect opportunity.

He wiped his hands and walked to the front door, opening it. "Hey, Candice."

"Hey…I assume you want to talk, finally," she said with a hand on her hip.

Bryson hid a smirk. His sister was the youngest of his siblings and she'd always complain about how unfair her life was because, not only did she have overprotective parents, she also had four older brothers who were just as protective of her. Bryson could admit that he was the most protective of his sister. He always reminded her how he was a teenager when she was born. He used to change her diapers. He fed her and rocked her to sleep. He would never allow anyone hurt his sister.

"How about you help me get this food prepared?" Bryson said. "We'll cook and talk."

"Whatever," she said, walking into the kitchen. She noticed a large pan of ham, green beans, mashed potatoes, corn, baked chicken and rolls. "Looks like you have everything covered."

"Well, I still have more chicken left to fry and I

need you to put the biscuits in the oven, but first, I want to say this, Candice. Yes, I told Quinton to leave you alone."

"Why?"

Bryson grimaced. He didn't want to hurt his sister which is the reason why he never told her what he'd discovered about Quinton. And he didn't want to tell her now, but he knew he had to.

"You told him to stop talking to me because you don't like him, right?" Candice asked. "Just like you didn't like Jamar. You promised me you would let me make my own decisions, Bryson. I'm aware that I'm younger than you and that you're playing the protective big brother role, but I can take care of myself."

"I'm sure you can, Candice, but if I see someone disrespecting you, I'm going to step in regardless." He took a breath. "I didn't want to tell you this because I knew how much you liked Quinton, but I saw him having dinner with another woman. And this wasn't a friend…they were holding hands, laughing…he even kissed her after he walked her to her car. So yeah, I told him to leave you alone and I would do it again, because you are my sister, I love you and I will never let a man disrespect you."

Candice blinked quickly to clear the water from her eyes. "You should've told me, Bryson. Why let me be angry at you for so long?" She dabbed her eyes.

"Like I said, I didn't want to hurt you." Bryson walked over to her, wrapped his arms around his sister and squeezed her. "And I'll never let anyone hurt you, Candy."

Candice sniffled. "I'm sorry for the things I said at dinner."

"Don't worry about it," Bryson said, breaking their hug. "Now go ahead and get crackin' on those biscuits before the family gets here."

"Okay. Let me wash my hands first." Candice walked over to the sink and after washing and drying her hands, she began kneading the biscuit batter, rolling small chunks into a ball, flattening them and placing them on the pan. "So, Bryce, are you serious about never being in a relationship again, or did you say that only because you were still hurt?"

"I'm not hurt. I was, but not anymore."

"Then why don't you date?" Candice opened the oven door and slid in the large pan of biscuits. She watched Bryson sprinkle salt on the corn.

"I don't have the time for it," he said.

"Oh, stop your fibbing. You have time to date."

"Well, I don't want to. Better?"

"Why not?"

"Because I didn't really want to get married anyway, Candice. It wasn't one of my life goals or plans…"

"Yet you and Felicia were married for six years. Not one, not two. Six."

"Your point?"

"Are you telling me it was an accident that you fell in love with Felicia?"

"No, it wasn't an accident but, now, I wish I never met her." He also wished he hadn't fallen for Kalina so quickly.

Candice carefully removed some chicken wings

from the deep fryer before she put the last batch in. Focusing her attention on Bryson again, she asked, "So if you don't want to date, what are you doing house hunting with Kalina Cooper?"

"And how do you know that?"

"I have my sources."

Bryson grinned and shook his head. "Kalina's a friend. I needed a woman's perspective on the houses I was looking at so I asked her to tag along. I would've asked you but you weren't too thrilled with me at the time."

"I see."

"Do you know Kalina?" he asked.

"I've never met her, but I feel like I know her. Her father talked about her so much...he would go on and on and on—"

Confusion washed over him. "You know Kalina's father?"

"Yeah. He was one of my college professors. He used to talk about her all the time...about how proud he was of her for starting her own business."

Kalina's father was a college professor? Bryson frowned. "Really?"

"Yeah."

"Interesting." Bryson couldn't fathom why Kalina's father would brag about her to his students when he had left Kalina and her mother to struggle. And he was a college professor? A well-educated man? Certainly he had some morals. Then again, just because a person had a level of intelligence didn't make them moral. Or maybe Candice was confusing the professor with someone else. To find out for sure, Bryson asked, "What's his name?"

"Stanley Dixon."

"Dixon? No, you must be talking about a different person. Kalina's father's last name is Cooper."

"Noo…it's Dixon. He was *my* professor, Bryson. Don't you think I would know the man's name?"

Yeah, she would know the man's name. "What else do you know about him?"

"Um…not much. He only talked about Kalina. I think he died a couple of years ago, though."

"He died?"

"I think I heard he had passed. He had cancer or something."

Surely if Kalina's father had died, she would've known, right? So there, it was settled. This person Candice was speaking of wasn't Kalina's father. Bryson felt a wave of relief at that realization. But to be one-hundred percent certain, he asked Candice a final question. "What did he say about Kalina…about what she did for a living?" Bryson paused, stirring the mashed potatoes, waiting intently for an answer.

"He said she owned some blog that she turned into a profitable business."

The sound of his heartbeat pounded in his ears. This was her father! But why would Kalina express so much hate for her father, talk about how he never called, never inquired about her and her mother as if the man was still alive? She said he was *living it up* with his new wife. She never said anything about him dying.

"Time check," Candice said.

Bryson glanced at his watch. "It's 5:15. We're

making good time. Just check the biscuits and make sure they don't burn. I'll be right back."

Bryson walked to his home office, closed the door behind himself then sat at his computer. He typed *Professor Stanley Dixon* in the Google search engine. The second search result was an obituary with the picture of a black man. Bryson continued to read through the obituary and saw that this Stanley Dixon was survived by a wife and one daughter.

"Why would she not have told me that her father was deceased?" Bryson asked in a monotone. The question nagged him. She told him everything else. Why not that?

"Why would you not tell me that, Kalina?" he asked, thinking out loud.

And then Stanley's last name was Dixon. Kalina's was Cooper. Since he knew her mother's last name was Cooper, it was possible she'd reverted back to her maiden name when Stanley left. It was also possible that Madeline and Stanley weren't married when Madeline gave birth to Kalina, thus, she'd kept the Cooper name.

Even so, even if that were all true, none of it helped to answer the question that nagged him. He leaned back in his chair, crossed his arms over his chest and asked aloud again, "Why would she not tell me that her father had died?" Then it dawned on him. He sat straight up in his chair and said, "She doesn't know!" That explained it all. She didn't tell him because she didn't know. That's why she talked about her father like he was still alive because, as far as she knew, he was.

Bryson thought about calling her, but after he'd already uninvited her to dinner, he didn't think it was an appropriate thing to do at the time. He'd wait to visit her in the morning instead, then he'd tell her about Stanley. If she knew her father was deceased, maybe she wouldn't hold on to the grudge she had against him and, by extension, every other man. She'd be open to dating and desiring love in her own life. And maybe, he would have a shot at winning her heart.

CHAPTER 33

In the morning, Kalina packed an overnight bag, before sitting down at the kitchen table, eating a bowl of Corn Flakes. She wondered how Bryson's family dinner had gone and why he had called to tell her not to come. Was it the kiss?

If it was, well, she didn't want to kiss him either, so why was he the one canceling plans like she was out of line somehow. *He* kissed *her* – not the other way around.

After breakfast, she set her bowl in the sink before running upstairs to the office to pack up her laptop bag and a few notebooks she needed. Finally, after placing her bags in the car, she was on the road, heading for Fayetteville. She was about to crank up the radio when she heard her phone. She quickly glanced at it and saw that the caller was Bryson.

She frowned behind her shades. Why was he calling now? To tell her how good his dinner was? She shook her head, turned the volume up on the radio and continued her drive.

* * *

Where was she? He'd tried calling her five times, back-to-back and didn't get an answer. He left an urgent voicemail, telling her to call him as soon as she got the message. He'd also sent a text message. He sighed. He needed to talk to her now.

He closed his office for lunch and drove to her house. He didn't see her car in the driveway, nor did he see Lizette's car. Today was a normal workday. Tuesday. Where was she?

Maybe she went to lunch, he thought. What if she had another lunch date with Isaiah? The thought of it angered him.

He dialed Edith and when she answered, he said, "Hi Edith."

"Hi Bryson."

"Is Kalina with you?" Bryson asked, getting straight to the point.

"No."

"Do you know where she is?"

"No. As far as I know, she's at home working. It is Tuesday."

"She didn't go to the hospital today to visit Madeline?"

"Not that I know of."

"Well, she's not at home. I just left her house. Her car is not there and Lizette's car isn't there either."

"Well, I can try to call her. Now you have me curious."

"Call her and give me a call back. I need to speak with her. It's urgent."

"All right. If I can get ahold of her, I will let her know."

"Thanks."

Thinking that she'd gone to lunch, he drove to

the only restaurant where he'd ever seen her out to lunch – when he'd saw her with Isaiah. He parked and even walked inside the restaurant, looking around, feeling disappointed when he didn't see her.

She must be at the hospital, he thought. That's where he would head next.

On the way out of the restaurant, he bumped into a woman. He looked at her to offer an apology and that's when he saw that it was Lizette.

"Hey, Bryson," Lizette said all cheery.

"Hi, is Kalina with you?"

"No. She's out of town."

"Out of town?" Bryson inquired.

"Yeah. She went to Fayetteville to visit her father."

"What?"

"She left this morning. I believe she's staying at the Courtyard."

"Okay. Thanks."

"No problem."

Bryson quickly returned to his car. He didn't think twice about what he was going to do next. He wouldn't take the time to pack a bag and he wouldn't go back to his office building to close it for the day. He'd have his secretary do that. He needed to get to Kalina as quickly as he could.

He blew a breath. What would make her want to go see her father anyway after she claimed to hate him so much? It wasn't like her to do something so spur-of-the-moment like that. She was the type to do research – to look Stanley up online, find out where he worked. Where he lived. Subsequently, she would've found out that he had passed. Why hadn't she done her homework before dashing off in a hurry?

An hour into his drive, Bryson heard his phone chiming in the passenger seat. He picked it up when he saw it was Edith.

"Hello."

"Bryson, were you able to reach Kalina?"

"No, I wasn't able reach Kalina, but I do know where she is."

"Where?"

"She's in Fayetteville. Do you know why she's in Fayetteville, Edith?"

"No. I didn't even know she was going there and—"

"So you have no clue why she would be going to Fayetteville?" he asked her again. She had to have known why. And she knew something else too – that Kalina's father had died, but for some strange, unsettling reason, she hadn't bother telling Kalina. "Let me ask you this, Edith…why didn't you tell Kalina her father died, because I know you knew. You knew, and you didn't tell her and now she's going there to talk to him and the man is dead."

"Oh no…what have I done?" Edith said.

Bryson shook his head in disappointment. "Edith, she's already depressed over her mother…when she finds out her father passed, she's going to be crushed."

"I…I never thought she wanted to see him. She was so angry with him, Bryson."

"You still could've told her that he'd died," Bryson said, in full protective mode now. "Why keep it a secret?"

"I didn't think she cared to know."

"Well, just so you know, I'm on my way there to find her. I'm hoping I find her and talk to her before she shows up at Stanley's house. I think it'll soften the blow if I tell her versus hearing it from Stanley's widow."

"Okay, well do what you can. I appreciate this, Bryson."

"Yep," Bryson said, ending the call. He tossed his phone in the passenger seat then hit the gas, speeding to get to Fayetteville.

CHAPTER 34

Kalina checked into the hotel then used the phone book in the room to look up her father's address, comparing it to the address she'd written down before leaving Wilmington. She grinned to herself about how old school that was – to search for someone in a phone book, but when she saw his name and his new wife's name, Martha, she knew he had the right Stanley Dixon.

Sliding the keycard in her pocket, she left the room in a hurry, driving straight for his home. She knew she probably should've called first, but in the heat of the moment, she didn't care. She only focused on getting there – on seeing her father's face when he finally realized who she was.

She wondered how he would react. Would he be surprised to see how she'd grown up? To see that she wasn't the little teenage girl that he left? Or would he open the front door and immediately slam it in her face?

Pulling up in front of his house, she double-checked the address from the page she ripped from the phone book to make sure she was at the right house. She was. She looked at the house again. It was fancy and looked to be in a ritzy, exclusive neighborhood. There was a silver BMW parked in the driveway.

Kalina pulled in a breath and braced herself saying, "Okay, here goes, Kalina." She opened the door, grabbed her purse and got out of the car, walking up to the massive house. She rang the doorbell and waited. Beside the loud chimes of the doorbell, she didn't hear much else – no TV, radio or any other sound that could indicate someone was home.

She rang the doorbell once more. This time, she heard the voice of a woman say, "Just a moment," before hearing the click of a deadbolt lock.

The woman opened the door and said, "Hi. Can I help you?"

She lost her words. Instead, Kalina studied the woman for a moment. She was dark-skinned with gray and black hair. She had on a navy blue business suit and looked sophisticated and sharp.

"Ms., can I help you?" she asked again.

"Oh, um…yes. Are you Martha Dixon?"

"Yes, I am. And who might you be, young lady?"

"I'm Kalina Cooper, your husband's daughter, and I was hoping I could speak to him if it's not too much trouble."

Martha brought her trembling hands to her face. Sadness filled her eyes. "Come in."

Kalina stepped in and when she heard Martha sniffle, she said, "I'm sorry, Martha. I didn't mean to upset you." She followed Martha into an antique-style living room and sat on the couch next to her. She saw pictures of Martha and her father, as a couple, on the walls and on the mantel.

"You didn't upset me dear. I'm just saddened

that you don't know."

"Don't know what?"

Martha dabbed her eyes and said, "Goodness, I don't know how to say this."

"You don't know how to say what? Please, tell me," Kalina said when she saw how disturbed Martha had become.

"Your father...he passed away two years ago."

"What?" Kalina said out of disbelief. She didn't feel any pain because she didn't know her father all that well. Still, she was surprised to find out he'd died. How had she not known that before? Shouldn't someone had notified her of his passing? After all, he was her father. He was a deadbeat father, but still...

Kalina didn't know what to say next. Her father had been dead for two years and she didn't know. Did Edith know? "Um...I hate to ask you this, Martha, because I know you're still grieving, but how did he die?"

"He had a heart attack...happened while he was sleeping." Martha dabbed her eyes more. "He battled cancer for years and finally when we thought he was making progress, the heart attack happened."

"I...I had no idea."

"Your father was a very troubled man, Kalina. He seemed to be bothered by his past."

"Bothered how?"

"He often talked about you...how he regretted leaving you and your mother."

Kalina shook her head. "If he regretted it so much, why didn't he try to contact me? It wasn't a difficult task. I still live in Wilmington. My mom is still there."

"I know. He talked about going back, but every time he got close he would back out. He really did want to see you though. He tried to keep track of you the best way he could. He went so far as to make a fake profile so he could follow you on Twitter. He was happy when you graduated from college and he used to brag to anyone who would listen about your blog."

Kalina frowned. Confused. He was bragging about her, but he didn't have the courage to come back to Wilmington to face her? She shook her head and said, "You know what, Martha...I'm not buying any of it. If he really wanted to see me and *follow* me, he knew exactly where I lived. He could've visited me and my mother. Instead, what did he do? He left us. Did he tell you why? Did he ever tell you that?"

"He told me he had to get away from it all. He didn't go into any details about why he left you and Edith. He just—"

"Me and Edith?" Kalina asked, frowning. "You mean Madeline. My mother's name is Madeline."

Martha dabbed her eyes and said, "Sorry. I must've got it mixed up. Like I said, he didn't talk much about it, but I knew it bothered him greatly. He had a guilty conscience until he died."

"Well, I guess this was a huge waste of time on my part and a great inconvenience for you." Kalina stood up and said, "I'm sorry to have disturbed you with all of this."

"No disturbance at all dear. I wish you would've

come years ago."

"Why?"

"Maybe you would've gotten the chance to talk to him and get the answers I know you're seeking."

"In life, I guess some questions are not supposed to be answered," Kalina responded, thinking about the illness that was taking her mother's life. That was a question she'd never get answers to. Maybe scientists didn't have a clue where the disease came from and maybe that's the way it was supposed to be.

Kalina reached for the knob at the front door. She could slap herself for making this trip to Fayetteville. The idea, after the fact, sucked big time because she should've taken her time and done some research before jumping up and taking off. But she hadn't done so. She just left.

"Wait, Kalina," Martha yelled out of the door.

Kalina was steps away from her car when she turned around to look at Martha. "Yes?"

"Hold on a minute…I have something to give you," Martha said before walking back inside of the house.

Kalina walked back to the door again and waited for Martha to return. *Where did you go, woman*, she thought when she'd been standing there for nearly five minutes. While she waited, she took out her cell phone and saw that Edith and Bryson had been trying to call. Between the two of them, they had called over twenty times, most of those being from Bryson. Why was he blowing up her phone?

"Here we go," Martha said, pushing the door open to step outside holding an envelope. "Your father put a will in place before he died. He wanted you to have this envelope."

"Why didn't someone mail it to me?"

"Because Stanley left instructions for it not to be mailed. He didn't want to risk it being lost, and he didn't want it to be intercepted by anyone. So, here it is and it's yours."

Kalina took the envelope from Martha's grasp, noticing that it was taped closed. "Thank you."

"Good luck, Kalina. I hope you find what you're looking for."

"Thanks, Martha. I appreciate this."

Kalina headed to her car again. She doubted she'd find what she was looking for now that she knew her father was deceased. She wanted to know why he left her and her mother. Seemed she was a little, too late.

CHAPTER 35

Back at the hotel, Kalina parked her car and sat there, thinking about her father and her mother. This was an absolute mess. Her father was dead. Her mother was near death. And she was…

What was she?

Kalina rubbed her eyes. She wasn't okay, so what was she? Alone in the world? Lost? Forgotten? A woman without a purpose? A family? Even though she had her aunt, she still felt alone. She leaned back in her seat.

What was she?

Kalina shook her head, got out of the car with the envelope Martha had given her, and continued on into the front entrance, through the lobby and when she turned the corner heading for the elevators, she saw Bryson standing there.

What is he doing here, she asked herself as she walked towards him. And how did he know to find her here? Did he come here specifically to see her? Surely he didn't make the drive to Fayetteville with the sole purpose of tracking her down because she was avoiding his phone calls. Would he do that?

She looked him up and down as she got closer. He wore a green work shirt, one that had his company's name printed on it, and his hands were hidden inside the front pockets of his khakis. As she approached, he shamelessly stared at her with a keenness that made her uncomfortable for a moment, like he wanted to question her. Like he had a right to do so.

Steps away from him, she asked, "Bryson, what are you doing here?" There was no other way to ask the question although she would have preferred not to ask it at all. Besides, he should not have been there.

"I could ask you the same thing, Kalina."

"You could, but you wouldn't get an answer because it's none of your business."

"That may be true from your perspective but it has no merit from mine."

Kalina blew an angry breath and pushed the elevator button. The elevator doors immediately slid open, allowing her to enter.

Bryson got in behind her and the doors eased closed.

Kalina pushed the button for the third floor then stood on the right side of the elevator, away from him.

Bryson had his eyes on her the moment the doors closed, silently analyzing her as they moved up to the third floor. "Where's your phone?" he asked.

Kalina looked at him and looked away, leaving his question unanswered.

"I've been trying to get in contact with you. Edith has been trying…where's your phone, Kalina?"

When the elevator opened to the third floor, Kalina brushed pass Bryson and continued on to her room.

"Unbelievable," she hissed in an angry, yet low tone and when she arrived to her room, she swiped the keycard and pushed the door open, not waiting for it to close before continuing inside and throwing her purse on the bed.

Before the door could completely close, Bryson had caught it and invited himself into her room. "Kalina—"

"Why are you here?" she asked, sitting in a chair at a small, round table near the windows, resting her elbows on the tabletop and massaging her temples.

"I wanted to make sure you were okay."

She frowned and looked up at him. "Make sure I was okay? Since when have you ever known me to be *okay*? I'm not okay. I'm never okay! So why would you come here to make sure I'm *okay* when you already know I'm not?" Kalina returned to massaging her temples. She was too frustrated to deal with him right now.

"First of all, you need to stop yelling."

"This is *my* room…I'll do whatever I want in it. I didn't invite you here. You took it upon yourself to show up. So if you don't want to hear me yell, leave!"

Bryson walked to the table where she was sitting and sat in the seat across from her. He inhaled a deep breath, got his thoughts together and said in a calm, soft tone, "I didn't come here to make you angry, Kalina."

"I know. You came here to make sure I was *okay*…like I believe that. You weren't worried about whether or not I was *okay* when you uninvited me to dinner."

Bryson shook his head. Was she angry about dinner? "Look, the bottom line is, I took time out of my day to come here to check on you. I was worried."

"Worried?" she said, a tear running down her face. "That would imply you actually care."

"I do care!"

"No, you don't," Kalina snapped. "Nobody does. I could drive my car off a cliff right now…you know who would be at my funeral? My aunt. That's all."

Bryson frowned. He never seen her behave this way before and he could recognize what it was – she was upset. Apparently, she had received the news he was rushing there to give her. So instead of irritating her any further, he sat there, looking at her as she sniffled and wiped her own tears away. He wanted to console her. He fought with himself to stay seated because, in this condition, she would only push him away.

Kalina dried her reddish, puffy eyes as best as she could with the backside of her hands, looked at him and asked, "Why did you not want me to come to dinner?"

"Now is not the time to discuss that, Kalina."

"Why did you not want me to come to dinner?" she repeated.

Bryson sighed. He didn't want to tell her the real reason he had changed his mind about her coming to his home for dinner. He had told her that he did it because he didn't want to take up her time – time she could spend with her mother and while that was partially true, it wasn't the whole truth. That's what she was seeking.

"Why?" she asked.

"Kalina—"

"Why?" she sniffled.

He grimaced, shook his head and finally responded, "I didn't want you to come because I didn't want to introduce my family to a woman who doesn't love, and who never would love me."

"Meaning what?"

"Meaning exactly what I said," he fired back. "It was a bad idea for me to invite you anyway, Kalina."

"Then why did you?"

"Because I wanted my family to meet you. At the last minute, I decided not to go through with it because, why should I put myself through the torture of bringing you into their life only for you to walk right back out of it?"

"And yet, you're here."

"Yes, I'm here because I care about you, but you know what, Kalina...I'm not going to sit here and listen to you belittle my feelings for you, just because you're incapable of having any for me." Bryson stood up and paced the floor for a few seconds trying to calm himself down. "I'm going to go get some air. Why don't you take a minute to get your thoughts in order? Take a shower to help yourself relax. Call your aunt. Why don't you do that instead of trying to think of clever ways to insult me?" Bryson walked towards the door and before exiting the room, he said, "I'll be back in an hour. If you don't open the door for me, I'll take the hint, but you can't say I wasn't here for you. That's for sure."

He walked away angry, the door slamming and locking behind him.

CHAPTER 36

The taps at the door took Kalina out of her nap. She had intended on taking a calming, warm shower, but she was so tired from the day's activities, she laid on the bed and went to sleep. At any rate, the little rest did her body good because her mood was better, even though her problems remained.

Boom, boom, boom.

A second round of knocks at the door had her scooting up from the bed and squinting through the peephole, she saw Bryson standing there with a white, plastic bag. She opened the door, watching him quietly walk in.

He walked to the table, set the bag there, then turned to her and said, "I brought dinner."

"Okay," she said softly.

He noticed she was a lot calmer than she was earlier. "Do you want to come and eat with me?"

"Sure." She walked over to the table and sat down. Before she opened her tray, she looked him in the eyes and said, "I'm sorry for the things I said earlier. I'm under a lot of stress, as you are very well aware, but that's no excuse for me to be rude to you. I'm sorry."

"Don't worry about it, Kalina. It's already forgiven."

She smiled and watched his lips slowly form into a smile as well. She opened her tray and saw a pulled pork sandwich, fries and coleslaw. "This smells really good."

"It better be good. I asked the locals what to order and they recommended it."

Kalina took a bite and mumbled, "Mmm, yes. Very good."

Bryson took a bite of his sandwich, agreeing with her. After a few more bites, he said, "I was trying to get to Fayetteville before you made it to your father's house. From our previous conversations, I knew you had no idea he had passed, and I didn't want you to be devastated to find out on your own. I wanted to tell you."

"How did you know?"

"My sister was one of his students. She told me."

"He was a teacher?"

Bryson nodded. "A college professor. She said he often mentioned you. Said he was proud of you and your accomplishments."

"That's what Martha said, too."

"Martha?"

"Yes. She's his widow. He had married her after he left my mom."

"Did you get a chance to sit down and talk with her?"

"For a few minutes. She told me my father was troubled. She said he created a fake Twitter account so he could follow me. That's how he stayed up-to-date with my life over the years."

"Wow. That's a little crazy."

Kalina grinned. "It baffles me why he didn't

reach out to me."

"He was probably ashamed to. Or maybe he didn't think you would accept him."

"And I probably wouldn't have." She took a sip of water. "Oh, I almost forgot…" Kalina stood up to get her purse from the nightstand, took the envelope from it and returned to the table. "Martha gave me this."

"What's that?"

She shrugged. "I don't know. I haven't opened it yet. Martha said my father wanted me to have it."

"Then what are you waiting for? Open it."

"All right, if you insist…" She took her time opening the envelope, sliding out a folded piece of paper. "It's a handwritten note."

"What does it say?"

"It says: 'If you're reading this, Kalina, then you've already taken the first step to find out who you really are and why I did the things I did. I'm sorry, sweetheart. I love you. Dad.'"

"Is that it?"

"Yep, and looks like he wrote a number behind his name. One thirty-three." She handed the note to Bryson.

Bryson skimmed over it and asked, "There's nothing else in the envelope?"

Kalina turned the envelope upside down and was a second away from saying *no* when a key fell out onto the table."

"A key?" Kalina said.

Bryson picked it up, looked at it and said, "It looks like a key that belongs to a safe deposit box." He handed the key to her. "And I bet the one thirty-three is the lockbox number."

Kalina analyzed the key and said, "It doesn't say what financial institution it belongs to, and he didn't leave it on the note. How do I know where to look?"

"Tomorrow morning, we'll have to ask Martha what bank he used."

Kalina beamed after hearing Bryson say *we'll* have to ask. He wasn't going anywhere.

"What?" Bryson asked when he saw her smiling.

"Nothing." Kalina studied him harder, watching him wipe a napkin across his lips – lips she remembered pressed against hers briefly.

"Did you call your aunt yet?" he inquired.

"No."

"Why not?"

"I will before bed…wasn't in the mood earlier."

Bryson took a sip of water and said, "I have to tell you something about her."

"About Edith?"

"Yes."

"What about her?"

"Well, she sort of encouraged me to talk to you."

Kalina grinned. "What are you talking about?"

"She told me you needed someone, so I made myself available to you."

"She told you I *needed* someone?"

"To talk to…to confide in and, yes, she told me about the bet, too. I hope you're not upset."

Kalina shook her head. "No. I'm not upset. Aunt Edith always try to do what's best for me."

Bryson grimaced, but nodded at the same time. Her aunt surely didn't tell her that her father had died. That wasn't what was best for her. But he left the subject alone because it wasn't his place to tell Kalina that. He did, however need to tell her the truth about how else he knew her – about the email Felicia had sent to her a little over two years ago seeking advice. He kept that email in his wallet, waiting for a moment like this.

"Kalina, I have something else to tell you."

"Okay…"

"I sort of knew you, well a little about you, when I first came across your blog two years ago."

"Two years ago?" she asked with bright eyes. "You knew about my blog?"

"Yes, and before you ask, I wasn't seeking any marital advice. I was looking at your site to find out who you were since I stumbled across an email you sent to Felicia."

Kalina frowned as she watched Bryson remove a folded piece of paper from his wallet and hand it to her. She quickly unfolded it and quietly read it:

From: Kalina Cooper
To: Anonymous
Subject: Torn

Hi Confused in Wilmington,

I can't say I understand exactly what you're going through, but I will say this. You've been married to this man for six years. That has to count for something. All too often people, men and women alike, are so quick to walk away from their relationships when they think that someone else can give them what their 'missing' in their current situation. And guess what…a few years from now, you're going to be feeling the exact same way about this strange man you've been dating. If you're bored within your marriage, you need to look within yourself, not into the eyes of another man to give you a feeling of excitement. Why don't you try to go away with your husband? You said you manage the household finances, so schedule a trip together. You better believe that there are plenty of women out here who would want a man like you have. Why not take the time to show your husband that you appreciate his hard work – providing you with the financial stability that enables you to get massages and manicures whenever you want? When was the last time you cooked a meal for him? Or surprised him at his office with lunch? Better yet, when was the last time you had an actual conversation with him, looked him into his eyes and really asked him if he was okay? When was the last time you told him you loved him? Try it. If nothing else I said has struck a chord with you, remember this – don't throw your marriage away because you think someone else can make you happy. Happiness starts within.

All the best,

--
Kalina Cooper
Editor | CEO
The Cooper Files

———

When she looked up at him, he asked, "Do you remember typing that?"

"I…I do. Oh my God…that…that was Felicia who wrote me?"

Bryson nodded.

"Jeez, I'm so sorry, Bryson."

"Why are you sorry? You gave her the best advice I think anyone could have given her, and I was so impressed with your response, I went to your website, read all about you and when I saw you in Edith's coffee shop, I asked Edith if she knew you and the rest is history."

"I…" Kalina said. "I…I don't know what to say."

"There's nothing to say, I guess. Like I said, I appreciated your words to her, but when a person has their heart set to do something, it's hard to convince the mind otherwise."

Kalina nodded. "That's true. The heart is treacherous, right?"

"Right, but not all hearts are disloyal, and I'm certain the heart of the woman who typed this email knows what loyalty means, knows how to treat a man. Only thing is, her heart isn't ready and it probably never will be."

Kalina smiled shyly, then shook her head. Speechless. He was right. Her heart wasn't ready. She stood up and said, "I think I'm going to take a shower, and afterwards, I'll call my aunt and go to bed. What are your plans?"

"What do you mean?"

"Are you staying? Going home?"

"I'm staying. You need me, remember?" He smirked.

Yes. I need you. She took her overnight bag into the bathroom before closing and locking the door.

CHAPTER 37

"Where on God's green earth have you been, Kalina?" Edith asked. "Bryson was looking for you, I was looking for you and—"

"Edith, I'm fine. I'm in Fayetteville and Bryson has already found me," she said, rubbing lotion on her legs while sitting at the foot of the bed.

Bryson had been watching TV before his attention was averted to her. She came out of the bathroom, wearing a pair of loose cotton shorts with the matching top – a comfortable pajama set for bed. Now, watching her rub lotion down her long legs and to her feet, he couldn't look at the TV if someone forced him to.

"Why are you there?" Edith asked.

"I was looking for my father. I wanted to talk to him, but I found out he passed two years ago. Why do I get the feeling you already knew that?"

Edith sighed. "Because I did know, Kalina. I'm sorry I didn't say anything about it. I assumed you didn't care to know anyway."

Bryson got up from his chair. He had enough of just watching her rub lotion on her legs while she struggled to hold her cell phone to her ear. So he stooped down in front of her, took the bottle of lotion from the bed, and after squeezing a little in his hands, he took over massaging her left leg – the one she has been trying to rub lotion on.

A whimper escaped her throat at the feel of his hands constricting around her leg.

"You okay, Kalina?" Edith asked.

"Oh…mmm…um...yes. Yes, I'm okay." *What were they talking about again? Oh, that's right…her dad.* "It's not like it would've mattered…he was never in my life anyway. It just…mmm…oh…seemed odd for you not to…to tell me. Anyway, enough about that. How's mom?"

"She's still the same. No changes."

Kalina threw her head back as she nibbled on her bottom lip, feeling Bryson's hands squeeze her thigh. This leg massage was pure bliss. And Bryson seemed to enjoy the fact that he'd made her whimper. "Have they…ah…um…have they spoken to you about when she's going to be leaving?"

"No, they haven't."

"Well, I'll be back tomorrow. I'm going to…to spend majority of the day with her, so if you have…umm…other things you need to do, just know I'll be there."

"Kalina, are you sure you're okay?"

"Yes. I'm fine," Kalina said, struggling to hold moans deep in her throat.

"Okay. I'll see you tomorrow then, sweetie."

"Okay. Bye."

Kalina placed her cell phone on the bed while Bryson began on her right leg.

"How's your mother?"

He had the nerve to ask her a question while he was massaging her leg – turning her words into mush?

"Edith said she was the same…I'm going to be there tomorrow so I'll see for myself."

"So, in the morning, we'll go to Martha's house and—"

"No, Bryson…I was thinking about what you said when I was in the shower."

"You were thinking about me in the shower?"

Kalina giggled. "No. You didn't let me finish."

"Okay. Continue."

"I was thinking that you don't have to come with me tomorrow. I appreciate your concern, but I'm capable of handling this on my own."

He stopped rubbing her leg and gave her his complete attention. "I know you are, Kalina. I just want to be there."

"Like I told you before, you have your own company to run."

"Yeah, and I have it covered. I'm concerned about you right now and it's not because your aunt asked me to help you. It's because I genuinely want to make sure you're okay."

"I appreciate that, Bryson." Kalina took the lotion and phone, placing them on the nightstand. Then she slid under the messy covers.

Bryson returned to the chair.

"Hey, Bryson," she said.

"Yes?"

"Where are you going to sleep?"

"I'm fine in this chair…not quite ready to go to sleep anyway."

"Okay, well, come lie next to me and keep me company."

"No…I don't think that's a good idea."

"It is a good idea. You're not doing anything else, now come here."

Bryson walked over to the bed, lying on top of the covers, facing her. "Is this better? Huh? Am I close enough now?"

Kalina giggled. "Yes, you are." Kalina gripped his hand, interlocking their fingers.

"What are you doing?" he asked, amused.

"I'm making sure you're not going to sneak my laptop out of my bag and attempt to do some work. You've answered enough emails for me, so don't even think about staying up tonight and working. Work can wait."

"Wait…I must be hearing things because I know Kalina Cooper didn't say *work can wait*."

Kalina laughed along with him before bursting into a yawn. "I did, and it can wait, especially considering all that's been going on in my life. I need a day off."

"I agree. You're the hardest working woman I've ever met."

Kalina smiled lazily and closed her eyes.

"Goodnight, Kalina." He pressed his lips against her forehead and felt her hand squeeze his tighter. He looked at her face after leaving the kiss and saw her eyes were open. "I thought you were sleep."

"I was," she said, groggy. "Your lips woke me up." She yawned and closed her eyes again. "Bryson."

"Yes?"

"The feelings you think you have for me, I need you to erase them."

Bryson smirked. "I can't do that." He used his

free hand to stroke her soft hair.

"You have to. You were right not to invite me to dinner. I can never fall in love with you or anyone else for that matter."

"You can if you try hard enough."

"No. I'm thirty years old. If I was going to fall in love, it would've happened by now."

"Not necessarily. Maybe you were waiting for the right person to come along…waiting for me."

She opened her eyes and their gazes locked. "While I would like to believe that, Bryson, I know it's not true. I've never been in love and have no intentions on falling in love because I don't have any feeling left in my body. I'm completely numb to a lot of things around me. My heart has been growing calloused since I first learned my mother had Alzheimer's disease and that's been years ago."

Still stroking her hair, Bryson asked, "You know what I wish?"

"What's that?" she asked, with Bryson hovering over her. She could feel the heat of his body radiating against hers, and his raw, manly smell of cologne and testosterone fusing into her nose. His scent was as calming as a lavender-scented aromatherapy candle.

"I wish I had the power to absorb all of your pain inside of my heart, so I can finally see you happy for once, Kalina."

Kalina opened her eyes, releasing a tear in the process, staring up into Bryson's eyes.

He lowered his mouth to her face, kissed the tear away before taking her lips, kissing her, feeling a strong current rip through his abdomen. He shifted his body on top of hers, feeling her hands settle at the back of his head while she opened her mouth, fully taking his lips. His kiss.

He felt her struggle for air, heard the moan that caught in her throat, so he stopped kissing her so she could breathe a moment. With their eyes connected, he wasted no time dipping his head and continuing where he'd left off, savoring her lips, then leaving kisses on her face, down to her neck. Her moans became louder. Her breathing, heavier.

"Make love to me, Bryson."

Struggling to catch his own breath, he stopped kissing her neck and looked at her, not believing those words floated between those lips he'd just kissed. He couldn't make love to her. He wanted to. Every cell in his body was urging him to. But he couldn't. He respected her too much, and she wasn't ready. Besides, she was the type of woman who deserved a man who'd actually wait for her. Wait until the time was right. Until they said vows. Vows? Why was he thinking about vows? Looking at her, he said, "Baby, I can't."

"You don't want me?" she asked, tearfully.

"I do," he admitted. "I do want you, but not like this. You're in pain and I can't...I won't do this to you, Kalina. And if I'm going to be your first, I'm going to be your last and it won't happen this way. It can't happen this way."

He rolled back to his position on the bed and pulled her into his arms, listening as she whimpered. "I love you, Kalina."

"I know," she said, tears rolling out of her eyes.

Bryson closed his eyes tight and let out a

distressful breath, because he knew he was in love with a woman who couldn't love him back.

CHAPTER 38

He wanted her to ride with him. Bryson had no idea what the envelope contained, and he wasn't about to let her drive. Her nerves were bad enough already. So after they'd dressed and she checked out of the hotel room, she threw her bag in the trunk of her car and left her vehicle parked at the hotel.

Bryson drove her to Martha's house and, after they received the name of the bank Stanley used, he drove her there. Now, they were sitting in the parking lot while Kalina braced herself. She was nervous about getting out, unsure of what she would discover.

She pulled in a deep breath and repeated the action five times over. Her eyes were closed.

"It'll be all right, Kalina," Bryson assured her. "You have me to support you. If you faint, I'll catch you, baby."

"I'm sure you would, Bryson," she said. "Um, listen…about last night—"

"Don't worry about it," he told her.

"But—"

"Kalina, don't worry about it."

"Bryson, I just want to apologize. I don't know what came over me last night and I shouldn't have come on to you so strongly. I've never done anything like that before."

"What part of *don't worry about* it, don't you understand?" he asked, then smiled. "Come on. Let's go."

"Okay." She reached for the door handle, finally stepping out of the car.

He got out, too, then they headed to the front entrance of the bank.

"This is a small bank, but a busy one," Bryson observed.

"Looks that way," Kalina said. Walking up to the customer service desk, she asked the gentleman where the safe deposit boxes were.

"First, I'll have to check to make sure your name is on the permission list to access the box," the man said. "I need your I.D., please?"

Kalina took her wallet from her purse, sliding out her driver's license. "Here you are," she said, handing it to him.

The man looked it over. "Thank you, Ms. Cooper." He returned her driver's license to her and said, "Right this way."

As if by instinct, Kalina clutched Bryson's hand, holding on tightly to it like it was her lifeline.

Bryson looked at her. He could feel the nervousness flowing through her veins – through her hands to his. She was already frazzled and scared, afraid of what she might discover in the box. Maybe it was a family heirloom her father wanted to pass down to her. Or it could've been old mementos of his that he only wanted her to have.

"Sir," the man said looking at Bryson.

"Yes?"

"I'm going to have to ask you to wait here. Only

one customer can be back here at a time."

"But he's with me," Kalina said. "We're together."

"I understand that, but we can only allow one customer back here."

"Okay," Bryson said. "That's fine. Go ahead, Kalina. You'll be fine."

She continued on with the guard, watching him pull the entire box out from the slot. He walked it over to a table, set it there and said, "Here you go, ma'am."

He walked back to the door and stood outside of it, giving her privacy to view the contents of the box. The only thing is, Kalina's hands were shaking so badly, she could barely put the key in the keyhole to unlock it.

Okay, Kalina. You can do this.

She pulled in a deep breath and braced herself, finally steadying her hands enough to unlock the box. She slowly opened it and removed a white, letter-sized envelope. That was the only thing in the box – an envelope. She slid it inside her purse, quickly leaving the room and thanking the guard for his time.

In the lobby, she met up with Bryson again, told him she was ready to go and when they were sitting in the car, he asked, "So?"

Kalina looked at him.

"What was it?" Bryson asked.

She unzipped her purse, removed the envelope and said, "This was the only thing in there."

"You didn't open it yet?"

"No. I'm too nervous to open it. Why would he

write me a letter and keep it in a safe deposit box, Bryson?"

"There's only one way to find out."

"I can't do it."

"Kalina—"

"Here," she said, handing the envelope to Bryson. "You open it."

He took it from her grasp. "Are you sure?"

"Yes. Open it."

"Okay." He slid his thumb underneath the flap that sealed the envelope together and slowly tore it open at the seam. When he had fully opened it, he immediately noticed a gold, diamond ring. He took it out and said, "Here's something." He handed the ring to her. "Must be an heirloom."

Kalina took the ring and analyzed it while Bryson removed the folded letter from the envelope. He unfolded it, noticing it was almost a full, typed page. He looked over at Kalina and said, "You want to read this."

"No. Read it to me," she told him.

"Kalina, your father went through the trouble of getting a safe deposit box for this letter. It was meant for your eyes only, dear. I think it'll be best if you read it."

"No. I want you to read it. Please, Bryson."

Bryson sighed. He didn't want to read her deceased father's words, but if this would help Kalina, he would do it. "Okay. It looks like he typed this letter eight years ago." Bryson cleared his throat and reluctantly began reading:

To my dearest daughter,

I want to start this letter off by saying that I love you very much and I'm sorry for how things turned out between your mother and I. I was sick for years, but then the cancer went into remission. That's when I met your mother. Boy was she a beautiful sight. I knew she was the one when I first laid eyes on her, and we were inseparable. Then something happened – she became pregnant. Pregnancy changed her. She told me right out the gate that she never—

Bryson stopped reading and turned to look at Kalina.

"Keep reading," she told him.

—she never wanted to have children. She wanted a career. She wanted success without a child being in the way so that's what divided us. You. I wouldn't let her give you up for adoption. I fought her tooth and nail and when that wasn't enough, that's when I knew I had to tell Madeline what was going on.

"Wait…what? That doesn't make any sense."

Eyebrows raised, Bryson said, "I'm reading it exactly as it's written, Kalina."

"I know you are, but it doesn't make sense to me."

"Okay, well let me keep reading and maybe it'll start making sense. All right, so where was I…oh, here we go."

I wouldn't let her give you up for adoption. I fought her tooth and nail and when that wasn't enough, that's when I knew I had to tell Madeline what was going on. It took a lot of courage on my part, because I knew I had done wrong and I knew it would break Madeline's heart for me to tell her what I had done, but I confessed that I'd had an

affair with her sister and she was pregnant. I told her that
Edi—

Bryson's voice trailed off before he could say
Edith's name because, now, he knew why her father
had placed the letter in a safe deposit box. Madeline
wasn't Kalina's birth mother. Edith was. When he
looked over at Kalina and saw tears traveling down
the length of her face, he knew she'd figured it out
as well.

"Do you want me to finish reading this, Kalina?"

She nodded.

"Okay."

I told her that Edith didn't want the baby and with tears
running down her face, she told me that we could adopt
the baby. You were that baby, Kalina. Madeline raised you
like you were her own daughter. She never did restore her
relationship with Edith. They were never close from the
start, but the affair pushed them even further apart. In a
way, I think you were more of a blessing to Madeline
because she couldn't have children and she desperately
wanted a child. In some weird, twisted way, you ended up
being a blessing to her.

I know I looked like a coward when I left after finding out
about Madeline's illness, but it was for your own good. I
knew that when the cancer came out of remission, I
wouldn't have long to live and I also knew the road
Madeline was going to face with Alzheimer's so I decided
to leave. I didn't want you to see the two people closest to
you die one after the other. I see now how poor of a
decision that was because I lost many years with you. I'm
sorry, daughter. I really am. I know I should've told you
this a long time ago, but it was a struggle to tell you that
the woman who raised you wasn't really your biological

mother. Still, that didn't prevent her from loving you like a mother.

I left a ring in this envelope. It was your grandmother's wedding ring. She passed it down to me and I was supposed to pass down to my firstborn, so now it's yours. I love you, Kalina and again, I'm sorry.

Bryson glanced over at Kalina watching her wipe her eyes and, when she lowered her hands from her face, he touched one of them and held it, not knowing what to say. "Um…that was it."

Kalina broke her hand away from him, dabbed her eyes again and said, "Can you take me to my car?"

He didn't want to do that. In his opinion, she was too distraught to drive or do anything else. "Kalina, I don't—"

"Please, just take me to my car, Bryson," she cried, sniffling.

"How about we go somewhere, sit down and have breakfast—?"

"Look at my face, Bryson."

He looked at her, feeling stabs to his heart. Her eyes were a reddish color and puffy, filled with tears. Her face was a teary mess.

"I'm not going to a restaurant to have breakfast like this! I'm not."

"Then I'll order breakfast and we can sit in the car and eat or go to a park or something, Kalina, but there's no way I'm going to let you drive like this. No way."

Kalina dug around in her purse for some tissue and when she found some, she dabbed her eyes and blew her nose.

Bryson folded the letter, slid it back inside the envelope and placed it in the center console. He started the car. Using his GPS, he found a restaurant, called in an order for the two of them then drove there and waited in the parking lot.

Kalina was quiet during the ten minute drive. She couldn't believe what her father had written – that Edith was her real mother. How could Edith deceive her like this? Did she not have a heart? A conscience? What kind of woman gives up her child because she doesn't want to be bothered? Doesn't want her success to be hindered by the care and attention it would take to raise a child?

Bryson looked over at her again. He wished they weren't sitting in the car so he could hold her close to his chest and ensure her everything would be all right, but he couldn't do that now. "Kalina, are you okay?"

She shook her head. "I honestly don't know how to feel, Bryson. This…this betrayal is on so many levels, I just want to walk away from it all and disappear…go somewhere where no one can find me."

"What would that solve?" he asked. "It would still leave you with anger."

"At least I'll have my sanity."

"*Would* you have your sanity?"

Kalina grinned through tears.

Bryson reached over, squeezed her thigh and said, "Wait here. I'll be right back."

While Bryson ran in to get the food, Kalina took the letter and reread it. She shook her head. How would she bring this to Edith? Should she say anything at all?

"Here we go," Bryson said, opening the door. He handed Kalina the coffee tray before sitting. Then he gave her a food tray. "Eat."

She opened it, reached for a French toast wedge, taking a bite.

Bryson felt comfortable eating now that he saw her attempting to eat, so he took a bite of toast as well. "So running away is not an option, sweetie," he told her. "I suggest you sit down with your aunt, well, mother and give her the opportunity to tell you the truth. Who knows, maybe she wanted to tell you all along. That's probably why she took you and Madeline in after Stanley left. Guilt."

"I can't believe she would do that to me. All these years she's been pretending she was my aunt...it never crossed her mind to tell me she was really my mother? Like how do I even begin to forgive someone who would do that to me, Bryson?"

Bryson shook his head. "It's going to take a lot...a whole lot, Kalina, but you have to face her. You can't deal with all of this on your own."

"I know." Kalina took a sip of coffee. "Thanks for convincing me to stay for breakfast."

"You're welcome. Oh, and that's decaf coffee, by the way. You need to start drinking more decaf...leave that dark, double-shot stuff alone."

"Why?"

"Because your hands tremble a lot when you're upset, scared or nervous about something and I don't like it."

269

Kalina turned to look at him. "You think you know me so well after what…"

"About a month and a half and, in that time, I've watched you drink more coffee than water."

Kalina giggled. "I have to drink something to stay awake."

"I know. You work so hard and you really need to stop and…you know…get your life in order. Especially after learning all of this."

Kalina nodded. "You know what the crazy thing is? I asked Edith why she had no love interest in her life…why she never married, settled down and had kids. She told me it wasn't for her…said she was success driven. So she gave me up because I didn't fit into her lifestyle, and I'm following her footsteps. My entire life is nothing but work."

"It doesn't have to be." Bryson finished up his food, closed the empty tray and said, "I want you to ride back to Wilmington with me, Kalina."

"I can't. I have to drive my car back, and don't worry. I'll be fine."

"Are you sure?"

"Yes. I'm sure."

Bryson released a worried sigh and said, "All right, but I'm going to be following you closely. If I see you running all across the lines and swerving, I'm pulling you over."

Kalina chuckled. "Yes, sir, Officer Blackstone," she quipped.

CHAPTER 39

At home, Kalina kicked off her shoes, dropped her overnight bag at the door next to a few pairs of shoes and sat on the couch.

Bryson sat down too.

"Go home, Bryson," Kalina said to him.

"I will after you get settled."

"It's going to take me a while to get settled. I have to do some work and—"

"All you need to do is relax. Don't think about work."

Kalina rubbed her eyes. She was tired but she wouldn't be able to sleep. Out of nowhere, she said, "She doesn't even look like me."

"Who? Edith?"

"Yes."

"That's because you look more like your father…must've had some strong genes."

Kalina turned to look at him and said, "How do you know how he looks?"

"I looked him up online."

"Oh."

"I feel so stupid for not doing that before I decided to go there on a whim."

"Why did you go there?"

"I told Lizette I wanted to do an article about marriage and what happens when the husband, or the wife, gets a serious illness…I wanted to see what kind of feedback I would get from the story. I was curious to know how many people out there, especially women, have been deserted by a man who said he'd love them forever, but when they became ill, the man ran for the hills." Kalina watched Bryson frown. "What's wrong, Bryson?"

"I was thinking you could change the article around to make it more positive. How about doing a story on the men, or women, who didn't desert their spouse, but stayed for the long haul?"

"I could do it that way, but I'm willing to bet there are more people who left than stayed."

"That's because you had a negative experience with it so you're already assuming the worst about everyone else, especially men."

Kalina shrugged. "Maybe you're right."

"So by your way of thinking, I should think all women cheat because Felicia was unfaithful."

"You may not think that *all* women cheat, but I'm sure you wouldn't be as trusting with women now that you've had the experience."

"See that's where you and I differ. I don't judge people based on what other people have done to me. I take them for who they are…judge them by their actions towards me and draw my own conclusions about the person."

"So you can honestly say you could trust another woman completely?"

"Yes, and don't get me wrong, Kalina. When Felicia cheated, I was hurt and I didn't pretend otherwise. Most men try to be all macho and pop their collars like it doesn't bother them, but I was with this woman for six years. It hurt me to my core to think she would do something like that to me, but I knew I had to move on, just like you have to find a way to move on from the things your father did. And Edith."

"I know. It's just…" Kalina sighed. "The woman I've been crying over my entire adult life isn't even my mother."

"But Madeline *is* your mother. She raised you, didn't she?"

"Yes."

"Then she's your mother. Edith may be your biological mother, but she hasn't earned any rights to be called your mother."

"None, whatsoever."

Bryson stood up and stretched. "All right, sweetheart. I need to run by the office, check in, make sure everything is kosher and then I can come back—"

"No. Go. I will be fine, Bryson," Kalina said standing. A few more steps and she was standing directly in front of him, close enough to lay her head against his chest and envelop her arms around him. Squeezing him. "Thank you for everything, Bryson."

"You're welcome," he said, squeezing her just as tightly. He released her, then gently touched her chin with his finger so she would look at him. "If you need anything, call me."

"I will."

He leaned forward, taking a small kiss from her lips. "I'll see you later."

"Okay."

With that, he turned away, walked out the door and drove away.

Kalina touched her lips, still feeling the warmth of Bryson's lips there. She couldn't deny she was feeling something for him. For a man to go all-out of his way for her was not normal and it felt good. She wasn't in the dark about what was happening. Bryson already told her how he felt – that he loved her – but even after all he'd done, she couldn't fathom giving her heart to a man, only to be disappointed in the end.

CHAPTER 40

She couldn't sleep much last night. She'd reread the letter from her father over and over again, staring at the gold ring he'd left in the envelope. And when she was tired of thinking about it, she began working to take her mind off of everything.

When she was up in the morning, she called Lizette to let her know to work from home again today and afterwards, she drove to the hospital to visit her mother. She sat in a chair, watching Madeline rest. Since she'd last saw her, she appeared to have lost a little more weight and her hair had thinned out more.

Kalina sighed, walked over to the bed and sat next to Madeline so as not to disturb her. She held her weak hand and, even though Madeline was asleep, Kalina said, "Hey, mom. It's Kalina. I'm back. I went to Fayetteville to visit dad but he...um...he wrote me a letter and told me everything. He told me how you took me in when Edith gave me away." Tears dropped from Kalina's eyes. "You raised me like I was your daughter and as far as I'm concerned, I *am* your daughter and you will always be my mother." Kalina took a breath when felt the slightest squeeze from Madeline's hand. With tears steadily falling from her eyes, she whimpered, "I love you, mommy."

Almost immediately after she uttered the words, the constant beeps from the heart monitor had ceased and now there was a loud, piercing, steady tone that remained constant. Flat. A few nurses and a doctor rushed into the room, doing what they could to revive Madeline. Another nurse escorted Kalina out into the hallway where she slid to the floor with her back against the wall, still crying. She didn't need someone telling her this was the end, that her mother was gone. She knew it already. Madeline had said her final goodbye with a gentle squeeze of her hand.

Too distraught to call anyone, Kalina told one of the nurses to call Edith. Wanting nothing other than to be alone, Kalina headed outside to her car and sat there, sobbing.

* * *

Edith had tried calling her an hour ago, but Kalina didn't answer. She didn't want to talk to Edith. Not now, but since she couldn't sit in the car forever, she went back inside of the hospital to find Edith sitting in a waiting room, in tears.

Edith looked up and saw her and said, "Oh, Kalina. I'm so sorry," rushing up to her to give her a hug.

Kalina's arms remained by her side as she tried with all of her might to hold in the anger building up inside of her.

Edith released her and said, "Were you here when it happened?"

Kalina nodded. "I got a chance to tell her I loved

her...that I appreciated her for taking care of me, even when my own mother didn't want me."

Edith's lips trembled. "You know?"

"I know everything, Edith. You should be ashamed of yourself." Kalina walked away from her and headed back outside to her car, driving away.

CHAPTER 41

Edith had tried to call Kalina on Friday. She even came over to her house, banged on the door, but Kalina wouldn't open it. She was in bed with a box of Kleenex, crying for most of the day until she'd had enough of feeling miserable. She wanted to talk to someone. Someone who knew what she was going through.

She took her phone from the bed then dialed June's number.

"Hey, girl," June answered.

"Hey, June. Um, what are you doing right now?"

"The guys are here about to play cards. I'm not doing anything. You want to come over?"

"No," Kalina said. She glanced at the clock. "Can you meet me at The Sandwich Shop in like an hour?"

"Sure. Is everything okay?"

"No, not really. That's what I want to talk to you about."

"Okay. I'll be there in an hour."

* * *

"Kalina, I'm so sorry to hear that," June said after Kalina informed her that Madeline had passed. "I know exactly what you're going through."

"It's been hard and, it doesn't help matters that I found out, a few days ago, that Madeline wasn't my real mother."

"What!"

"I mean, she raised me, but she's not my biological mother."

June frowned. "Do you know your biological mother?"

"Yes. My aunt Edith."

"What?" June said, shocked. "Oh my gosh!"

"Edith couldn't find it in herself to tell me the truth after all these years."

"So does that mean your father had an affair with his wife's sister?"

"That's exactly what it means. Edith ended up getting pregnant, told my father she didn't want the baby and was going to give me up for adoption until my father stepped in. He said he confessed to Madeline what he'd done, and Madeline agreed to raise me as her own daughter."

"Wow. That's…goodness…I can't even find the words. It sucks you have to deal with that and Madeline's death all at the same time."

Kalina nodded.

"Have you made arrangements and everything for the funeral service and—"

"She didn't want a service. And she wanted to be cremated." A tear rolled down Kalina's face. "So…um…Edith is taking care of that."

"Oh."

"Anyway, I wanted to talk because it's been a struggle trying to deal with all of this, you know."

June nodded. "One thing that helped me deal

with the loss of my mother was knowing I was there for her. Even though you just learned that Madeline wasn't your biological mother, she was still your mother. She cared for you, took you in and loved you."

"I know."

"And I think you need to stay with someone, Kalina. I know everything inside of you is telling you to shut everybody out and mourn in silence, but you need support right now."

"Well, Edith is all the family I have and I'm definitely not staying with her."

"Then come stay with me and Everson."

Kalina shook her head. "That's kind of you to offer, but I can't do that, June."

"What about Bryson? You two seem to be close. Stay with him."

"Bryson has done enough for me already."

"But—"

"June, I'll be fine. I promise I will call you if I feel like I'm going to have a meltdown."

"Okay, Kalina," June said, reaching for her hand.

CHAPTER 42

"Hey, babe," Everson said as he watched June walk in. He was still sitting at the kitchen table, playing cards with Garrison, Bryson, Barringer, Rexford and Colton. "Everything okay?" he asked when he saw a hint of sadness in her eyes. He knew his wife well. Very well. They'd dated for two years before they married and in those years, he grew to learn the woman he loved.

"Yes, everything's fine."

June leaned down to give him a quick kiss on the lips. "You sure?" Everson asked.

"Yes."

"Where are you coming from?"

"The Sandwich Shop. I was talking with Kalina for a while and all those emotions I felt when *my* mother died came back."

Bryson looked up when he heard her mention Kalina's name. He was shuffling cards, but had since dropped the deck on the table.

June continued, "Bryson, I told her she shouldn't be alone right now."

Bryson frowned. "What do you mean?"

June looked confused. "She didn't tell you?"

"Tell me what, June?"

"Her mother passed yesterday."

"What!" Bryson said, standing up quickly.

"Bryson, I thought you knew."

Without saying a word more, Bryson quickly left. Too many thoughts were running through his mind for him to even think about paying attention to the speed limit. He had to get to Kalina's house now. Why didn't she call to tell him about Madeline?

He rang the doorbell and banged on the door as hard as he could, saying her name. He waited a few seconds and repeated his actions. "Kalina, open the door, please."

He doubted she'd be sleeping nine at night and even if she was, she was going to get up. He wasn't going to leave until he spoke with her. Bryson pressed the doorbell again, then he heard her unlocking the door. She pulled the door open, standing there in a robe and messy hair.

He stepped in, walked up to her and took her into his arms, embracing her tightly while feeling her whimper against his chest. "I'm so sorry, baby," he said. "I'm sorry."

He held her for a while more until her crying ceased. When they were sitting on the couch, he asked, "Why didn't you tell me, Kalina?"

"I didn't want to bother you."

"Bother me? You're not a bother to me." He released a frustrated sigh and said, "Please let me be there for you. I don't know how many times I have to tell you that."

"You have your own life to be occupied with, Bryson. I'm not going to burden you with mine."

"Kalina—"

"No listen to me," she said loudly. "You have

your business, you have your brothers...you have a loving, caring family, Bryson. You still have a shot at a normal life without having to concern yourself with my screwed-up life."

"I *want* to concern myself with your life. Jeez, Kalina. When June told me what happened, I broke my neck to get over here to you." Bryson ran his hand over his head, frustrated. "Gosh, Kalina. Can't you see how much I love you?"

Kalina closed her eyes and shook her head.

"Why are you shaking your head? You don't believe that I love you?"

"I do believe you, Bryson, but it's unfortunate you feel that way about me because I can't love you back. I'm in no condition to love anyone. That's why I didn't call you."

"Kalina, baby," Bryson said, lowering himself to his knees in front of her while she remained sitting on the couch. "I don't want to talk about whether or not you love me. I'm here because I care about you and I want to make sure you're okay."

"And I'm telling you I don't want you doing that anymore, Bryson," she cried. "I can't be the woman you want me to be. I'll never be that woman. You know about my issues...my past. I don't want to make you feel like there could ever be anything between us when there never will be."

Given the circumstances, Bryson didn't want to discuss this now, but she was forcing him to. So with pain radiating from his eyes that matched the sadness in his voice, he asked, "You don't trust me?"

"Bryson, can you please just go?"

"You don't trust me, Kalina?"

"I told you from the start I didn't trust men and—"

Bryson placed his hands against the sides of her face and said, "I'm not talking about men. I'm talking about *me*. Do you trust *me*, Kalina?"

Bryson watched her lips tremble. As it was, she was grieving the loss of the woman who she thought was her mother and now she was crying over this separation between them. For her sake, he wanted to take himself out of the equation. "Kalina, I'm going to say this and then I'm going to go. I know you love me. I know you do. And I know you're afraid and I know you have trust issues. But I've never done anything to hurt you, or to make you *not* trust me. So, I'm going to go. I hope you find someone to help you deal with your anxiety, and I wish you nothing but the best." With a heavy heart, Bryson stood up and exited out of the front door.

More tears poured out of Kalina's eyes after he left. Bryson had been nothing but a gentleman to her. He helped her with work. He honestly and genuinely cared for her. Yet, she couldn't find it in her heart to tell him how she really felt about him.

CHAPTER 43

With puffy eyes, Kalina sat on her couch, listening to Edith give the full history about how she and Stanley had fell in love. She went on and on as she tried to explain her actions.

"So you decided you didn't want me because I didn't fit into your lifestyle," Kalina said.

"Kalina—"

"Just tell the truth, Edith! I'm so tired of people lying to me."

"I told you before that I didn't want children and I didn't. So when I got pregnant with you, I was devastated."

"Devastated," Kalina said, rolling her sad eyes. "You should be *devastated* to lose a child...not to find out you're bringing one into the world! I trusted you, Edith, and here I am thinking you're the hero in all of this by taking me and my mom in and now I understand you're the cause of it. Of everything! Not only did you have an affair...you had to sleep with *my* father...your sister's husband! And to add insult to injury, you didn't want me. Now you're trying to justify this?"

"Kalina—"

"All these years you had me believing my father was the enemy and, while he played a role in this too, you were the prime suspect. That's why you didn't tell me he passed. You weren't sure whether or not he'd left something like this letter to tell me the truth." Kalina sniffled and angrily swiped tears away from her face.

"I'm sorry, Kalina. I—"

"Do you realize what you've done to me? Because of you...because of all of this, I don't know who to trust anymore. I can't even bring myself to tell Bryson that I love him...the man who has been there for me throughout this...this crisis, because I'm afraid he'll end up hurting me like everybody else in my life! I'm so tired of being hurt by people who claim they love me."

"People make mistakes, Kalina," Edith said. "I take full responsibility for what I've done—"

"You haven't taken full responsibility. If you had, you would've told me what you did. I had to find this out on my own."

"Okay, I know forgiveness won't happen overnight and I know what I did was wrong, but when Stanley left, I took responsibility by taking you and Madeline in to live with me. I did that, Kalina. I didn't have to, but I did," Edith said, in tears. "And I took care of Madeline for years before she went into that facility. You don't think it pained me to see my sister literally break down in front of my eyes? You don't think it hurt me to watch you spoon-feed her? I carried so much guilt with me and—"

"Answer me this...why didn't you tell me that you were my real mother?"

"I wanted to. I really wanted to, but I didn't want to take that privileged title away from Madeline.

She had suffered enough and you were the only thing she had left to be proud of."

Kalina dabbed her eyes. "And you really didn't want me? You were going to give me up for adoption?"

"Kalina, I didn't know what to do with a baby. I never wanted children. I was never the kind of woman to grow up and want a family. I didn't want that responsibility."

"But yet you ended up taking care of Madeline and me."

Edith nodded. "I did. I guess I saw it as a way to correct my wrongs. It was a way for me to be close to my sister again. When her memory faded, she'd forgotten what I'd done and I felt like we could be sisters again. But even still, even after the Alzheimer's, Madeline was more of a mother to you than I could've ever been. She loved you dearly."

"Until the end," Kalina said, wiping her eyes, remembering how Madeline had squeezed her hand before she passed.

"Yes…until the end," Edith responded. She stood up and said, "I know you want to get to bed, but before I go, I want to say that Bryson is a good man, Kalina. I actually coached him to talk to you because I knew you needed help and I knew you would need someone to confide in, especially when you found out who I really was. If you love him, you need to let him know. Some of us are not lucky enough to find the one person we were meant to be with and I know you're afraid, especially since you've never been down this road before, but the road less traveled is the very road you need to be on. Talk to him. Don't let the circumstances in your life destroy your chance at happiness. I may not be much of a mother, but the least I can do is not let you repeat my mistakes." Edith turned to head for the door.

"Edith," Kalina said, getting up from the couch.

Edith turned around to look at her.

Kalina took a deep breath. "I've been holding on to too many things for too long and I'm not going to let grudges continue to dominate my life. I didn't get a chance to make things right with my father, but I still have a chance with you." Kalina wrapped her arms around Edith, feeling Edith's body tremble as she broke down and cried.

"I'm sorry about everything, Kalina. I'm so sorry," Edith cried.

"I know. We'll work through it, okay? I can't promise you that I'll be happy to see you some days, but we'll get through it."

"Okay, honey."

With that, Edith continued on to her car.

Kalina closed the door when she drove away and sat on the couch again, grabbing a pillow and wrapping her arms around it. She wondered what Bryon was doing this very second and for a moment, she thought about calling him. She needed to apologize. She needed to tell him the truth about how she felt for him. But she couldn't do it over the phone. She would have to talk to him face-to-face, if she could work up the nerve to do so.

CHAPTER 44

A Week Later

Bryson was standing in his kitchen, making potato salad. He had a feeling these family dinners was his mother's way of making sure all her children learned how to cook. After he'd placed the boiled white potatoes in a bowl, he added two dollops of Miracle Whip before pausing, thinking about a family. He thought he would have a family with Felicia but that didn't turn out so well. After the divorce, he swore he'd never marry again. He killed his dreams of having children. And he even wanted to sell his house. That was all before he met Kalina.

Never once did he think he'd meet another woman who would make him consider wanting to marry again, but Kalina was different.

"Um…that potato salad ain't going to make itself, Bryce," Candice said. She was helping him prepare their Monday night family feast again.

Bryson glanced up at Candice and said, "Yeah…I suppose it won't."

Candice closed the oven after she was done checking on the lemon-pepper chicken. She looked at Bryson again. "Okay, you better get out of that funky mood if you don't want everybody drilling you at dinner."

"I'm fine."

"No, you're not. You've been extremely quiet. What's bothering you?"

"Nothing, lil' girl. You just make sure that chicken doesn't burn."

"I know how to cook chicken. Everybody raved over my chicken last week, didn't they?" Candice took a bottle of water from the refrigerator. "So what's on your mind?"

"Nothing. I'm good, Candy."

"All right. Suit yourself, but when you get slammed with twenty-one questions at dinner, don't say I didn't warn you."

* * *

Nobody questioned him at dinner. As a matter of fact, this was one of the smoothest, most relaxing dinners the family had ever had. It was also an eye-opening dinner for Bryson, watching his brothers and their wives interact. There was Garrison who was the happiest he'd ever been, rubbing Vivienne's belly – anticipating the arrival of their first child who would be the first grandchild of the Blackstone family. Everson and June were still in the honeymoon phase of their marriage and Barringer and Calista, though they were going through some things, still loved each other.

Bryson was the only single brother. The divorced brother. In the presence of family, he liked to pretend it didn't bother him, but it did, especially now that he was in love. But the woman he wanted was unavailable and now, he was left crushed. Again.

But what was a man supposed to do? Sit in solitude and allow depression to take over? Men didn't do that. Men sucked it up, shoved all of their feelings aside and moved on the best way they knew how. That's what he was doing. Well, that's what he was trying to do until he realized he couldn't.

A few days ago, he'd been out buying groceries when he walked pass a vintage shop he must've passed a million times before. In the display window, he saw a porcelain jewelry box, one he remembered Kalina had described to him – one like Madeline had given her. He remembered how upset Kalina was that she'd broken it so he turned around, went back to the store and bought it. He kept it in the passenger seat of his car – a small piece of her. A memory of her. One day, he hoped to be able to give it to her one day.

While the women were busy in the kitchen getting plates and spoons ready for dessert – French vanilla ice cream and apple pie – Bryson stepped outside for a moment, standing in his drive way, leaned up against the body of his Mercedes with his hands in his pockets, legs crossed at the ankles, staring up into the night sky. He enjoyed the time he spent with his family, but tonight, as was the case with many other nights, he was here, but his heart was someplace else.

He watched his father come out of the front door and descend the stairs. At sixty-two years of age, his father was efficiently mobile, highly intelligent and still worked from time-to-time at the company he started – Blackstone Financial Services Group. When he retired, Barringer was named as the C.E.O., Garrison was the Director of Finance and Candice took on the role as Customer Relations Manager.

Bryson started his own company. He admired his father for doing that very thing and so he followed in his footsteps, building his own legacy to have something to pass down to his children.

Children…

"How ya doing, son?" Theodore asked.

Bryson cracked a half smile. "I'm okay…thought I'd come out here and get some air."

"Too bad there's not much air stirring tonight, huh."

Bryson inhaled a deep breath and said, "Yeah."

"Listen, son…um…I know when something is wrong with my boys, especially you. You know why?"

"Why's that?"

"Because you're the most like me. When I'm bothered by something, I'm usually quiet, not much for company. I just want to be to myself. Sound familiar?"

"I'm fine, dad."

"Okay, but let me say this. I know the divorce put a strain on you, son. I couldn't imagine what I would've done had your mother done something like that to me. But at some point, you have to let go of things and move on with life."

"Trust me, I let that go a long time ago."

"You have?" Theodore asked, frowning.

"Yes. I have no ill feelings towards Felicia. It wasn't meant to be, so it's over."

"And are you still trying to sell this beautiful house?" Theodore asked, turning to look at Bryson's home.

Bryson looked at it too. "No, pops. I changed my mind about that. This is my home...I won't let a failed marriage run me away from it."

Theodore patted Bryson on the shoulder and said, "That's my boy." He turned to go back inside and said, "Come on, Bryson. Candice has been bragging about her apple pies and I want to make sure I get a slice."

"Hey, pops, I do have a question before you go back inside."

Theodore turned around and said, "Okay."

"You always used to tell us that you knew mom was the one."

"Oh yes, she was and she still is," Theodore said.

"Well, let's say, when you met mom, she brushed you off and told you she wasn't ready for a relationship. What would you have done? Would you have given her space, or—?"

Theodore chuckled. "It's funny you mention that because something like that happened when I met your mother. She told me she'd just gotten out of a relationship and didn't want to jump into anything else. I was crushed."

"So what did you do?"

"I made her see things my way. I bought her flowers, I went out of my way to see her...I made sure she knew I wouldn't stop until she was mine. And I didn't stop, and I still love her to this very day, as much as I did on the first day I laid eyes on her."

Bryson nodded. He knew how much his parents loved each other. They'd made it a practice to show that love in front of the children so they could see what real love looked like, especially in this day in age when lust was more common than love.

Theodore pat Bryson on the shoulder again and said, "Come on, son. Let's go get some of that dessert."

"I'll get some later. Right now, I have some place I need to be."

CHAPTER 45

Some days proved to be more difficult than others, but with a lot of prayer, exercise and a healthier diet, Kalina managed to get through the hard times. She took care of herself and as a dear friend had suggested a while ago, she switched from regular to decaf and eventually, she'd stopped drinking coffee altogether. Now, she preferred green tea instead.

Sitting at her table in Edith's Café, she reflected on how, just a week ago, she was furious with Edith for deceiving her. Now, they were at a good place. Things between them wasn't quite normal yet, but at least they had started somewhere. Besides, they had to be each other's support for the loss of one of the sweetest women to ever walk the earth – Madeline Cooper.

Kalina took a sip of tea and clicked on an email, reading it. Her inbox wasn't stuffed to capacity with hundreds of emails, especially since she'd hired a blog designer to completely revamp and overhaul her blog. Now, she was limiting the amount of emails from readers to fifty per week and, since noticing that a lot of the questions were redundant, she started a question and answer section of her blog. That way, readers could have their questions answered without having to email her, thus cutting out the stress of the job.

When the door chimed, signaling someone was entering, she did something she barely had time to do before – she looked up. When she did, she caught the gaze of Bryson Blackstone. She hadn't seen him in over a week and she doubted she would ever see him again, especially here at the café, but here he was, on a Monday, holding a small black bag. Wasn't he supposed to be at a family dinner? What was he doing here?

Kalina returned her focus back to her computer and began typing when she felt him getting closer and closer until he pulled out a chair and sat down. At her table. In front of her.

She instantly felt herself become woozy by his scent – a scent she missed so much. She took long, savoring breaths of him, enjoying the way her body relaxed with his presence alone. She looked up, held his gaze and saw something familiar in his eyes. Care. Concern. Love. Deciding to break the silence, she said, "Hi, Bryson."

"Hi, Kalina." His eyes swept every inch of her face – the dark berry lipstick on her lips, the hint of color on her cheeks, the long eyelashes that curved up and those big, innocent eyes that could convince a person of anything. He looked at her hair, hanging around her shoulders, framing her face. She had on a V-neck, black blouse and around her neck, she wore a gold necklace with the name 'Madeline' engraved on a small pendant.

"What are you doing here, Bryson?"

Instead of answering her, he stared into her eyes, trying to read her, looking for indication of how she'd been for the last week. He'd been worrying about her. Even after she told him she could never love him, he was still worrying about her. Still thinking about her.

Finally, he asked, "How have you been holding up after everything?"

"It's a struggle, but I'm surviving."

"And what about Edith? How are things with her?"

"We have a long way to go, but we're trying. It's hard to think about at times."

"That's understandable. I see she's not working tonight?"

"Edith takes Mondays off now."

"Oh. That must be nice."

"Yeah…she enjoys it."

After a few moments of passing silence, Bryson asked, "Did you get the flowers I sent you for the service?"

Kalina nodded. Even though there wasn't an official funeral for Madeline, Bryson had still sent flowers to the funeral home on the day Kalina and Edith said their final goodbyes. "Yes, I did. Thank you."

"You're welcome," he said, watching her type something now. "Still busy sending emails, I see."

"Yes," she said, glancing up at him. "My eyes are not *glued* to my computer screen anymore, though."

She watched him smile, then said, "I'm actually enjoying my work again."

"Good," Bryson said, "Because I have a question…a relationship question I need an expert opinion on."

Kalina smirked. "What's your question?"

He gave her a long, piercing, heated stare. "I've been seeing this woman…this beautiful, breathtaking, sophisticated woman, and I told her that I love her and she didn't say it back to me. So my question is, do you think that, since she didn't say it, she doesn't love me, or do you think she's afraid I would hurt her if she admitted she really *did* love me?"

Kalina froze, not knowing how to respond. She knew he was speaking of her and she thought about how much she missed him – his comforting hugs and kind words. He seemed to know all the right things to say to help fix her moods and for a little over a week, she didn't have that. Didn't have him. So, being real with herself, she held his gaze and answered truthfully, "I think she's afraid you would hurt her."

"I wonder why she would be afraid I would hurt her, though, because I don't have a history of hurting her. All I've ever done was love her. Now granted, my relationship with her started off a little rocky, but once I got to know her, I fell in love with her."

"How do you know you love this woman?" she asked him.

Bryson's lips curve to a smile. "This is the part where you're supposed to tell me to dig deeper."

She smiled, her eyes brimming with tears.

Bryson continued, "I know I love her because I think about her all the time. I worry about her. When I don't see her or talk to her, I feel a loss…like something is missing in my life. And when I finally do see her again and get to talk to her, my heart smiles. My mood instantly improves and I know that whatever problems I have, whatever is going on in my life, it'll all be okay because of her."

Kalina swallowed the lump in her throat and opened her mouth to ask him another question but before she could say a word, Bryson said, "I thought I never wanted to remarry but I do want to marry again. I want her. I thought I didn't want children, but I do want children. I want her to have my babies. I want a life with her. I want everything with her but only if she wants everything with me and it all begins with an *I love you*. Only thing is, she won't say it."

A small tear crawled down Kalina's face. Bryson wasn't giving up on her and she recognized that he loved her a long time ago. If he was willing to be vulnerable and put his feelings out on the table, she could do the same. So, folding her laptop closed, she held his vision and said, "I love you, Bryson. And I miss you. I do."

He smiled wide. He'd waited to hear these words and now that he finally did, he closed his eyes and felt the highest feeling of satisfaction he'd ever experienced. "I have something for you," he said, handing her the small gift bag.

"What's this, Bryson?"

"Open it, baby."

Kalina opened the bag, removing the jewelry box. More tears fell from her eyes. The jewelry box looked almost identical to the one Madeline had given her.

"It's…it's beautiful, Bryson," she said, her hands trembling. Lips quivering. "I can't believe…you…you remembered this."

"I remember everything where you are concerned, future Mrs. Kalina Blackstone," Bryson said, standing tall, before lowering himself to his knees in front of her, turning her chair, while she was still in it, to face him.

"Open it, Kalina."

Kalina looked at him, not fully comprehending what he was asking of her. Apparently, this was a lot for her to take in.

"Open the jewelry box, sweetheart."

She nervously opened the box and saw a ring, resting at the bottom of it. She took it out, looked at it through her tears and, looking at Bryson again, she said, "Is this—"

Bryson took the jewelry box from her and placed it on the table. Then, taking the ring in his hand, he looked at it for a moment, looked back at her and said, "I never thought I wanted to do this again and I told myself I never would, but I didn't count on meeting a woman as special as you." He paused to take a breath. "I love spending time with you and I know you never wanted this, but I'm asking you to make an exception for me because I'm convinced I can't be without you." Bryson took her left hand into his hand, kissed the backside of it, before sliding the white gold, princess-cut diamond onto her finger. "Kalina, will you marry me?"

Like the sunshine bursting through gray clouds, a smile came to her teary face. "Yes, I will marry you, Bryson."

Bryson stood up, taking her hands so she could stand, then kissed her, sealing their engagement and wrapping his arms tight around her.

"I love you so much, Bryson."

"I love you too, Kalina. Now pack up your things, because I need to take you somewhere and do something I should've done a long time ago."

"And what's that?"

"I need you to meet the rest of my family...of our family."

CHAPTER 46

Bryson was elated when Kalina pulled into the driveway behind him. "Welcome home, baby," he told her before taking a kiss from her lips again. He gripped her hand and interlocked their fingers while they walked up the stairs to join the family.

All eyes were on them when they stepped into the dining room. A second ago, the room was noisy, filled with laughter and conversation. Now, there was complete silence.

"Hi, everyone," Bryson said. "Most of you know Kalina, and if you don't know her, you'll get to know her over the years because we're engaged."

"Yes!" June said, standing up and throwing both of her arms in the air. She ran to give Kalina a hug. "You two are so perfect for each other. I'm soo happy for you!"

Barringer, Garrison and Everson looked like they were in shock, especially since knowing that Bryson didn't want to marry again.

Candice smiled then ran over to Bryson and wrapped her arms around him. "Congratulations, Bryson. I knew you could do it." Candice looked at Kalina and said, "You don't know me but I'm Candice." She threw her arms around Kalina. "Welcome to the family, sis."

Calista was happy for Bryson and his new

beginning, but she felt like she needed one of her own. She contemplated telling Kalina that she had written to *The Cooper Files* about three months ago, asking for advice since Barringer seemed to be changing his mind about wanting to have children. She definitely wouldn't tell her tonight, but when they got to know each other better, she would, and maybe Kalina could give her even more advice.

His parents were elated. They didn't know Kalina either, but what they did know was the smile on Bryson's face was authentic – one they hadn't seen in a while. Their son was happy for the first time in a long time. Elowyn, a romantic at heart, was afraid her oldest son had given up on love, but here he was, starting over.

While the women all gathered around Kalina, introducing themselves and gawking at her ring, the brothers pulled Bryson off to the side.

"I knew this was coming," Everson said. "I knew it, I knew it, I knew it! Happy for you, bro."

"Whatever, Everson," Barringer said. "There's no way you knew."

"I did," Everson responded. "I knew it the day when Bryce and I had lunch together and he couldn't take his eyes off her."

"Oh, and remember when Kalina came over one day when we were playing cards?" Garrison said. "Bryson kissed her hand…talking about they *work* together. Yeah, you were *working* all right…"

Bryson grinned. "We were working together, Gary, and now—" Bryson turned to look at Kalina, thinking about all she'd been through over the last couple of months. About how the independent, thirty-year-old, beautiful entrepreneur had managed to avoid relationships for her entire life, but how she was willing to take a chance with him. He swallowed hard and said, "Now, she's going to be my wife."

Bryson smiled when Kalina looked up at him, watching her return a smile his way. It had been a difficult journey for him to take as well, having been heartbroken in the past, betrayed by infidelity, but he would give marriage another chance, not because he was lonely. Not because his brothers were married and he wanted to fit in. He would do it because he wanted to give Kalina a life she deserved. He wanted her to finally have something her heart desired more than anything – true love and a family. And as her man, her lover, her confidant, her husband, he would forever take any pain she felt in her heart and absorb it in his. He now had that power, and he would use it to make her happy for the rest of their days.

EPILOGUE

Two Months Later

Every one of her married children had exchanged vows at their waterfront home in Wilmington, North Carolina and, sticking to tradition, Theodore and Elowyn had prepared the beach for yet another Blackstone wedding, and today, a beautiful, flawless, sunny day in September, Bryson and Kalina stood at the altar, holding hands and repeating vows.

"You may now kiss the bride."

Bryson released Kalina's hands, brushed tears away from her eyes with his thumbs and holding her head between his strong hands, he pressed his lips against hers, taking his time to seal this moment in their minds. Even among the applause, cheers and whistles, he kept on kissing his beautiful bride, deepening the kiss when he slipped his tongue inside her mouth and greedily kissed her, listening to the slightest whimpers escape her throat.

"Ahem," Barringer said, clearing his throat, signaling Bryson to end the kiss.

Bryson pulled away from Kalina and whispered, "I love you, Mrs. Blackstone."

"I love you, Mr. Blackstone."

Bryson took her hand again and they turned to look at the guests – close to a hundred family and friends, all gathered to see two people in love declare it before God.

The minister said, "I present to you Bryson and Kalina Blackstone."

More cheers and whistles roared from the ecstatic crowd as Bryson and Kalina walked down the aisle again, this time as husband and wife.

Round tables covered with white tablecloths and candles were strategically set up around a wide open space for dancing. After they ate dinner together, Bryson took Kalina by the hand and said, "It's time for our dance, my lady."

Kalina took his hand and he led her to the dance floor as the area cleared for them. The DJ announced that it was time for the couple to share a dance and then he played their song – *All of Me*, by John Legend. With their hands interlocked, they swayed to the music while Bryson softly sung the song to her.

Beautiful.

When the song was over, the crowd applauded and he whispered, "I will always love you, Kalina."

"And I will always love you, Bryson."

Next came the cutting of the cake. Kalina cut a small piece of vanilla cake with buttercream frosting, picked it up with her fingers and held it in front of Bryson's mouth.

Bryson opened his mouth wide, taking the piece of cake and her fingers along with it, licking frosting from her fingers. And when he gave her a piece, she did the same and he kissed her, tasting frosting on her tongue.

"Let's sit down for a moment," Bryson said,

taking her hand and sitting at the head table. Once they were seated, he said, "I hope you're not overwhelmed by all of this. My mother likes to throw big weddings."

"It's fine, Bryson. Elowyn warned me during the planning stages of the wedding that she liked to go all-out for family."

"And she was not lying. There were over six-hundred people at Everson's wedding."

"Six hundred?"

"Yep, but that's partially because no one could believe he was actually getting married. He was Mr.-Player-For-Life until he met June."

"Aw...she's a good person. He definitely settled down with a winner."

Bryson nodded, then saw Vivienne on the floor trying to dance. "Vivienne looks like she can go in labor any minute now."

Kalina smiled, watching Garrison place his hands on Vivienne's stomach as they danced. "She does, and that's going to one gorgeous little boy."

"Yeah. We're going to have some beautiful children, too," Bryson said, then kissed her lips briefly.

"Yes we are," Kalina responded, "Although, we never said how many."

"I don't think we should put a number on it. Let's just see what happens."

Kalina nodded. "I like that idea." After noticing Calista sitting alone, while Barringer stood near the bar with a drink, she asked, "Hey, what's going on with Calista and Barringer?"

"Barringer says Calista is ready to have a baby,

but he was having second thoughts about children and—"

Kalina looked at Bryson with a wide-opened mouth. "Oh my God…the email! I bet it was from Calista."

"What email, baby?"

"You remember…the one I told you to answer when we met. It was the first email you ever answered for me. The woman asked if she should give her husband an ultimatum…"

"Oh, I remember. You're right. It could've been from Calista."

"You don't think she'll actually leave him do you?"

Bryson looked across the room at Calista. "I don't know. She certainly doesn't look too happy right now. I'm going to have a conversation with Barringer real soon."

Kalina took a sip of champagne, noticing Rexford and Colton by the bar. "Hey, Bryson, take a look at your cousins."

Bryson grinned. "They do this at every wedding…stand back and check out the single ladies."

"I better tell Lizette to watch out," Kalina said, then laughed. "And who is that talking to Candice?"

Bryson frowned. "I don't know, but I'm definitely going to find out before this night is over."

Kalina found his overprotectiveness endearing. "You love your little sister, don't you?"

"I do, and I tend to be very protective of the people I love."

"I like that about you." She kissed him on the lips again, smiling at how good it felt to do so.

"I'm glad Edith was able to make it," Bryson said.

"I am too. She seems happy for us."

"Well, she is the reason we got together, right?"

"Yes. That is right. Even after everything she's done, I can still be grateful to her for introducing me to my best friend."

Bryson locked eyes with Kalina and stared. "Keep talking like that and we're going to go on home and really get this party started."

Kalina giggled. "Hey, I'm down for that. Most of the guests have already left anyway."

Bryson stood up, took Kalina by the hands again and said, "Then let's go home, baby."

"Let's."

Hand-in-hand he walked with her to the limo and, after they got inside, Bryson gave the driver his address. Then, he took Kalina in his arms, and they kissed all the way home.

* ~ *

Enjoyed, *Evenings With Bryson*? Keep reading for a BONUS chapter, *After The Wedding*, beginning on the next page!

Look for book two in the **Blackstone Family Series** titled, *Leaving Barringer,* which will tell the story of Barringer and Calista Blackstone.

All books in the **Blackstone Family Series** are standalone books and can be read in any order. Visit www.tinamartin.net for regular updates and, while you're there, subscribe to my newsletter.

Evenings With Bryson, Book Extra
After The Wedding...

Bryson scooped Kalina up – her and all of her dress – carrying her inside of the house.

"I'm so glad we decided to spend a week here instead of rushing off to Maldives right away," Kalina said.

"Me too," Bryson told her. "It'll give you a chance to familiarize yourself with every aspect of our home, especially since we didn't live together pre-marriage."

Kalina nodded. She was glad Bryson didn't pressure her into moving in with him or do anything else to make her feel uncomfortable. He was a true gentleman.

Standing in front of her, he stared in awe, remembering the time they'd spent together in the past and how quickly he'd fallen in love with her.

"You look like you're in love," Kalina said. "I see a sparkle in your eye."

"You learned that in college, or by the way I put these lips on you?" Bryson asked, but not waiting for a reply. He pressed his lips against hers and savored the feeling of being in love again.

When they parted, he picked her up again, carried her up the stairs and into the master bedroom. His phobia of sleeping there had been resolved. This time, he knew he had the right woman by his side.

Bryson lowered her to the bed, watching her fall back, her face towards the ceiling.

"Finally, we're home," she said. "It's 3:00 a.m., but we're home."

"Yes we are, baby. We are home." Bryson loosened his bow tie and unbuttoned his shirt.

Kalina kicked off her shoes and said, "It was truly the happiest day of my life."

"Mine too, and I'm looking forward to creating even more happy days with you."

Kalina sat up on the bed and that's when she saw he'd taken off his shirt. It was the first time she'd ever laid eyes on him, shirtless, his chocolate abs exposed for eyes only.

"Something wrong?" he asked.

"No. Um...no, everything's...fine."

He grinned. "I know you well, Kalina. Very well." He sat next to her on the bed and continued, "Baby, we do not have to make love tonight or, shall I say, this morning. Don't worry."

"That's not what I was thinking, Bryson."

"Then why did you look so nervous all of a sudden?"

Kalina giggled. "I wasn't nervous...I was in awe. You *do* realize this is the first time I've seen you without a shirt on."

"Then don't let the six pack scare you, baby. I'm a gentle giant." He smiled.

So did she.

"Seriously though, sweetheart...I know you're

tired. So, what I would like to do is get some rest, talk each other to sleep and hold you in my arms. That's what I want to do more than anything."

"Okay," Kalina said. "I'm going to step in the bathroom and get out of this dress."

"All right, baby."

After taking off the beautiful gown, she kept on the slip she wore underneath. Tonight, it would have to suffice as her nightgown since she had no other clothes at Bryson's house. She washed makeup from her face and pulled the hairpins out of her hair, letting curls bounce all over.

When she stepped back inside of the bedroom, Bryson had since turned off the primary light source in the room, settling for the natural light of the moon illuminating through the bedroom windows. He almost lost his breath when he saw Kalina emerge from the bathroom in a thin gown. He lifted the covers and said, "I have a spot right here waiting for you."

"Perfect," she said, playfully jumping in bed, sliding closer to him.

"Hey, baby," Bryson said, taking a kiss from her lips.

"Hey, you." She slid a leg between his powerfully strong thighs and rubbed her fingertips across his head. "This is nice."

"It is nice...and to think you were giving me such a hard time when we met."

Kalina smiled. "I know. I'm sorry."

"I'm just teasing you, sweetheart," he said, finding her hand and interlocking their fingers.

"I never told you this, Bryson, but that week I

went without you, the week after my mom died…it was horrible."

Bryson brought her hand up to his mouth and kissed it. "It was for me, too."

"I wanted to feel your arms around me…consoling me," Kalina said. "No matter how bad things were for me, you were there and I'd never had that before you…never gave anyone a chance to be there for me. Only you. That's how I knew we were meant to be together. That you were the man I was meant to be with. That I will love forever."

Bryson gently rolled against her, slowly maneuvering his body underneath the covers so he could cover her like a blanket. He lowered his lips to hers, took a tender kiss before leaving a kiss on her nose. On her cheeks. Her chin. Her forehead.

"Bryson?"

"Yes, sweetheart."

"There's something else I want you to know."

"What's that, baby?" he asked before dipping his head and kissing her neck, feeling her body jerk.

"I want you to know that I will never betray your love. I promise to always be true to you and our marriage. I will never hurt you, or give you a reason to believe I would because I love you too much to ever cause you pain."

"I love you the same, Kalina," Bryson said before taking more kisses, from her lips this time, feeling his body yearn for her. He knew he said they would rest, but now, rest was the furthest thing from his mind. He wanted to make love to her.

Kalina closed her eyes when she felt the

warmness of his breath, his lips around her neck. He kissed her tenderly, leaving trails of his lips, marking his territory.

"I know I'm kissing you, baby, but I meant what I said. We don't have to make love."

"I want to," Kalina whispered into the darkness.

And he wanted her too, as evident by how quickly he'd helped her out of her slip. With their souls, skin-to-skin a sensation neither of them had felt with each other before, Bryson took his time analyzing her body, every inch of it, touching her soft skin until he needed something else – until he needed to connect their souls and truly make her his. But first, he whispered, "If I'm going to be your first, I'm going to be your last." Then he slowly introduced his body to hers, inviting her into a world of passion she had yet to experience with anyone. She would experience it with him – only him. He would be the only man to ever make love to her.

Slowly descending, he listened while moans escaped her lips and when he'd nestled comfortably he looked at her. Studied her. He wanted to know if she was okay. Her needs, her feelings, her desires would always come before his.

"Kalina," his said softly until he saw her open her eyes, a hint of despair on her face.

"Yes, Bryson?" she whispered in a lingering moan.

"Are you okay?"

"Yes. I'm okay," she replied, her fingertips stroking his back.

"All right, baby," Bryson said, kissing her again,

submerging his hands in her hair, making love to her slowly. Passionately. Purposefully. She needed to know what this was like…what it felt like to truly be loved. She'd had enough pain and heartache in her life from parents who didn't accept her – a father who deserted her and a mother who didn't claim her. She had a right to be skeptical about love, but now that she'd taken the leap of faith and fully committed herself to him, Bryson was intent on showing her exactly what love felt like in its expressive, physical form. When he felt her body quiver underneath him, he knew he was doing just that.

"Look at me, baby," he told her.

She opened her eyes, holding his gaze for as long as she could until she had to close them again, belting out sweet sounds of ecstasy.

"Oh, Kalina. I love you," Bryson said, before he soared off into a lover's abyss, plummeting to depths unknown, then rising again before falling once more. He leaned his head down to capture her lips, completely enamored, in love, intoxicated and obsessed with *his* Kalina.

"I love you, too, Bryson Blackstone."

Completely spent, Kalina rested against his chest, feeling his arms tight around her. She thought about how they'd met, fallen in love and had gotten married. She smiled, thinking how ironic it was that something they both didn't want ended up being the very thing they needed – love, happiness and a wonderful marriage. All those evenings they'd spent together at the café had led to this, marital bliss, and she looked forward to spending not just evenings, but mornings, afternoons, nights – every single day of her life, with Bryson.

* ~ *

Discover other books by Tina Martin:

Been In Love With You (Mine By Default Mini-Series, #1)
When Hearts Cry (Mine By Default Mini-Series, #2)
You Belong To Me (Mine By Default Mini-Series, #3)

Evenings With Bryson (The Blackstone Family)
Leaving Barringer (The Blackstone Family)

His Paradise Wife (The Champion Brothers)
When A Champion Wants You (The Champion Brothers)
The Best Thing He Never Knew He Needed (The Champion Brothers)

Accidental Deception, The Accidental Series, Book 1
Accidental Heartbreak, The Accidental Series, Book 2
Accidental Lovers, The Accidental Series, Book 3
What Donovan Wants, The Accidental Series, Book 4

The Millionaire's Arranged Marriage (The Alexanders, Book 1)
Watch Me Take Your Girl (The Alexanders, Book 2)
Her Premarital Ex (The Alexanders, Book 3)
The Object of His Obsession (The Alexanders, Book 4)
Dilvan's Redemption (The Alexanders, Book 5)
His Charity Challenge (The Alexanders, Book 6)

Dying To Love Her
Dying To Love Her 2
Dying To Love Her 3

Secrets On Lake Drive
Can't Just Be His Friend
All Falls Down
Falling Again
Just Like New to the Next Man
Vacation Interrupted
The Crush

For more information about the author and upcoming releases, visit her website at www.tinamartin.net.

WITHDRAWN

42996196R00194

Made in the USA
Middletown, DE
19 April 2019